DARKLING I LISTEN

DARKLING I LISTEN

David Fiore

Writers Club Press

San Jose New York Lincoln Shanghai

Darkling I Listen

Writers Club Press
an imprint of iUniverse, Inc.

For information address:
iUniverse, Inc.
5220 S. 16th St., Suite 200
Lincoln, NE 68512
www.iuniverse.com

ISBN: 0-595-22303-6

Printed in the United States of America

To Kim.

Darkling I listen; and for many a time
I have been half in love with easeful Death,
Call'd him soft names in many a mused rhyme,
To take into the air my quiet breath;
Now more than ever seems it rich to die,
To cease upon the midnight with no pain,
While thou art pouring forth thy soul abroad
In such an ecstasy!
Still wouldst thou sing, and I have ears in vain
To thy high requiem become a sod.

—John Keats, *Ode To a Nightingale*

Maybe I am a fool, but I want to go in for bulb culture. Oh, I know there is no money in it! I know that I shall just get attached to the bulbs when I shall have to give them away to somebody who wants them to grow into crocuses or tulips or something, and there I shall be, alone in that great, big, lonely house that my grandfather, the Duke, left me.

—Robert Benchley, *The Menace of Buttered Toast*

The hardest part is things already said.

—Sleater-Kinney, "Good Things"

Though he saw not the person from whom it came, and though the voice was wholly strange to him, yet the sudden shriek seemed to split its way clean through his heart, and leave a yawning gap there.

—Herman Melville, *Pierre, or the Ambiguities*

God delights to isolate us every day, and hide from us the past and the future. We would look about us, but with grand politeness he draws before us an impenetrable screen of purest sky, and another behind us of purest sky. 'You will not remember,' he seems to say, 'and you will not expect.'

—Ralph Waldo Emerson, "Experience"

Her lips were waitin'
Her eyes looked sad
The dreams of a lifetime
A year gone bad
The dreams of a lifetime
Told me wrong

Everything is all right
And now it's gone
Don't blame me
Please be strong I know I'm not wrong

       —Fleetwood Mac, "I Know I'm Not Wrong"

BOOK ONE

CHAPTER I

---▼---

"Hello, my name is Mike. I'm a twenty year old film student. I'm five-foot-five and weigh about one-sixty…I have dark hair and green eyes…I have many interests, and I think I'm a fun person to be with. I love old movies, jazz music, Charles Dickens, and my cats…I'd like to meet an attractive, intelligent, creative woman who will inspire me, and be inspired by me…Obviously, none of that can happen overnight, but let's not waste any more time than we have to! If you like my ad, get in touch with me at box #10843. Bye…" (*Actually, I'm only nineteen, and my studies are—informal. Did I mention I was a virgin?*)

*   *   *   *

Mike Borden cradled the receiver and stretched out. He had cued the *Jerome Kern Songbook* to 'I'm Old Fashioned'—setting the tone for his debut on 'Dial-A-M8: Montreal's number one talk personals system.' Mike closed his eyes and listened to the rest of the song. He liked that the meaning of "old fashioned" never changed. Rita Hayworth had been "old fashioned" when she had lip-synched to the tune in 1942; Ella had been "old fashioned" during her recording session in 1964; and he, lying on a half-dead air-mattress in August 1993, was "old fashioned" too.

The next track was 'Remind Me'—not one of Mike's favorites, but he was too lazy to reach for the skip button. He opened his eyes, contrasting his Puritan clubhouse with the suave ad. The four white walls were blank, except for the gray streaks that had built up on them since the all-purpose cleaner had run out. Mike wondered if it was too early to put up the Christmas tree.

Would Miss Dial-A-M8 find his way of life endearingly quirky? Or would she write him off as just another brute without a futon? He wondered if she'd come at all. Had he sounded calm and nonchalant? Or had his inexperience clung to the carefully chosen words of his ad like a sickly-sweet film of cherry-flavored cough syrup?

A knock at Mike's door signaled his sister's return. She would bug him for not taking the steak out of the freezer, as per her instructions. She would ask him if he had done anything productive with his "free time". Then they would settle down in front of the television and order a large mushroom pizza.

Mike grabbed his coffee, got up, and blew a kiss toward the telephone. Opening the door, he put on a playfully patronizing grin.

Diane looked impeccable. Black hair in a bun overlooked a pale cheekside. Her eyes were silvery-gray chrome fenders. Mike scanned her forehead for perspiration, but her thin vee-brows trumped the weather. She wore a light beige blouse and a pair of dark gray slacks that flared conservatively near the bottoms. Mike was proud of his sister. She had the kind of face that gets turned to in emergencies.

Mike froze in the doorway. His grin dribbled into the coffee. Diane had brought a guest.

"Anna," she announced, "this is my little brother, Michael."

Mike shook a handful of lacquered fingernails.

"Anna is the newest employee of La Paz Incorporated: Fine Coffees…We had to stop by to get a 'New Recruit' package. They're in my room, I'll be right back…"

Mike smiled weakly at the girl. The black talons on her heels, the chemical gleam of her lips, and the neon blue smudges above her opaque brown eyes gave her the look of some brittle, poisonous creature from a nature special. He wondered what she looked like in her pyjamas, waiting outside the washroom in the morning, frantically pleading with some relative: "*I have to put my face on!*" He thought he saw a freckle near the left corner of her small, rounded nose—beneath a layer of foundation—and he focused on that.

"S-so," he sputtered, "uh, have you been out of work long?"

"Oh no," she replied, "I have a job at a restaurant, but I'm not getting enough hours."

"Oh," he nodded unconvincingly, "not enough hours…"

"Mm-hmm."

She looked around the room, avoiding his eyes.

"Well! Diane'll keep you busy, she's a workaholic too."

"I'm not a workaholic," Anna snorted, "but I've got bills, y'know."

"Sorry…"

"No problem."

Mike noticed that her brown curls were frizzing in the humidity. He was about to take a shot at the weather, when Diane returned with an official-looking yellow envelope. "Here you go," she handed it to Anna. "I want you to read this very carefully over the weekend. If you have any questions, my home phone number is in there. If not, I'll see you on Monday morning."

"Sure," Anna replied, "thanks Miss—uh—thanks Diane…"

Diane patted her on the back and led her to the door. Mike flopped himself onto the circular blue couch, next to a beige kitten with a long tail and a Golden Retriever smile. He decided that he had just had the most worthless conversation in history and wondered whose fault it was. He buried his face in Marbles' fur.

Diane closed the door and walked over to the couch, which she had made the centerpiece of the living room. The subdued blue melted seamlessly into the spongy gray carpet, perfectly complementing the winter landscapes hung at regular intervals on the walls. Diane clicked on the news, lit a cigarette and poked Mike's soft midsection.

"So. What're we gonna eat?" she asked. "Or have you already gone through your daily box of cereal?"

Mike flipped over and beamed at her: "Pizza!"

"I guess," she turned away from him, smiling. "What have you been doing all day, Michael? You didn't even wash the dishes."

"I had a weird dream last night," he whispered, sitting up thoughtfully.

"So?" She rummaged through the menus, piled neatly next to the magazines on the glass coffee table.

"I've been thinking about it…"

"What?"

"You know: trying to make sense of it."

He stared at her for a full minute, then explained: "I was strolling in a forest. It must have been early autumn, judging by the number of brilliant leaves still clinging to their branches. It was a mixed forest. There were evergreens too. All the colors were represented. The thin vegetable blanket on the ground was just soft enough to protect my feet (I wasn't wearing any shoes); just crisp enough to produce music as I walked. There were birds, beautiful birds, singing to each other. I felt like an eavesdropper. The whole scene was swathed in gray clouds, and that misty October air which carries sweet fragrances from an unseen censer. I just rambled on, wondering, with every step, how much longer it could possibly go on. A long time…The sights never grew monotonous. Every tree was unique, but always rendered in a similar style. Then, I happened upon a capybara and her offspring…"

"A what?" Diane interrupted.

"A capybara. You remember: from the Biodome. The giant South American rodents…"

"The big gerbils? Those things are scary…"

"Well," he continued, "I scratched the coarse fur under her chin, and tickled her webbed paws. The young ones rubbed their snouts against my legs. They walked with me for a while down the path, then scurried off into the brush; looking for their river-home, I suppose.

"Eventually, I emerged from the woods, finding myself in an apple orchard. Row upon row of fruit-trees marched into the horizon. They were Mackintoshes, I think. Bright red. I reached for one. Instead, I found a graceful woman, perched on a bough. She leapt down to my level, pulling my eyes with her. She was an impressionist painting—vivid colors exploding out of muted softness. Her eyes were aqua comets, with cores of molten gold to match her hair. Her lips were like the Mackintoshes. Her smooth white cheeks made a perfect canvass. She wore jeans and a blue-check flannel shirt. I don't know how I knew her name was Gwendolyn.

"She led me away from the orchard, toward a pool. I caressed her back, her hips, with visionary ardor. By the water, she took my hand in hers and bade me kneel beside her. We watched bright fish at play beneath the surface and then, out of the corner of my eye, I glimpsed, in reflection, our kiss…She noticed me looking into the pool, and rivulets started down her cheeks…Somehow, the water engulfed us; I flailed about and looked for her and woke up in a sweat…"

"That's quite a dream, Michael," Diane sighed. "What do you want on the pizza?"

CHAPTER 2

▼

Mike's dream intrigued Eric Lantz. He leaned back in his chair and absorbed the details, with his eyelids pressed together. He drained every symbol of its significance, washing down the refined product with a foamy glass of *Boréal Rousse*.

In high school, Mike and Eric had usually spent Sunday afternoons chatting in the basement, playing Strat-O-Matic baseball; their every need catered to by Mrs. Lantz, who hovered over them like a kindly humming-bird, in curlers and a kimono. Their friendship was built on board games. In grade seven, this had seemed more important than the differences between them. Mike spent his teens brooding in his room, questing after perfect self-control. Eric opened himself up to everything the After School Specials warn kids about, but an instinctive moderation saved his body and mind from the worst ravages of hedonism. An exceptional athlete, he had straight teeth, a clear complexion, and the kind of confidence that doesn't need deodorant.

Mike enjoyed playing the martyred outcast, but he liked an occasional break from the role; and Eric welcomed a friend who was not a follower. At first, they had discussed things like the ideal characteristics of lead-off men and the relative merits of Raymond Chandler and Dashiell Hammett. Gradually, they had moved on to bigger words and wilder speculations.

Mike liked meeting at "The Bell Jar": it was close to his apartment, the coffee was usually free, they never played dance music, and, in case boredom set in, they had games. It had taken them about twenty minutes to find a table in the smoky green labyrinth, writhing with plaid shirts and young faces straining after seriousness. Grunge rock provided the appropriate ambiance. They had placed their orders with a pale waitress, all in purple, with poppy-seed dots of mascara around her eyes. Then Mike had described his vision of Gwendolyn.

"Listen to your subconscious," Eric announced.

"What do you mean?"

"I mean," Eric lit a cigarette, "you're telling yourself things *I've* had to learn through experience."

"Like what, for instance?"

"Like: romantic love is a sham. Love ought to be completely unselfish. But have you ever seen anything more selfish than a monogamous relationship? Egoism always gets in the way. Look—in your dream— you're too preoccupied with your own image to kiss her properly. Her possessive instincts are inflamed by your distant attitude. And then those crocodile tears start falling…"

"No," Mike shook his head, "you've got it wrong. I'm not staring at *myself* in the pool. I'm staring at the kiss."

"And what do you think *that* means?"

"I have no idea. I just think it was beautiful…"

"Believe me, Romeo, there's a lot of grunt-work involved. At a certain point, you just get tired of it."

"What are you getting at?"

"Well…I broke up with Wendy today."

"What!?" Mike choked on smoke and surprise. Eric had been dating Wendy Szabo for four years. They had gone to the prom together. She had also been kind enough to speak to Mike, every once in a while. "How come?"

"I dunno man," Eric sighed, "it's been obvious for a while; to me anyway. I start at university on September 4th; I'm moving downtown next week; she just doesn't fit into the equation."

"Hunh?"

"Jesus!" Eric stared at his empty glass. "How'm I supposed to make sense of Plato—not to mention Kant—with Wendy draped over my shoulders, hinting at marriage?"

Mike sighed: "You enroll in the philosophy program, and now you're a monk?"

"Trust me," Eric smiled, his eyes fixed on the waitress, approaching their table, "I'd make a very bad monk..."

They each requested refills. After Eric had done some flirting (the lady's name was Pamela), Mike took a wry tone: "So! You want to sleep around. Why didn't you just say so? Instead of dragging Immanuel Kant into the mire with you..."

"You think I'm a casuist?" Eric sounded hurt.

"Of course you are."

"That's so unfair! I'm telling you: I've honestly come to the conclusion that romantic love poisons the soul. What right do I have to possess a woman's body? There's no way in Hell she'll ever possess mine! That doesn't mean I'm going to give up sex. It just means that I'm free to do as I please; and, from now on, I'll require the same of my companions..."

"Isn't it possible that two people could—of their own free will—choose to be together, always?"

Eric chuckled: "A self-sufficient love, eh? There's no such thing Michael. You watch too many old movies..."

"If I stopped believing in that, I wouldn't know what to live for..."

"You're just sitting around, waiting for a beautiful blonde, and a swell in the soundtrack?"

"Sounds about right..."

"That's pathological, Michael. I'm serious; you can't go on thinking that way. Every day of your life must feel like a slap in the face."

"Kind of," Mike nodded, "but there's always the hope that I'll be vindicated, eventually. What keeps *you* going?"

"Are you kidding? I *know* where I'm going! Guys as intelligent as *we* are have a duty to develop to our full potential, Michael. Otherwise…well, there are plenty of mediocre people ready to take up the slack."

"And what, *exactly*, constitutes mediocrity?"

"Lack of…life-force, I guess. What Nietzsche would call the will-to-power. Good song!" he exclaimed. Nirvana's *Breed* roared through the room.

"I don't think I want to read Nietzsche. He sounds like an ego-maniac. What's *his* claim to superiority?"

"He cultivated his soul, Michael. And he left a monument of his existence. That's what I plan to do."

"You're going to rebuild the world in your image?" Mike sneered.

"No," Eric shook his head, "but I promise you: I'll be part of the decision-making process within twenty-five years."

"And that'll satisfy you?" Mike asked.

"It's my *duty* to make a public contribution."

"Don't you think that power corrupts?"

"Not if it's wielded in the best interests of all."

Pamela returned with their drinks. Eric took a swig of beer and brushed the sandy bangs out of his varnished brown eyes, strafing the waitress' body. She wiped a bit of foam off his upper lip and ran her fingers along the contours of his jaw.

Mike sipped his coffee. He scanned the bar for attractive women, wishing that just one of them would pay attention to him. He knew he was not the sort of guy that makes conquests upon sight. He was a born observer, and he had about as little mystique as a fly on the wall. People with mystique didn't need "Dial-A-M8". He wanted to tell Eric about his new experiment, but when Pamela dashed off to another table, he remembered their debate.

"Eric Lantz," Mike spoke with mock-solemnity, "man of the hour. Knows just what all of the little people want, especially Pamela…"

"You think I don't know I sound arrogant?" Eric countered. "Look. I'd rather go down in flames than stay on the sidelines; pretending that everyone is equal, that everything is wonderful; carping at the people who assume their share of responsibility."

"Responsibility? What about the responsibility of being a good friend? A good spouse? That's more than enough for most people…"

"Maybe. But not for us…"

"*Us!*" Mike exclaimed. "What does *that* mean?"

"You're going to be a great filmmaker, someday; if you can pull yourself out of the treacly melodramas you create in your head. It's an important role in the modern world."

"Very kind of you sir. But I'd prefer to create my own private world, with a woman I love…"

"A declaration of independence, sponsored by Harlequin! Now *that's* arrogance. I'd rather put my finger on the pulse of society, than on some woman's clit!"

"You're above that sort of thing?"

"I've *transcended* selfish relationships," Eric glowed.

"Fine," Mike smiled, "could I have Wendy's number?"

"Fuck you," Eric muttered.

CHAPTER 3

▼

Mike woke up with a headache. Seven coffees had taken their toll. He made out a blurry green 6:12 on the VCR clock, as he clawed at the glue between his eyelids. The debate with Eric had gone on until closing. As usual, nothing was decided; but each friend had sharpened his position, ever so slightly. At three o'clock, Pamela had gone with them to a twenty-four hour breakfast place. They had swallowed eggs, greasy home-fries, and superfluous coffees. Then Eric had taken Pamela's arm and marched home with her.

Mike never got Wendy's number. He had floated back to his apartment on a crisp breeze, ripped off his clothes in the living room (Diane spent the weekends with her boyfriend—Vito—at his condo in Laval, an island pock-marked with mini-malls and dance-clubs, just north of Montreal), lolled with Marbles and Pandora on the couch, and read a few stanzas of Shelley. He had gone to bed sometime around eight in the morning.

Mike rolled off his air mattress onto a pile of clothes that still reeked of cigarette smoke. He stood up, grabbed the clothes, and threw them onto the floor of his cupboard—a makeshift hamper. He herded his cats into the kitchen and filled their bowl with pellets. He replaced the cat food on the top shelf of the pantry, next to a fresh box of "Cracklin' Oat Bran". Mike gripped the blue cardboard between his fingers and shook firecracker noises out of the package. He drowned a bowlful in milk, plugged in the electric kettle, and fidgeted in front of the stove.

There were no chairs in the kitchen. It was a small, light-gray room, with minimal cupboard space and the usual appliances. The linoleum floor had a sickly olive-green tinge that disturbed Mike. He could have used some aspirin, but the bottle in the pantry was empty. He waited for the coffee.

A couple of minutes later, he was back in his room, dialing for a mate. A robotic, vaguely feminine voice answered the call. She asked Mike to enter his box number, and he eagerly complied. An eerie fanfare accompanied the announcement that he had "five—messages—waiting." He pressed "3" to hear these auditions for the role of sweetheart. The first was from an eighteen year-old girl named Angela. She described herself as "open-minded, down-to-earth, and easy-going." This sounded fine to Mike. He listened on. Her physical description was vaguely interesting: she was "five-foot-two, one-hundred-and-twenty pounds, with long brown hair and hazel eyes," but he told himself that these details were beneath him. Angela listed "dancing, playing pool, and listening to R&B" as her favorite activities. Mike didn't like any of these things and could not, in good conscience, respond to her message.

Next, he heard from Shelly, a nineteen year-old who also described herself as "open-minded, easy-going, and down-to-earth." Although she preferred listening to rap music, it occurred to Mike that she and Angela could have a really pleasant time, dancing and playing pool together. He never reached Shelly's physical description. He decided to press onward when she mentioned that she "loves to party." The use of "party" as a verb was a pet-peeve of his.

Amber—a twenty year-old university student with black hair and green eyes—was next. She wrote poetry, painted, and liked to read. However, she harped on the fact that she dressed entirely in black, had many body-piercings, and a tattoo of a dragon on her back. She labeled herself a "Goth" and showed no interest in meeting "people who wouldn't understand her". Mike wondered why she had picked *him*.

Next, he encountered an anonymous girl who hated *Oliver Twist*. She complained at length about Dickens's tedious descriptions and expressed contempt for the entire cast of the novel. She pointed out how short Mike was, guessed that "one-hundred-and-sixty sounds kinda pudgy on your frame," and said: "the way you talk about your cats, you sound like a fag." She suggested that he switch to a gay dating service and hung up. For this advice, Mike had paid a dollar.

The final message was from Monica, a twenty year-old who was "easy-going and open-minded," but not "down-to-earth." She claimed to love "books, music of all types, and movies." She described herself as "blonde, with eyes that change from brown to green, and a good body." She said that she had seen a Marilyn Monroe movie once, and had enjoyed it. She thought Mike had a nice voice.

Mike considered her words carefully. She seemed an unlikely soul-mate, but she liked his voice. He told himself that they had made a *connection*. He pressed "1" to reply. After several takes, each of which cost him a dollar, he abandoned all hope of sounding coherent, and pressed "#" to send. The product of all this deliberation was a hectic list of questions, such as: "What is your favorite movie?"; "What is your favorite book?"; "What are you looking for in a guy?"; "What kind of music *don't* you like?"; and "Do you like animals?"

After a minute or so, he received Monica's response: "Hello Mike! How are ya? Listen. I don't have time to answer all of your questions right now—I'm at work. But I'd like to talk later—maybe at the La Paz café on McGill College? Say, when I get off? Around eleven? You sound like a nice guy—let me know if you can do it, okay?"

"That sounds great!" he ejaculated into the receiver. "I guess I'll see you later…at eleven. Bye Monica—um, have a good evening at work…Oh, I'll be wearing jeans and a green T-shirt. And I'll carry a book of Shelley's poetry. Bye!" He pressed "#" and tenderly hung up the phone. He devoured the bowl of cereal, spilling milk everywhere.

Mike cleaned himself off with a towel from the hamper. The VCR clock read 6:43. He had time to watch a movie before getting ready.

He needed a romantic comedy, but there were many of those, among his three-hundred videos. He scoured his boxes for just the right film. *The Philadelphia Story?* (No. He wasn't in the mood for romantic quadrangles. He wanted something simple.) *Love Crazy?* (No. The slapstick antics in the insane asylum would only aggravate him.) *The Awful Truth?* (No. A divorce/reconciliation comedy was inappropriate.) *The Talk of the Town?* (No. It had too much intellectual debate, too little romantic banter.) *You Can't Take It With You?* (No. He had watched it three days before, as part of an all-night Capra marathon.) *Platinum Blonde?* (No. Ditto.) *Holiday?* (No. It was probably his favorite romantic comedy, but he knew the dialogue by heart; he wanted something *new*—like the awesome blank that loomed on the far side of eleven o'clock—yet comforting.)

He settled on *Lucky Partners*, a 1940 film starring Ginger Rogers and Ronald Colman. He had taped it off PBS when he was thirteen, and hadn't seen it since. He dashed to the kitchen, turned another spoonful of crystals into liquid energy, summoned the cats to his side, turned out the lights, and pressed "play."

A throbbing signal tower flashed onto the screen. Beneath it, the northern hemisphere swirled like a merry-go-round. A backdrop of cumulous clouds insulated the picture. The words "An RKO Radio Picture" appeared inside circular sound waves emanating from the tower. The names of Jack Carson, Spring Byington, and Harry Davenport trailed after those of the stars. The director was Lewis Milestone, whom Mike associated with "serious stuff," like *All Quiet on the Western Front* and Popular Front Communism. He wondered why the "socially conscious" *auteur* had been assigned to a "trifle" like *Lucky Partners*. (When thinking about the cinema—he didn't know anyone he could *talk* about it with—Mike always sandwiched loaded critical terms between quotation marks. It made him feel subversive.)

The action began: a whistling loafer and a determined errand-girl (*Ginger a brunette?* Mike missed her usual blondeness) cross paths on a Greenwich Village street. On a whim, he wishes her "good luck". She thinks him fresh, but changes her mind when a customer gives her a $300 dress. Convinced that he can manipulate probabilities, she hunts him down and asks him to go halves on a sweepstakes ticket. Colman, a Bohemian artist, asks her *why* she wants the money. Reluctantly, she explains that she's engaged to be married. An "independent" woman, she won't abandon her job (and move to upstate New York) without some "insurance" in the bank. Colman disapproves, asking why he should abet a man who, after a brief ceremony, will whisk her off to Poughkeepsie—"and apparently keep her there"? She is furious, especially when he demands the privilege of taking her on a consolation "honeymoon", with his half of the proceeds, should they win; however, the entire film spools out from this zany kernel.

Mike was delighted. *Lucky Partners* was an archetypal romantic comedy. (Had he been in university, he would have written an essay on the topic). All the elements were in place: the unorthodox protagonists seeking wholeness; the non-conformist value-system; the convivial settings (Colman's garret, Rogers' second-hand 'Book Nook'); the Dickensian supporting cast (a dithering aunt, a pair of English-mangling restaurateurs named Nick and Nick, a leering hotel clerk, a nervous maid, a kindly old judge, an old couple who write fairy tales); the loutish fiancée, who represents the tyranny of the majority; and the *picaresque* adventure (which Colman dubs a "journey into the absurd"), ending in a regenerative embrace. Mike particularly enjoyed the *double-entendre* at the heart of the story: Colman literally "charms" Rogers away from a fate worse than death—marriage to Jack Carson's businessman-philistine.

The couple's relationship comes into focus, under moonbeams, on the terrace of their Niagara Falls hotel. Mike was struck, as always, by the poetic mingling of shadows and shimmer that distinguishes Studio-Age night-scenes. He watched as the pair, seeking the solitude of a garden, glided over a small bridge, and came upon a wishing-well. The scene was a silvery gloss upon reality. Later, he would try to approximate the effect by casting sidelong glances at his bathroom mirror.

The experiment only made shaving more difficult. He showered the blood off his cheeks, slipped into baggy clothes and turned off the light-switches in each room. He felt like chugging a bottle of antacid. He grabbed his keys, wallet, bus pass and book, and said goodnight to the cats. He jogged down the emergency stairs to street level, not chancing his stomach on the elevator.

The night air was pleasant enough, not too humid for September 1st in Montreal. His hair was still wet from the shower. Later, he knew, the moisture would be sweat. He decided to kill some time on Mount Royal. It was a five minute walk from Mike's apartment. He often went there, to be alone, with several hundred other Montrealers who had the same idea. He strolled up Peel street to the decaying stairway. He hopped up, two steps at a time, eager to reach a less crowded altitude. He cursed himself, when he saw a squirrel, for forgetting to bring peanuts. Not that the squirrel looked hungry. He followed a path to the chalet/observatory, then abandoned it, in favor of the woods.

He nearly tripped over a middle-aged couple, making out, beneath a young oak tree. Still listening to the score of the movie, he didn't hear the friction of their bodies. They laughed, but he didn't. The incident forced him to think about his meeting with Monica. He had never kissed anyone. Would he want to kiss her? Would he know how? He wanted to want to. He hoped he'd know how.

He perched on a flattish rock, between two lopsided pines. He listened to the sounds of engines on the street below and grackles in their nests. Suddenly, the pines turned to palms, reaching to suffocate him. Images of frozen lips and palsied tongues paraded before him. He saw himself mummified; lying eviscerated, next to a beautiful woman with flashing eyes and silken flesh. He watched her caress his tightly wrapped body, but felt nothing. *"These bandages come off,"* he tried to scream, but dried blood in his throat blocked the sound. The black sky dilated in his eyes.

He cracked open his book and tried to read *Mont Blanc*. He couldn't concentrate, so he stood up and retraced his steps back into the city. He started to jog, thinking that he might like Monica. It was possible. *Anything was possible.*

He reached the meeting-place at 10:46. He ordered a cappuccino and sat down, spreading the volume of Shelley conspicuously in front of his eyes. He read *Love's Philosophy*, a smarmy poem of seduction, and tried to imagine himself saying: "nothing in the world is single; all things by a law divine; in one spirit meet and mingle. Why not I with thine?" (He couldn't.)

A fingernail caressed the spot between his shoulder blades. Mike put down the book and turned to greet his date. She was a thin woman, about his height, with long blonde hair and a toothy smile. She wore a tight black tank-top and platform shoes. The rest of her, from her bony ankles to her boyish hips, was saran-wrapped in gaudy silver stretch-pants. Her eyes were a tired and watered-down version of the coffee in her mug.

"I've never read Shelley. Is he any good?"

"Uh, yeah," Mike replied, "he's great."

"Hmm," she mused, running her fingers along the spine of the book, then stretching them toward Mike. "Hi! I'm Monica."

"It's nice to meet you," he took her hand, "I'm, uh, Mike."

"Yes, you are," she smiled, sipping her coffee.

"So," he tried to sound interested, "what do you do, Monica?"

"Oh," she sighed, "I'm a telemarketer."

"Really?"

"Yeah, really. It sucks, I know. There's nothing to say about it…"

"Well, uh, my job's not any better. I'm a temp…"

"Oh?"

"But," he flushed, "I'm going to make movies someday."

"That's cool," she sucked her mug dry, "you wanna get out of here?"

"Um," he was puzzled, "where would we go?" His eyes pulsed hopefully: "Mount Royal?"

"Mount Royal?" she sneered. "What? So you can rip off my clothes, fuck my ass, and leave me for dead?"

"No!" he got up to leave.

"Hey," she grabbed his arm, "I was just kidding! Man, you're sensitive!" She looked at him, thoughtfully, "You didn't lie in your description. You look exactly like you said you would. You *actually* have green eyes."

"Sure," he muttered, "why would I lie?"

"I dunno, but a lot of them do. Now, you might think *I* was lying, about my eye-color, I mean; but they really do turn green—when I'm really horny."

"Uh," he blushed, "that's—uh—that's interesting…"

"You'll see," she pressed hard on his middle knuckle with a long fingernail.

"But, uh," he pulled his hand back.

"Listen Mike," she dead-panned, "I had a tough day today; I wanna get fucked tonight; I think you're cute enough…What's the problem?"

"I—I," he dropped his book on the floor, then picked it up. "I have to be home by midnight. I'm…taping a really good movie. Bye Monica."

CHAPTER 4

▼

On Sunday evening, Mike knelt next to the VCR, holding a cassette labeled "The Killers (1946)". He thrust the tape into its slot, turned up the volume, and sagged horizontally. The melodramatic score filled his ears. Another studio globe—this time accompanied by "Universal International," scrawled in white—spun into view, then blacked out. Hard faces looked out from the dark screen. Mike gritted his teeth and stared back.

He watched two gunmen walk into a cozy lunch stand and riddle the place with tough banter. They order dinner, insult the owner, then pull out their guns and wait for their quarry: the Swede. The execution stalls. The condemned man never shows up. Then the camera finds Burt Lancaster, lying in a murky rented cell and moaning: "I did something wrong, once." The gunmen aren't far behind. They light up the room with murderous torches, leaving a mangled Swede on his cot. An insurance investigator named Riordan inherits the case and starts hunting for pieces to puzzle over.

Mike loved the flashback technique. He loved the fractured narrative of film noir. He identified with the Swede, a nice boxer with a busted fist who drifts into bad company. Mike felt like he had been born injured.

Like any good film noir, *The Killers* had a *femme fatale*: Kitty Collins. From the swamp of Swede's wasted life, Riordan dredges up the wreck of a recollection: a party at a big-time gangster's apartment, soft music rising from a grand piano, and a torch-song gurgling from the porcelain volcano of Ava Gardner's body. Mike joined the Swede in admiring her. Her eyes were green in black-and-white. Dark waves of hair lapped at her bare shoulders. The wry corners of her smile rested on plush cheeks. But there was nothing tender about her. She was a boxing glove: luxurious material wrapped around a clench-fisted soul. Her love-taps dazed the Swede, laying him out on the mat: a welcome target for the killers of the opening scene. Mike wondered how far he'd stick out his own chin, for the privilege of being slugged so silkily. He thought he would rather be preyed upon than ignored. He didn't see any other options. If the film was right—if everyone *was* wearing a mask—they weren't doing it for his benefit. He was just a kibitzer. He had nothing to ante, nothing to be suckered out of. At least, nothing that showed.

Whenever Mike despaired of finding a silvery Eden, he settled for a gray Hell, lit up by deceit. He longed for some treacherous con to make a play for his soul. The encounter with Monica didn't count. She wasn't evil. Just bored. And lonely. Even more pathetic than he was. It had been no trick to resist what passed for her charms.

Mike projected himself onto the screen and drew strength from the exercise. He patted himself on the back for resisting Ava Gardner's eyes. He got better at it with every scene. Of course, he couldn't smell her skin. That made it easier.

The film's ironic ending undercuts Riordan's tense inquiry. He straightens out a very twisted plot; exposes a whole gang of cynical masqueraders (including Kitty), and recovers the quarter of a million dollars they stole, with only a few dim memories to guide him. Back at the insurance company, his boss notes: "Congratulations! Due to your efforts, next years' premiums will probably drop one-tenth of a cent."

Refreshed, Mike listened to the tape rewind. Film noir always brightened his mood. He tossed "The Essential Glenn Miller" on the CD player and pondered his next move. He was whistling the "Song of the Volga Boatmen" when he heard a knock at his door. He bounced out of the room to greet Diane.

He found her fiddling with hangers in the living-room cupboard. Her long black hair was brushed out. She was wearing a pair of dark slacks and her favourite sweater: a crisp nightshade vee-neck. Her limbs moved happily.

"Jacket-weather?" he asked.

"Uh-huh," she turned, smiling at him, "you haven't been out yet, have you?"

"No," he sighed. "Only got up a couple of hours ago…"

"Unbelievable," she shrugged, grabbing the remote and pressing 'power.'

"What's unbelievable?" boomed a voice, chugging down the hallway from the bathroom.

"Nothing sweetie," she murmured.

"Hey!" Diane's boyfriend burst into the living room, ready to throttle Mike's hand with his gold-encrusted fingers. Vito's large frame bristled with sharp attributes. His dark blue blazer complemented a white shirt and a black tie covered with blue triangles. There was stuff in his hair to make it look alive. His big teeth had a predatory friendliness that brought out the rabbit in Mike. "That's pretty cool," he bobbed his head in time with "Tuxedo Junction", which pulsed behind Mike's door. "Bet you dance around a lot, when you're alone."

"No," Mike replied, pulling out of Vito's metallic grip, "I just listen."

"Your brother's funny," Vito smiled, nestling with Diane on the blue couch. His large brown eyes flooded with dew whenever he looked at her. Their relationship made no sense to Mike. He couldn't picture his sister with an auditor, fresh from the Commerce department. Still, it was clear that Vito loved Diane, and that she was comfortable with him.

"What did you guys do this weekend?" Mike asked, half-interested.

"Hmm?" Diane was preoccupied. "Oh, we went to the casino yesterday…"

"It was great," Vito added. "You should come with us some time, Mike."

"Did you win anything?" Mike directed his question at Diane, but Vito was the only one listening.

"Did we win anything, babe?" he took the remote away from her.

"We broke even."

"Yeah. I ran our winnings up to a thou, and then your sister lost the pile at the roulette table," Vito snickered.

"Really?" Mike was intrigued. "Are you developing a gambling problem Di?"

"Hey! The only gambling problem is a losing streak," Vito grinned at Diane. "There's nothin' on TV babe…You wanna watch a movie, Mike? We rented *Scent of a Woman*."

Mike started to decline the invitation.

"You're wasting your breath, Vee," Diane warned, playfully grasping for the remote. "Michael only likes black-and-whites."

"That's not true," Mike shook his head. "Just because I have standards…"

"What's your standard?" Diane asked. "The older the better?"

"I'm not going to argue," he sighed. "I guess you like watching middle-aged hams yell at people. I don't."

"Hey!" Vito joined the conversation. "You callin' Pacino a ham?"

"Mm-hmm," Mike nodded. "I swear to God, I don't know how his eyeballs stay in his head."

"Fair enough," Vito got up to put the tape in Diane's high-tech VCR. "You don't mind if *we* watch it?"

"Of course not."

"You're strange Michael," Diane made a face at him.

"I think he's funny," Vito chuckled, from the other side of the room.

"Don't press play yet, Vee," she ordered, then turned back to her brother: "Any messages?"

"Couple on the machine."

"What did you do this weekend?"

"Oh," he yawned, "not much. Went to 'The Bell Jar' on Friday. Watched a lot of movies. *Black-and-white ones!*"

"Big surprise," she rose to give him a hug. "I missed you."

"Me too Di," he smiled. "Good night guys."

"G'night," Vito pressed play and turned out the lights.

Mike grabbed Marbles and wandered back to his bedroom. The CD had reached "Elmer's Tune". He sank into his mattress and picked up the phone.

CHAPTER 5

▼

"Hello?" Eric sounded out of breath.

"Oh," Mike choked on a mouthful of Ovaltine. "I was expecting the answering machine."

"You almost got it. It picks up on the fourth ring…I was getting my books in order…Man! Moving out was a great idea Mike!"

"Guess so," Mike drained his mug and placed it on a cardboard box. He was propped up against a pillow on his wall. Both cats were somewhere deep in his sleeping bag, which was zippered to his throat. It was a cold night. Big crisp drops of rain that was almost sleet splashed against Mike's window.

"What's up?" Eric yawned. "I called you earlier."

"I know. I was out. I had dinner with a girl named Susan…"

"Really?"

"Yeah. It was weird. I met her at Berri metro, and we went to Da Giovanni's. You know: the place with the great sauce and the geriatric waitresses…"

"Uh-huh."

"Well. We sat down. I ordered gnocchi with tomato sauce. She ordered spaghetti with Caruso sauce. Anyway, while we were waiting for the food, she asked what I did. I wasn't particularly interested in discussing the life of a temp, so I told her what I *want* to do. Make movies. She listened with a smile (it was a nice smile). Until she realized that I wasn't talking about documentary film. That's the only kind

of movie she likes. She said: 'Why would you want to make things up?'
Just like that. As if the imagination was a cancerous growth. She's in
her last year of pure-and-applied at Marianopolis. She wants to do
medical research. Apparently, that's the only way for a person to serve
humanity. That and making documentary film. She explained it to me:
'The real world is so fascinating Mike. You should make reality your
subject.' I started to say that I don't have any idea what *reality* is, so I
wouldn't know where to point the camera. But I decided it wasn't
worth it, and asked her what her favorite documentary was. (I've seen a
few.) You know what she said?"

"What?"

"*Unsolved Mysteries*, with Robert Stack."

. "What!?"

"Yeah. I said: '*That's* reality?' She said: 'Sure. What's more real than
death?' I wasn't prepared for that. Her getting philosophical about
Robert Stack, I mean. Our food arrived. I took a tangy bite and told
her: 'You can't mix Robert Stack and existential angst, it doesn't work.'
She was offended. I quickly realized that she has some kind of crush on
the old guy. I wanted to make sure. I said: 'What's with you and Robert Stack?' 'I think he's sexy,' she admitted. 'You know, he's almost
eighty,' I informed her. You should've seen her face. She was livid. Her
idol, a doddering octogenarian? 'You're *lying*!' she almost yelled. I
couldn't help myself. I said: 'Uh-uh. I'm telling you: He gave Deanna
Durban her first screen kiss. In *1939*! He's an old man!' We didn't talk
much after that. I asked her about Marianopolis, but she just grumbled
and ate faster. We finished our food and walked to the metro. She took
the orange line. I took the green. I guess I'll never see *her* again."

"Forget that! Where the hell did she come from Mike? You've never
been on a *date*!"

Mike was impressed by his friend's restraint.

"Oh, I met her on 'Dial-A-M8'."

"The telephone date thing?"

"Uh-huh."

"How long have you been using *that*?"

"About a week."

"That's incredible…Is she the first person you've met?"

"No. The fourth."

"And you didn't mention it 'till now? It must be going badly."

"Uh-huh."

"Still," Eric mused, "I'm impressed, Mike. It's proactive. You're usually so passive. You have to challenge the world. Make an effort to get the things you want. This is a positive change. I really didn't expect it…"

"I'm a surprising guy," Mike chuckled. "But I don't think 'Dial-A-M8' is gonna work out."

"Why not?"

"Because the other dates were even more awkward than the one I just told you about…"

"So what? Don't do this thing half-assed Mike. You've got to keep at it."

"Why?"

"I know you, man. You don't ask for advice. You've already made up your mind. My arguments aren't going to influence you. Besides, I'm sure you could've guessed what I would say. So just tell me. Are you giving up already?"

"I'm really not sure. This is the most confusing thing that's ever happened to me. I mean: the idea is so tempting. I get so riled up thinking about the possibilities. But it falls apart when I meet them. I don't even feel anxious. Just numb. I don't know if it's me or her or the situation."

"Or some combination of all three?"

"Probably," Mike agreed.

"Tell me more about the others. It's interesting."

"Hmm. Well, the first one was just ridiculous. I hope she was kidding, but I get the feeling she wasn't. She asked me to have sex with her before I'd finished my coffee…"

"What?"

"Yeah."

"What did you do?"

"I—uh—kind of ran away."

"Hmm. Well. Whatever. And the other two?"

"Uh. Well, I met a girl named Shauna on Monday."

"What was she like?"

"Physically?"

"In general."

"There was nothing wrong with her. She's studying Early Child-hood Education. She's cute. She has curly black hair, nice brown eyes, and chipmunk cheeks. No makeup. That's always a plus. We planned a picnic at Mount Royal. It was cloudy, but it didn't rain. It was humid though. I was sweating a lot by the time we got to the Cross. She must've been worse. She had on a lot more clothes than I did. And some really hard-core leather boots. I talked more to the squirrels than to Shauna on the way up. I don't know what the problem was. We had spoken on the phone that morning, and I had enjoyed it. But my enthusiasm dried up as soon as I met her. It happened with the first girl too, but Shauna really *was* attractive. Maybe I can't be romantic unless I'm alone…"

"Did she seem interested in you?"

"Not particularly. Although I'm not sure if I could tell…"

"Hmm. So, you had the picnic and came home?"

"No. We made an evening of it. We walked around downtown, ate at the 49¢ pizza place and then went to Hurley's. She had a few pints of Guiness. I had two coffees. We talked mostly about how humid it was; how much we both liked autumn; and how nice Mount Royal was. It was basically the same conversation we had had on the phone, but it wasn't fun the second time around. Neither of us seemed able to pull the plug. I even walked her home, around one in the morning. We did the two-cheek kiss thing. I have her number. She's got mine. We haven't spoken since…Have you ever had a date like that?"

"Not exactly," Eric replied, "but there have been times when I've forced something that wasn't really there. At least you showed restraint."

"Restraint? I guess you could say that. If you were determined to be kind. And you are. But restraint implies a struggle of some sort."

"So there was no chemistry. That happens. How about the third date?"

"It was pretty lame too. But not as long. We had dinner at Da Giovanni's last night. Her name was Patricia. She's in the journalism program at Concordia. I was anxious to meet her. But it was the same old story. She had sharp features—which you know I'm not partial to—and her eyes were a little too steely for me, but I suppose she was good-looking. She had the syllabus from her Wednesday class with her and she paid more attention to it than to me. She wasn't easy to talk to. Not that I tried very hard. I don't know whether she was bored or nervous or just neurotic, but at one point she started sliding pieces of napkin under the lids of the hot pepper and parmesan shakers. Her idea of a joke. She smiled strangely and said: 'I always do this at restaurants, don't you.' I just shook my head. I really didn't care what she did. When she went to the washroom, I unscrewed the lids and pocketed the napkin bits. Then I paid my bill and walked out."

"Wow," Eric whistled, "maybe you're right in giving up on this thing."

"I didn't say I had."

"That's true. You didn't."

"I'll probably try again this weekend."

"Oh…You know, I'm starting to think this wasn't much of a departure for you."

"You noticed that too, huh?"

CHAPTER 6

▼

The alarm bored into Mike's eight-AM funk like a crew of termites with a deadline. He felt like a piece of driftwood. Not a very buoyant piece. It was Friday morning. A phonebook-sized pile of general ledger entries awaited him, next to a gray keyboard and a gray terminal with gray icons on it, at the "MarcoSport" Head Office. It was a typical work-day. Mike had only gotten three hours of sleep and his fatigue carried him along, past the brink of lateness. The alarm sounded like the score of *Psycho*. Some mornings, Mike would have rather gone under the knife than the shower.

He switched the alarm off, got into his housecoat, and tried to rinse the red from his eyes. It was there to stay. He listened to the weather and the sports and the news on the radio and decided, since he was late anyway, to play just *one* song from the *Showboat* soundtrack ("Ol' Man River" by Paul Robeson). He listened to it twice.

At the metro-station dépanneur, he bought a maple muffin. The clock, which jutted out at a right-angle over the platform, said 8:52. Mike found a comfortable spot on the wall next to a billboard that announced an upcoming Céline Dion concert. Céline looked like a hatrack with a jack-in-the box head and a brown Ronald McDonald wig. He finished his muffin before the blue-and-white metal worm slithered into view. He tossed the sticky paper packaging into the garbage just as the doors slid open.

Once the ride began, he focused on avoiding the sleepy elbows aimed directly at his head. It wasn't easy. Somehow, the track had bumps in it. He could feel the muffin decomposing in his stomach, and his brain needed soaking in coffee. A woman with overcast blue eyes and frizzy brown hair kept scraping Mike's knuckle with her ring as she wrestled with a black knapsack strap that kept slipping off her shoulder. Each time, he smiled chivalrously at her; just to show her he could spare the skin.

He transferred to the orange line at Berri. There was no place for him to anchor himself on the sweat-stained poles of the car. He tried to keep steady by suctioning his palms to the glass panes of the door. He was pressed up so close that he could see the reflection of the window in the reflection of his eyes. He glanced down at his favorite metro sign. It read: "*Attention aux portes/* Watch the doors." Mike had a weakness for inept translations. This one paled in comparison to the package of rice noodles from Chinatown that proclaimed itself "good for dinner, or as a gift"; but it amused him, nonetheless.

He stumbled out at Cremazie and followed the beaten path to the escalator. On the foggy street above, he squeezed into another blue and white receptacle, the 146 bus. His stomach roiled some more as the bus driver handled sharp turns like a Nintendo player and nailed every pothole in his path.

Mike got off at De Louvain street, the heart of the garment district—a ten-block warehouse. He wouldn't see a patch of grass again until six o'clock that night. He kicked a rock along the sidewalk as he walked; until he lost the rock in a sewer grate. He frowned and moved on. He strolled into the "MarcoSport" building at 9:20. The receptionist, Marie, good-naturedly tapped the face of her watch and blinked her concern.

"Got up late," he mumbled, and headed for the cafeteria. He liked Marie, but he had liked her predecessor, Karine, even more. She had accomplished the feat of looking beautiful in a clunky head-set. It was the hair, he decided. Marie's intricate red curls just didn't hold up under the strain as well as Karine's straight, chestnut waves. Unfortunately, Karine had recently joined the army.

There was a line-up at the coffee trough. Mike grabbed a mug and joined the procession. The billing girls—Marie-France, Emilie, and Nancy—were trying to guess which employee would get pregnant next. Nancy indicated her willingness to hear his thoughts on the subject, with a thin smile. He shrugged. All he knew was that the baby wouldn't be his. He studied the bottom of his empty mug and the brick wall in front of the cafeteria window, while he waited his turn.

Finally, he reached the machine, pulled the lever, and caught the brown shower in his cracked porcelain cistern. The coffee at "MarcoSport" tasted like bilgewater strained through cat litter, but Mike couldn't work without it. Taking his first sip as he wandered toward the accounting department, he swore he would get up early enough to make his own coffee next time. He had made the same vow every work-morning for a year.

He perched on his swivel-chair and switched on his computer. Blurry numbers in the lower right-hand corner of the screen said it was 9:30. On the radio, Barry Manilow crooned "Mandy." All around the room—which held twelve people and their electronic life-support—phones rang, heads bobbed and fingers flew. Mike cracked his knuckles and ran his thumb up and down a four-inch thick block of computer paper: the record of general ledger transactions for Period 8, 1993. All the data had to be entered by 5:00 PM, or the accounting department would self-destruct. No one had ever explained to him why things had to be done this way. He took a deep breath and placed his ruler under line one of page one. He looked for a pencil. There were several on Tanya's desk, next to his. She was on the phone with her mother, so he just took one. He started typing.

A strong gust of perfume and a tap on his shoulder stopped his fingers. It was Nathalie, his boss. "Salut Mike. Un peu en retard n'est-ce pas?" she asked in her most subtly reproachful tone. It was supposed to make him feel bad for forcing her to exercise her authority. It almost worked.

"J'l'sais. J'm'excuse," he replied, hiding as much of his face as he could with his mug.

"It iz not good, Mike," she switched to English. She only did that when she was really disappointed in him.

"I know."

"You are going to try 'arder?" She smiled. Her mouth and cheeks were so taut that Mike often wondered if she had had her face lifted. But she was only twenty-six. Her blue eyes keyed up a notch. She had the accountant's habit of always conserving as much of her energy as possible. The only time they lit up to their full capacity was when the auditors descended upon the building. "You know I tink you are a good worker."

"I know," he smiled back. He liked her. She was nicer to him than was really necessary, from an office-efficiency point-of-view. It wasn't her fault that he wanted to make movies. "I'll get it done."

"Vas-y," she patted him on the back and returned to her sanctum, a large glass-walled office just beyond Tanya's station.

He resumed typing. Mariah Carey had taken over on the radio. He blocked the squealing out and settled into a groove. Tanya said good-bye to her mother and called another number.

"Hey babe," she spoke into the receiver, "ma wants us for dinner on Sunday."

She listened for half a minute. She didn't look happy. She coiled the phone wire around red fingernails and blinked quizzically at her computer. Her screen-saver was an irritating kaleidoscope of bouncing chimpanzees. Mike shook his head at it.

"You think it's dumb?" she asked him, then spoke into the phone: "no babe, I was talking to Mike."

"It's pretty bad," he answered.

She held up her hand to stop him and mumbled a few "uh-huhs" to her husband. Then she smiled and said: "Okay babe. It'll be fine. I'll just tell her to have the food ready an hour earlier. Okay. Love ya. Bye."

She hung up the phone and looked at Mike. "Sorry Mike, just had to get that straightened out..."

"That's alright."

She pressed on her mouse to banish the chimpanzees and swivelled excitedly. "He's taking me to a show on Sunday night! He was hoping to surprise me, but my mother's dinner invitation forced him into the open."

"That's great," Mike replied, flipping a page over.

"Yeah. You think I should get my hair done?"

"I don't know." He looked at her brown ringlets. Her hair already looked "done". "I guess you should—if you want to—but it looks fine..."

"You're sweet Mike."

"Yeah?" He blushed. "Uh, what's the show?"

"He didn't say, but I guess it's *Phantom*."

"Oh," he choked back the special bile he reserved for Andrew Lloyd Webber, "cool."

"Uh-hunh," she opened up a Word file and assumed a professional air. "I've got a great husband."

Mike finished another page and got up to get another coffee. He came back with it and buzz-sawed through fifty more pages before lunch at 12:30.

He burrowed into a corner of the cafeteria, with a spinach-and-tomato-on-rye sandwich and a copy of *Wuthering Heights*. He concentrated, but the hum of three microwaves and the constant ringing of the phone limited reading comprehension. There were seven tables in the room. At each one, a different television show dominated the conversation. Mike sat at the *Beverly Hills 90210* table. (With Marie-France, Emilie, Nancy, Tanya, and another girl that he didn't know by name.) He was comfortable among them. They got such pleasure out of debating who was in love with who, and who was too old to be playing a teenager, that Mike had been forced to abandon his belief that they were wasting their time. Still, he felt no urge to join in.

"I thought you were reading Shelley?" Nancy asked him.

He looked up: "That was last week."

"How often do you work anyway Mike?"

"A couple of days a week, usually."

"Why?"

He shrugged.

Tanya said: "Nancy, the real question is: why are the rest of us here every day?"

"Is that what you think Mike?" Nancy demanded. "That we're all just a bunch of office zombies?"

"We are," Tanya replied firmly.

"Hmmph!" Nancy was miffed.

"Don't get mad at *me* Nancy," Mike pleaded. "I-I admit that I couldn't do this every day. But that doesn't mean I'm laughing at people who do…A-are you happy?"

"Sure I am."

"Then…you shouldn't worry about what Tanya thinks I think," he shot Tanya a mock-glare.

She was smirking behind a spoonful of light yogurt. She swallowed it and tossed the container into the garbage, along with the plastic spoon. "You're funny Mike."

Nancy decided to change the subject: "What's *Wuthering Heights* about? I've heard of it, of course, but…"

Mike smiled: "I'm not sure what it's about. But I know that Dylan's all *wrong* for Kelly…"

Everyone laughed. Everyone agreed that Mike was very funny. Then they resumed discussing the show. He got up to use the phone. He called 'Dial-A-M8' to check his messages. There were no interesting ones. Just a lonely middle-aged woman, a lonelier middle-aged couple, and another girl who liked to "party".

He went back to his desk at 1:30. The data-weed had grown in his absence. He attacked it; gave himself up to the process. He set little challenges for himself. How many lines could he enter in a minute? Could he type accurately without looking at the screen?

The pile expired too early—four o'clock. Mike scanned the room. Nathalie looked like she was getting ready to ask him to do some filing. He got up and went to the washroom.

He stood in the little windowless box and stared at himself in the mirror. Invoice numbers and tax codes blocked his view. He unleashed a flood of cold water from the tap and pressed his face into cupped palms. When he looked up again his cheeks had a blue tinge. His pen had burst and there was ink on his hands. He preened for ten minutes; just trying to get back to the dubious condition he had woken up in.

By the time he got back to his desk, the accountants were in an analytical blood-frenzy. They attacked the numbers he had entered from every conceivable angle. Nathalie walked up to him and said: "Bien fait, Mike. Mais on a pu de travail pour vous aujourd'hui."

He smiled. He loved being dismissed early. He grabbed his book. "C'est correct."

"I know," she replied. "But I must first sign your time-sheet."

"Oh yeah." He produced it. She reached over his shoulder and scrawled something illegible on the paper. Her perfume was still too strong. The computer-clock read 4:25 just before he switched it off.

He didn't bother saying good-bye to anyone, except for the receptionist. They were too busy. He thought about his quiet room and re-reading the first few chapters of *Wuthering Heights*. He was feeling a little better when the 146 splashed mud on an elm in front of the metro station.

CHAPTER 7

▼

Mike was a hundred pages deep in the book when the doorbell rang. He had been considering quoting from Brontë on 'Dial-A-M8', but he feared it would only provoke snickering. He prayed that love was as intense as the novel made out. He doubted that it could ever become so dark. Where was the line between love and hate in Brontë? Mike added it himself, commenting on the implausibility of the Cathy-Heathcliff relationship, in the margins.

He folded the book over his index finger and walked to the door. He opened it and found Eric in the corridor, holding a six-pack of Sleeman's. Eric followed Mike into the living-room, placed the yellow box on the coffee-table, pulled out a beer, and twisted the cap off. He took a swig and smiled: "So Mike, you met any interesting strangers since we spoke?"

"I worked all day."

"Why don't you hook up with a girl from the office?" Eric asked, dropping onto the blue couch.

Mike shrugged. "They wouldn't have anything to do with me. They think I'm sweet."

"I see. And you're just dying to date a secretary, aren't you?"

"What?"

"You're a snob, Mike. Admit it."

"I'm too pathetic to be a snob."

"Everyone's pathetic Mike. But some people are desperate. You're not desperate. You're holding out for something. If a girl at the office took a shine to you, you'd find a way to squirm out of it…"

"What are you talking about?"

"Don't worry. Keep up this 'pathetic' thing. It's great…Whacha reading?"

"*Wuthering Heights.*"

"Perfect."

"Are you gonna be the Riddler all night?" Mike sat on the other side of the couch, next to Marbles, who started purring.

"No. I'll be more direct if you like. This 'Dial-A-M8' thing, and our talk last week…"

"You *remember* that?" Mike interrupted.

"Perfectly."

"Oh."

"Anyway. I've been thinking. This nineteen-year old virgin act is getting stale man. There's no earthly reason why you shouldn't be getting laid. You discourage it."

"Why would I do that? Don't you think I'm interested in sex?"

"Sure. But only with—what's her name? Gwendolyn? And even there, all you did was kiss her, right?"

Mike blushed, then gritted his teeth. "Maybe you'd be happy to know I had an orgasm."

"Only you could make a virtue of prematurely ejaculating in a dream."

"You know, it *is* possible to hurt my feelings."

"Actually," Eric leaned forward, "it isn't. You're so convinced that you're one of God's little cherubs that nothing gets to you. You're the teflon angel."

Mike shrugged: "Hmmph."

"Mike, it's tough having a best friend that forgets to be human."

Mike got up and stared out of the window. A seagull with a french-fry in its beak flew by. "Why do you think I decided to try 'Dial-A-M8'? Isn't that human enough?"

"It won't work. You said it yourself. You've just brought the act on a road trip."

Mike sat back down. "Believe me Eric, I'm tired of the act too. But the problem is: it's not an act. And I *can't* act until I have feelings to act upon. You wouldn't believe how worked up I get, worrying that I don't get worked up about anything..."

"Now who's playing word-games..."

"If I am, it's because this is too serious *not* to joke about. I don't *discourage* women. I just don't know how to *en*courage them."

"I think it just happens..."

"Me too," Mike nodded, "but it never happens to me. I can't even encourage myself, outside of my room..."

"I'm not surprised. Considering the people you meet. Why the fuck aren't you in school Mike? That's where the inspiration is. And I'm not just talking about the women."

"Yeah?"

"I'm serious." Eric opened another beer. "You've gotta at least start sitting in on my classes, on your days off. They're incredible!"

"Tell me about them."

"I'm taking this course on Greek philosophy. The syllabus'd blow your mind man. We're covering everything. And the professor seems like someone I could really learn from. We've only had one class, but everyone was mesmerized, just by his introductory remarks. He could be a demagogue, man. It's a lucky thing he decided to teach philosophy instead..."

"Sounds cool."

"It is. But there *are* some things that are going to be hard to take."

"Like what?"

"Oh...The pretentiousness. The ivory-tower do-gooderism. Activist *chic*. I hung out with a bunch of environmentalist types today. They have a little space all of their own, paid for by the University, where they can gather and feel pure. I've never seen so many piercings in one room in my life. Why is that radical, exactly? Anyway, they all seemed pretty sure about the root of all the world's problems. It's The Man. The Establishment. Get rid of it man. Then everyone would settle down for a good old-fashioned snuggle-fest. Just like in pre-historic times..."

"Sounds a little naive."

"I haven't even told you the worst part."

"What's that?"

"Almost all of them were part-timers, registered for one class. *One* class! And they probably won't even go to that one. It's just a formality. The University is part of The Establishment. The written word is a tool of the patriarchy. Every sign in the room had spelling mistakes. And my ham sandwich went over really badly..."

Mike wagged a finger: "What'd you expect?"

"A dialogue," Eric replied.

"How can you have a dialogue about vegetarianism? Either you think it's the right thing or you don't."

"And why do *you* remain friends with me?"

"Because I like you, and I've got better things to worry about than whether you're going to Hell. Besides, the meat is already dead. But don't ever try to shoot a duck in front of me. You'll find out how strong my convictions are..."

"Interesting...That's not what I expected you to say...Anyway, you'd hate these people Mike..."

"I don't *hate* anyone. I only hate bad ideas..."

"Then you'd hate their ideas...They consider pet-ownership an affront to Mother Nature."

"Maybe we should commit species suicide."

"That's where their logic leads...Man! I wish you were at school with me Mike! Why the fuck aren't you?"

A key turned in the lock and Diane walked through the door. On a Friday night. Mike couldn't remember the last time that had happened. She had on a simple black dress and black heels. "Hello boys. How are you Eric?" she asked, removing her shoes and placing them carefully on the closet floor.

Eric winked at Mike and replied: "Fine. You still working for The Man?"

"Uh-huh," she closed the closet and folded her arms across her chest, "you still plotting The Revolution?"

"Only if I can make you my puppet monarch."

She shot him a silent raspberry and wandered down the hallway to the kitchen.

"Why are you home Di?" Mike called to her. "You're forty-eight hours early."

Diane returned with a glass of water. She said: "My brother thinks I'm an automaton, just because my life is in order…"

Eric patted the middle cushion of the couch. "I hate to interrupt, but you're neglecting the beer…"

"Yeah," she nodded, "I saw it. I guess I'll have one. I only had two glasses of wine at the restaurant." She walked over, sat between them, and pulled a bottle out of the box.

"Where's Vito?" Mike nudged her shoulder.

"On a plane to Toronto. I just saw him off. We had dinner. It's an important trip. There may be a promotion in it."

"Great," Eric twirled a finger in the air.

She ignored the comment. "So I came home to spend some quality time with my brother. I figured we'd watch a movie or two…When's *he* leaving?" She pointed at Eric.

"I just got here," Eric settled back on the couch.

"Why aren't you out with Wendy? It's Friday night."

"Didn't Mike tell you? Wendy and I broke up."

"Actually," Mike added, "*he* broke up with Wendy."

Diane frowned. "That's too bad. I liked her."

"Me too," Mike said.

"That makes three of us," Eric sighed, "but it just didn't work out, y'know."

"He needs time to read Plato," Mike explained.

"Fuck you, you little bitch," Eric glared at him. "Bottom line: Wendy is still the perfect girlfriend for a fifteen year-old boy. All she wants to do is go out, gossip, and plan future weddings..."

"Whereas you need to talk about philosophy?" Diane inferred.

"Among other things. I need to be stimulated..."

"Wendy's smart," Mike asserted.

"Sure. But she doesn't like to *think*."

"Well," Diane mused, "Vito's not exactly a thinker, but we manage to have a good time..."

"Yeah?" Eric shrugged. He scanned the living-room wall. The winter landscapes all had little DB's in their corners. Once, Eric had tried to explain his fascination with them to Mike. They were bleak. There were no people in them. No animals. Just snow, bare trees, and rocks. But there was something about that snow, those trees, those rocks, that made them seem like more than just building blocks for a void. The tree-roots bulged up in defiant white humps. The rocks were a reddish-brown colour that made him think of lava. Diane's dead world was strangely alive. "I love your work Di. When's the last time you did one? These all look pretty familiar..."

"Very subtle," she shook her head.

"What?"

"It's not Vito."

"Hunh?"

"He isn't the reason I quit painting."

"Oh."

"Maybe I've said everything I needed to say."

"Or maybe not."

"Maybe. I'm not dead yet." She smiled. Mike thought it was a strange smile, for Diane. The corners of her mouth weren't sharp and her lips hesitated too long before unveiling her big white teeth. He stroked Marbles's ears and thought about his own creative project, a half-finished screenplay lying fallow on his bedroom floor. "Anyway," Diane resumed, "Vito and I have a good time. And I *like* managing the café."

"Mm-hmm," Eric snickered, "it really allows you to develop those skills you learned in art school..."

"Actually, it does," Diane snapped. "The owner let me redesign the whole place...Stop looking at other people's lives through the lens of your ambition, Eric. It's a bad habit..."

Eric bit his tongue. "The plants are doing great." He pointed at a pair of geraniums hanging from the ceiling in front of the largest window of the living-room.

She nodded. "There are a lot more in the kitchen. But they get pissed on sometimes..."

She frowned at Marbles.

"Fuckin' cats," Eric shook his head.

Mike covered Marbles's ears and pleaded: "He's no different from the rest of us. He wants a nice fresh plot of earth to call his own..."

"Well he's invading *my* earth," Diane waggled her finger. "Next time he might step on a land mine."

"Hey," Mike soothed, "he's not destroying your winter grain stores. It's just a plant."

"Plants animate a house," Eric declared. "And they do it without messing up your stuff while you're out, or ruining your clothes." He plucked beige fur off his dark blue sweater.

"But they don't snuggle with you at night," Mike parried.

"Mm," Diane shrugged. "Is that a bad thing?"

"Yeah," Eric agreed. "Animals are needy. They just keep me awake...Plants are different. You set them up with dirt and sun and water and they do the rest. I think I'll get some geraniums for my new place..."

"Hey!" Diane exclaimed, "you just moved, didn't you?"

"Uh-huh."

"How come Mike didn't help out?"

Eric shrugged. "*Look* at him."

Mike cupped his heart in his palm. "You never asked me."

"You never offered."

"No. I had other things to do. And I know you know stronger people than me…"

"Great friend…What was so important?" Diane asked.

Mike was in no mood to bring up 'Dial-A-M8'. "My screenplay," he replied.

"Oh," she muttered, "*that*. How long have you been working on it?"

"It *has* been a long time, hasn't it?" Eric concurred. "And you never talk about it in detail. You just say you're really excited and I'll see it when it's done."

"What *is* it about, Michael?" Diane poked him.

"If you really want me to, I'll summarize the plot for you guys. But I warn you: it's not the kind of thing that will appeal to either of you…"

"Why's that?" Diane smirked. "Because it isn't any good?"

"Because it's hopeful," Mike replied.

"Just tell us about it," Eric urged. "You can't play the misunderstood artist until you've produced something."

"Alright," Mike sighed. "Well, it's called *A Matter of Time*. It's a time-travel story cast in the form of a romantic-comedy. It's about a shy young dépanneur clerk who stumbles through a strange portal into the past and finds himself in 1930's New York…"

"A strange portal?" Eric crinkled his forehead. "Where does it come from?"

"I don't know. It's not important. Anyway. So he's in Depression-era New York, and—I think this is a new wrinkle—he's *really* happy to be there. It turns out he's an aficionado of studio-age movies, and he welcomes the opportunity to see them in the theatre. Plus there's absolutely nothing he'll miss about his life in the nineties. The first thing he does is sell his digital watch to a credulous pawn-broker for a lot of money. Then he goes to the movies…It's October 1936, so I think he'll go see *Mr. Deeds Goes to Town, The Petrified Forest, Swing Time, Libeled Lady,* and *Fury;* but I have to check the release dates for those.

"Then he gets himself a room at a boarding-house in Greenwich Village and goes to eat at a local tavern. A huge fight starts somehow, and he meets a beautiful blonde waitress while hiding under a table waiting for the violence to die down. He tries to strike up a conversation. She stops him cold. He is undaunted, for the first time in his life."

"Encouraged?" Eric asked.

"Uh-hunh," Mike nodded.

Diane looked confused. "What's that? A code?"

Mike continued: "So. He secures a job at the tavern as a bus-boy and keeps working on getting to know her. One day, he finds her reciting lines from *The Petrified Forest* in the cellar. It turns out she's an actress, and has an audition that night. The hero knows the dialogue, and cues her from the stairs. She softens toward him. She agrees to have dinner with him after the audition. She doesn't get the part, but he buys her a phonograph and a record with songs from *Swing Time.* He sings along with "The Way You Look Tonight" and they dance around her living-room. A wonderful romance ensues…The only problem is, at some point, he starts to get pulled back to his own time. There is some plotty nonsense I have to work out, which involves magical antiques and mediums, but the upshot is: someone has to go in his place. Conveniently, a no-nonsense older waitress at the tavern—I think I'll call her Diane—makes the sacrifice. She's a lesbian, and will be much happier in today's more liberated climate. So everyone gets what they want…"

"That's," Diane hesitated, "quite something Michael…"

"It's a romantic-comedy," he countered pugnaciously.

"Hmm," she looked at her watch, "it's midnight. I have to call the store. Make sure they closed properly."

She walked down the hall to her room.

"What do *you* think Eric?" Mike asked.

"I think people might like it. This *is* the post-modern era. It's all movie-references…"

"Yeah, but?"

"Well," Eric shook his head, "I have to say: I expect more from someone of your intelligence, Mike. You treat joy like it's something you found on an archeological dig."

"There's too much sediment on my sentiment?" Mike grinned.

"Yeah," Eric chuckled, "that's it."

"Maybe you're right," Mike nodded. "But what can I do?"

CHAPTER 8

▼

The telephone rang. Mike rushed for it. After nearly two months of waiting in his 'Dial-A-M8' box, he had changed his strategy. Now he sifted through the new ads daily and left his phone number with every woman who sounded remotely interesting.

"Hello?" He answered hopefully.

"Hey. What's up?"

It was Eric.

"Not much," Mike replied. "Trying to decide what to do tonight."

"Aren't you coming to Derek's party?"

"I don't know…A Hallowe'en party?"

"What do you mean: *a Hallowe'en party?* You act like there's something strange about that…"

"I just can't really picture myself there."

"Well," Eric sighed, "try harder. It starts at nine. You know where Derek lives?"

"Yeah."

"I'll see you there?"

"Oh, probably."

"Good." Eric hung up.

Mike put down the receiver. He had been planning to watch a movie—*Arsenic and Old Lace*, or *Meet Me in St. Louis*, just to acknowledge the thirty-first of October—but now he wasn't sure. He didn't *want* to go to the party, but he felt like he ought to get away from the phone. It was seven o'clock, so he had two hours to decide. Derek's place was only a few blocks away.

He wandered out of his room, headed for the shower. Diane had her coat on. "What're you doing tonight?" she asked.

"Looks like I'm going to a Hallowe'en party…"

"That sounds like fun," she said, making a loom with her fingers. "D'you want me to help you with your costume? I don't *have* to leave for Vito's right away. He'll get an extra half-hour's nap in. We're going to hand out candy; but only to kids that have made a real effort."

"No thanks Di, I'm not planning to wear one."

"What? Why? You're *supposed* to, you know."

"Sure, but I don't like the idea. If anyone asks, I'll just tell them I'm actually six-feet tall. That'll keep them busy…"

"Yeah. They'll wonder why you bothered to come."

"They'll be reading my mind…"

"Alright Michael," she hugged him and walked to the door, "I'll see you on Sunday."

"Bye Di."

He cleaned himself up, got dressed—in jeans and a light gray sweater—and left. A brisk wind played games with candy-wrappers on the sidewalk. It pushed him toward Mount Royal. He hadn't been there since his first 'Dial-A-M8' encounter. It always surprised him how quickly the days rearranged the sets of life. Not that he minded the mountain's fall wardrobe. The red, orange, and yellow leaves radiated warmth without the summer stickiness. Every inch of the landscape was fresh and on its steel against the cold weather. And the rodents were friendlier than usual. Mike walked slowly along the muddy trails, tossing peanuts to gray squirrels.

Crowds of starlings monitored his progress. Mike stared back at them. They had traded in their oil-slick rainbow black coats for white-speckled ensembles. Even their beaks had gone from yellow to brown. Mike resented the change. On summer nights, their bright-beaked scurrying for seeds looked like stars shooting along the ground.

He pulled the last peanut out of the bag and aimed at a chipmunk sitting on a log twenty feet away. He threw a bullet through squirrelly interference and smiled as his target retired with the manna. Out of ammunition, he turned back.

The streets teemed with sweet-toothed marauders. Their costumes varied in professionalism and originality. Mike passed scissor-hole phantoms, brill-cream vampires, and old-hankie desperadoes on his way to the party. He also saw a miniature Chairman Mao and a picture-perfect Bride of Frankenstein. He pitied the pre-fab Teenage Mutant Ninja Turtles who dared to show their plasticky green faces at Vito's door.

Mike wandered into Derek Frazier's tastefully macabre bourgeois Inferno at 9:15. Blood-red velvet covered the walls, and mail-order wooden demons, with dainty *fondue* pitchforks, hung from the ceilings. The living room fireplace blazed. There were *hors d'oeuvres* on the coffee table. Mike calculated the number of movies he could have bought with the small fortune that had financed the spread. Soon it would all be soaked in beer and ashes, and left on the curb.

Derek didn't worry about such things. His father was V.P. of something-or-other, and, as a matter of course, he had been set up in a stylish pad in the McGill ghetto, upon entering the Engineering program in September. He and Mike weren't friends. But everyone who knew Eric Lantz wanted him at their parties. Inviting Mike was part of the deal.

Derek came out of the kitchen, holding an imported beer. In the crimson livery of Lucifer, he looked even more than usual like a sleep-walking inquisitor. He had grown a goatee for the occasion and pasted *papier mâchée* horns to his forehead. He shook Mike's hand and said: "Hey Mike. You don't have a costume?"

"No."

"Oh. Uh. Have a beer?"

"No thanks, Derek."

"Uh, well, make yourself at home."

Derek returned to the kitchen.

Mike went into the living room, which was empty, and sat on the black leather couch. He ate raw broccoli and planned his escape. The room filled up gradually. Mike remained focused on the *crudités*. Graham Blair, dressed as a satyr, sat next to him and said: "Hey Mike, lotta hot girls here tonight…"

A tall, skinny red-head in a tutu and her friend in a Marge Simpson wig overheard the remark. They snickered in unison. Mike did not appreciate the attention. He prided himself upon his inconspicuousness. A scared little smile vibrated on his lips. "Why don't you nab one Graham?"

"Oh, I'm working on it." Graham picked up a glass of something-and-ginger ale from the coffee table and finished it. Mike watched another ring of putrid dew form on the glass surface.

"Yeah? How?"

"There was this girl in the kitchen. I didn't get her name. *Huge* tits. She said I could go and get her some broccoli." His words weren't slurred, but they were too loud.

"Sounds promising," Mike nodded. He waved magically toward the plate of vegetables and hoped that Graham would disappear. Mike felt implicated somehow in Graham's desperation. He looked around the room and saw weakness in infra-red. Beneath the costumes, too much id showed. Human beings never seemed more naked than when they dressed up and went out on the town. And everyone looked so much uglier than he wanted them to. Carefully developed strategies for dealing with life dissolved in just a couple of rounds. Of course, he reminded himself, the dissolution *was* a strategy. Mike often wondered what he'd be like if he drank. He figured he'd probably cry a lot and get pushed around. So he didn't drink.

Graham grabbed some broccoli and got up. The leer of an old letch and the dilated pupils of a child lost in a shopping mall shared his face. "Wish me luck Mike. At least I'm trying…"

"Good luck Graham."

Mike was about to leave when Eric showed up. He had on a spi-der-man costume, without the mask. Pamela was with him. Mike guessed that she was dressed as Elvira. She looked pretty much the same as she always did.

"Hey Mike!" Eric hollered, "having fun?"

"No."

"Of course not," he shook his head. "How could *anyone* have fun at a *Hallowe'en* party?"

"Looks like most people can. Hello Pamela."

"H'lo," she replied. She poked Eric: "So this guy's got free booze?"

"Mm-hmm. In the kitchen." He pointed the way. "Get me some-thing too hunh?"

"Yeah." She walked off.

"What's wrong with her?" Mike whispered.

"I dunno," Eric shrugged, "fucked up childhood, or something. I'm not *with* her, you know…"

"Poor Pamela…"

"You should go for her Mike. She told me she thought you were lovely."

"Great. I must look even more like a cadaver than I thought."

"Hey. No one's forcing you."

Pamela returned with two beers. She seemed a little happier. Eric was staring at the soundsystem, which had finally gotten around to playing Mike's choice, Public Enemy's *Apocalypse '91*. "Has Derek been playing this shit all night?" Eric demanded rhetorically. "We need something we can dance to!" He reached into his knapsack and pulled out a bunch of CDs. He looked at Pamela.

"I-I don't dance," she said.

"Neither does Mike," Eric pointed at his friend and dashed off. Soon techno music was blaring, and gyrating bodies had pushed Mike and Pamela into the hallway.

"Eric's so great," she sucked down half her beer.

"I think so too," Mike nodded, "sometimes."

He waved goodbye and walked to the door. She kept drinking her beer.

CHAPTER 9

▼

The day after the party, Mike stared at the advancing grime on his walls for the better part of an hour and decided it *was* time to put up the Christmas tree. He threw a Nat King Cole album on the CD player and tried to remember where he had stashed the portable evergreen. He found the boxfull of mirth pushed up against the wall of the hall closet. He lugged it to his room and pulled out the instructions. He set up the base and hunted down each colour-coded branch, humming along with *The First Noël* and *The Christmas Song*.

Marbles and Pandora bounced in and out of the box, enjoying the rustling sounds they made. Mike lifted them out whenever they threatened to destroy something, or swallow tinsel. Before doing the lights, Mike needed hot chocolate and pumpkin pie. He dashed to the grocery store to get some.

He found an expired pie, with cheap drawings of gourds on the package, in the discount bin. He hoped it would be wonderful. He waited cheerfully in the eight-items-or-less aisle, whistling the remaining tracks of the Christmas album. He envisioned the tree as a completed work and thought about how happy it would make him. The line moved slowly. Everyone seemed to want lottery tickets. He grabbed a *TV Guide* and looked through the movie section for promising showings. He noted that PBS was playing *Meet John Doe* at eleven on November third, put the guide back, and paid the cashier.

He ran home, heated up the pie in the microwave, made hot chocolate, and sat down amongst the ornaments the cats had strewn on his
floor. He put on *Ella Wishes You A Swingin' Christmas*. He finished the
slice in five bites and set the plate aside. He connected three sets of
white lights to each other and wound them around the tree. He had to
start over several times, until he figured out how to stretch the plug to
the wall outlet.

The phone rang. He grabbed it and said: "Hello."

"Hi Michael. How was the party?" Diane asked.

"Oh. It was about what I expected."

"You say that more than anyone I know…What are you doing?"

"Putting up the tree."

"Michael! Really?"

"Yeah, but don't worry, I'm setting it up in my room. We can move
it out when you're ready…"

"O-kay…Have fun."

"I will."

"Bye Michael."

"Bye."

He went back to his room and grabbed a handful of candycanes
from the box. He unwrapped one, licked it, remembered how much he
disliked peppermint, and threw it out. The rest he hooked onto
branches of the tree. Next he pulled out balls and stars and snowflakes
and reindeer. Everything was silver.

The phone rang again.

Again, he rushed to answer it: "Hello?"

"Hi. Could I speak to Mike, please?" A high-pitched voice asked.

"Speaking." He twirled a silver snowflake in the air.

"Oh, uh, hi Mike. This is Judith. You sent me a message."

"Hi Judith. You were…in Liberal Arts, right?"

"Uh, that's right…Is that Christmas music I hear?"

"Uh-huh. It's Ella Fitzgerald. *Rudolph the Red-Nosed Reindeer*."

"Oh. Why are you listening to that?"

"Because it makes me feel good. Don't you think it's a great song?" The snowflake began to lose momentum. He twirled it again.

"I never thought about it one way or another...It's not exactly the *Ode to Joy*..."

"Oh. Classical music reference. I know you're in Liberal Arts. You don't have to remind me..."

"I don't know if you realize it," she snipped, "but this is not the way to impress the ladies."

"I guess not. Well, I have to go Judith. I'm putting up my tree."

Mike hung up and put the snowflake where it belonged. He pressed "search" to give Ella another chance to sing Rudolph. She rose to the occasion. He decided he wouldn't answer the phone for the rest of the evening. He wouldn't even leave his room. Everything he needed was there. He felt badly about his dismissal of Judith, but he couldn't help resenting her attitude. He had pegged her straight-off as an academic elitist, and she had done nothing, during their brief conversation, to change his mind. "That's why I'm not in school," he muttered to himself.

He finished loading the branches and pulled out several yards of thick, silvery garland. He wrapped it around the tree. His anticipation was peaking. The idea of having his own Christmas tree had been in his head since kindergarten. Now it was about to become a reality. He would never take it down, he thought. It would stand forever as proof of his goodwill toward the universe. He didn't blame anyone for his parents' drinking, or his loneliness, or the short life-spans of cats, or the problems with his script, or Liberal Arts, or Barry Manilow. That was just how things were. All it took to rise above it was a little tinsel, Ella Fitzgerald, and an unexpectedly fresh pumpkin pie. He pictured himself watching *It's A Wonderful Life* by the light of the tree and almost evaporated through his pores.

Only the angel remained. Mike unwrapped the protective layer of newspaper and looked at her. She had on a flowing white robe with silver trimmings. She had a halo. A real angel wouldn't need a halo, Mike thought. There were faint smudges of ink on her face and left wing. He cleaned her off with some spittle on his finger. He stood on the tips of his toes and floated her into position.

He closed his eyes, backed up, and turned out the lights. The CD ended. He opened his eyes. He thought the tree looked fine. He picked up his dirty dishes and took them into the kitchen. He even considered washing them.

The phone rang. Mike dropped the dishes into the sink and answered the call: "Hello."

"Hi. Mike. It's Judith again."

"Hi Judith. I'm sorry about before…"

"You should be. I'm sorry too though. I guess I *did* sound pompous…"

"You did."

"Hmm…Well. I was thinking we should meet for a coffee sometime. I think you're interesting, in a prickly Care Bear sort of way."

"How about right now?"

"Now?" Judith sounded surprised.

"Sure," he replied, "I'm not doing anything."

"What about your tree?"

"Oh. That's over."

"Well, I *can't* do it now. I have too much studying to do."

"That's alright, some other time…"

"Sure."

"Goodnight Judith."

"Goodnight."

Mike cradled the phone and went back to the kitchen. He put the kettle on and did some dishes while he waited for it to boil. It was better than nothing, he told himself. And Diane would be proud of him.

Book Two

CHAPTER 10

$\triangledown$

♫I'm dreamin' of a white Christmas
Just like the ones I used to know... ♫

"This *fuckin'* song," Eric sighed. He threw a thin, black wallet back into a leathery pile in a bin. "I'm so *sick* of this fuckin' song..."

Mike stopped whistling and smiled: "You don't like Bing?"

"I can't judge anymore. I've lost all perspective. I've heard it a thousand times in the past two months. And most of the damage was done at your house."

"It's a beautiful song."

"It's the *best-selling* song of all time."

"So?"

"It's a cash-cow."

"Are you trying to say that you can't touch people and make money at the same time?"

"Maybe if you're a pickpocket."

"Whatever...It's not inappropriate *now*. It's Christmas Eve Eve..."

"God! Soon that'll be on the calendar...And they won't stop there...There'll be a whole gaudy month of days leading up to December 25th, and there'll be something to buy on each of them...Look at this place! It's a big green spider's web. And every fly it traps leaves more green behind."

"Canadian money isn't green."

"You know what I mean...Look at all these big fake smiles. And the little kids being indoctrinated by Santa. And the golden wrapping paper next to every cash. Listen to that *music*." He rolled his eyes at a speaker, now playing Judy Garland's 'Have Yourself a Merry Little Christmas'. "There's nothing Christian about any of it."

Mike leaned against a shelf of loafers and put his finger to his lips. "Shh. This is the best."

Eric continued sifting through the wallets. When the song was over, Mike said: "I know you don't believe this, but I think some of these people are happy. What's wrong with a holiday *evolving*?"

"Nothing. But it's evolved into something ugly. We're all little drummer boys with purchasing power and no saviour."

"Speak for yourself. I have no gifts to buy. I'm just here for the ambiance."

"Ambiance!" Eric exclaimed. "It's a bright object twirling before our eyes. In January, the credit card companies snap their fingers and we wake up walking funny. All the way to the poor house." He picked up a square, brown wallet.

Mike said: "That's a nice one."

"Yeah," Eric held onto it.

Mike straightened up. "It's interesting to watch you choke on your principles just to keep your dad's money snug and comfy."

"*Having* principles makes life more interesting..."

"Ah." Mike started walking.

Eric joined him and asked: "What'll your family say when they find nothing 'from: Mike' under the tree?"

"No one expects *anything* from me. You know that."

"It's true...*Everyone* seems to want something from *me*..."

"Well, cheer up," Mike smirked, "at least you don't have to buy anything for Wendy this year."

Eric stopped walking. "I saw her yesterday. On the bus back into the city. She looked good, you know. But not once she saw me. Then she got the same look she had the last day…Like there was a flood coming. But it didn't come this time. The energy turned into electric hate…Don't ever make anyone cry Mike…"

Mike put his hand on Eric's shoulder and said: "Sorry man…I thought it was fair game."

Eric took a deep breath. "Did I say it wasn't?"

"No."

Mike watched his friend, staring at a mannequin in a plaid bathrobe. His eyes were marble dikes. Mike tried to empathize but couldn't. He couldn't imagine himself making a woman cry. The realization cheered and then sickened him. He envied Eric every hate-ridden moment of that bus ride.

Mike felt shabby. About his dream of vulturing Wendy's emotions like the second-lead in a movie. About triggering Eric's grief and then resenting him for it. He wanted to bandage the scar with a debate, but the logistics of the segue were difficult.

"So, uh, you're done with school," Mike said.

"Yeah," Eric nodded slowly. "It was a great semester. I had to work pretty hard though…"

"No kidding. I haven't seen you much lately."

"Essays," Eric sighed. "I have to stop obsessing over every word. What'll I do when I have to write my thesis?"

"You'll develop a system. It's what you do best."

"Hunh?"

"Channeling your energy. I'm no good at it…"

"What *have* you been doing?"

"Oh. You know. Working as little as possible. Watching movies. Running down blind-date alleys." He motioned toward the cash-register barricades on the threshold of the street. Andy Williams was singing 'The Most Wonderful Time of the Year.' Even Mike was reluctant to defend Andy. "Shouldn't we go? God may smite these people any minute."

"It could happen," Eric smiled.

While waiting in line, Eric flopped the wallet open and shut. "I'll put a family photo in it," he mused.

"That'll be nice," Mike nodded.

Eric paid for the gift, refused the standard wrapping, and asked: "You wanna get a coffee?"

"I can't. I've got to be in NDG by seven o'clock."

Eric looked at his watch. It was six-twenty. They walked out into the off-white city. It was snowing a little. "What's going on there?"

"This girl Priscilla said she'd watch *It's A Wonderful Life* with me."

"Oh yeah? When did you meet her?"

"I haven't yet."

"She just invited you over?"

"Uh-huh."

"That's crazy!"

"I'm not expecting a rocket scientist. But Frank Capra's always good company."

"Maybe too good," Eric said. They reached a metro station. "Well, I'm gonna keep walking. Maybe she'll surprise you."

"That *would* surprise me," Mike smirked.

"What are you doing for Christmas?"

"The usual. Add booze and stir. Di would kill me if I didn't go."

"Let's do something after."

"Sure."

Mike walked through the airlock metro door and stepped onto a crowded escalator. Several people jostled him in frantic efforts to get down two seconds faster. Mike shook his head and felt the inside pocket of his gray coat. The movie and the directions to Priscilla's house were still there. He slid his bus pass through the slot in front of the attendant and got to the platform just in time to catch the train. He pulled out the *It's A Wonderful Life* box (it was the 45th anniversary edition) and read the back for the one-thousandth time. He murmured: "After 45 years it remains as powerful and moving as the day it was made." Mike's eyes wandered to the top of the box, where three stills made the point that the hackneyed copy aimed at.

The first was from his favorite scene, where George and Mary flirt in the moonlight after falling into a swimming pool at a graduation dance. Jimmy Stewart looks ridiculous in the football jersey he borrows to replace his wet clothes—like a giraffe in a straight-jacket. And his contribution to the duet of 'Buffalo Gals' is pitiful. Yet Donna Reed looks at him like he's the prize in a Cracker-Jack box. This was the romance that Mike liked. The kind that winks at faults. Not the kind that magnifies them.

Mike switched to the orange line at Lionel-Groulx. It was unfamiliar territory. He pulled out a torn paper with faint pencil marks on it. Priscilla had instructed him, in her nervous monotone, to get off at Vendome and catch the 105 bus. He did so. The clock in the lobby of her building said 7:01 when he rang the buzzer.

"Yes?" she asked through the intercom.

"It's Mike Borden."

"Come up! Seventh floor."

A sick-duck noise followed and he pulled the door open. The lobby was nice. There were rubber plants in large brown urns and mirrors everywhere. He looked into one and thought about sucking in his stomach. He didn't bother, but on the elevator ride he brushed his overlong bangs out of his eyes. He batted his lashes and patted the movie pressed against his chest.

Priscilla's apartment was 727. He found the number and tapped the wood beneath it. The door swung open. Huge teeth ripped through thin bloodless gums and caught Mike's attention. The black flaps under Priscilla's jellyfish-blue eyes cried out for a mortician's touch. "Hello Mike," she said.

"Hi," he extended his hand.

"Uh," she hesitated before touching him, "come in."

"Thanks," Mike withdrew his hand quickly. He didn't like the way her skin felt, or rather the bones beneath her skin. Her fingers were little quills tipped with anxiety.

At Priscilla's suggestion, he hung his coat on a rack next to the bathroom door. She took a couple of steps forward and spread her arms: "Well, this is my place!"

There was only one room. On Mike's right, a sink overflowed with dishes, forks, and thick water that smelled of decaying cheese. In front of that was a small melamine table. It held a glass candleholder covered in waxy red residue, an open box of salt, and a plate full of steaming Kraft Dinner. Beyond that was a wall unit with a TV, a VCR, and two books on its shelves. A large window overlooked the parking lot. Directly facing the TV was a big waterbed smothered in a heavy pastel comforter. There was a person on it.

She had on baggy green jogging pants and a plaid shirt that was buttoned about two-thirds of the way up. She wore no socks and her toes moved vaguely in time with a Smashing Pumpkins song on MuchMusic. She was spooning large heaps of chocolate ice cream into a rosy mouth. The rest of her profile hid behind thick auburn hair that swirled patternlessly about her head and hugged her throat.

"This is my friend Tina," Priscilla explained. "She's here to protect me in case you're an axe-murderer."

Tina put the ice cream on the bedside table and faced them. She blinked dark bicycle-reflectors. Faint russet drops speckled her cheeks and the skin between her shirt-buttons. She licked a bit of chocolate off her upper lip and showed white teeth.

"Anything up your sleeve Mike?" she asked.

"No," he smiled back, "in my coat."

"You mean the movie...right Mike?" Priscilla rattled.

"Uh-huh," he nodded, without turning toward her.

"Great," Tina yawned, "I could use some culture." Her arms floated into the air and her eyes focused on a spider on the ceiling. Her body remained arched as she watched it crawl toward the wall unit. Mike tried not to notice that she wasn't wearing a bra. He cleared his throat.

"*It's A Wonderful Life* isn't *culture*. Not the way *you* mean it. It's just a beautiful Christmas movie. I'm not into old movies because they're *arty*. I love them 'cause they're *not*."

"Tina's just teasing," Priscilla explained.

"He knows." Tina lost interest in the spider and stretched out on the bed.

"Do you want something to drink Mike?" Priscilla asked.

"Yes please. I'm thirsty."

She walked over to the fridge, next to the sink. Mike inspected the books on the shelf. There was a Webster's Collegiate Dictionary and a Home-Diagnosis Guide, which he cracked open.

"There's no entry for hypochondria," he complained.

Tina chuckled. The mattress rippled beneath her body. "They couldn't. They'd have to list themselves as a symptom."

Priscilla handed Mike a cold glass of water. She put her hands on her hips and said: "You wouldn't laugh if you had as many problems as I do…"

Tina propped herself on one elbow. "You know why I've got this whole vat of ice cream to myself Mike? It's because Pris forgot to read the ingredients. It's a good thing I noticed the 'may contain peanuts' clause. If I hadn't, this little date might have ended in the emergency ward."

Mike put the book down. "Can I try some?"

"Be my guest," Tina shrugged. "I don't need all five-thousand calories."

"Is there another spoon?" he asked.

"In this place? Not unless you wash it yourself."

She handed him the container and the spoon and he took a bite. "It's really good."

Priscilla let out a long-suffering sigh.

"Oh stop whining Pris. You've got your Kraft Dinner…"

"That's true," Priscilla's skeletal grin widened. She grabbed her plate. Between mouthfuls, she said: "You know, I wish you wouldn't call me Pris. It's not exactly flattering."

"Get a shorter name," Tina took the spoon back from Mike.

"How about 'Scilla?" he interjected. "You know, like in Scylla and Charibdys."

"What?" both women asked.

"They were monsters that threatened Odysseus and his crew. It would give you a dangerous mystique."

Priscilla beamed. Tina sighed: "*More* culture…"

"Maybe we'd better watch the movie," Mike decided.

"Good idea," Tina yawned again.

Mike got the cassette out of his coat and shoved it into the VCR slot. Priscilla switched off the lights and pulled out a hard plastic chair for Mike. Tina watched through slits in her eyelids. "You're giving him the chair?" she needled Priscilla. "Follow my example, Mike. I don't come here unless she lets me on the bed."

He blushed, pressed play, and sat down. "This'll be fine."

Capra's Liberty Films bell-logo swung onto the screen. The Christmas-card credits rolled. A sub-aquatic harp version of "Buffalo Gals" accompanied them. The Norman-Rockwell-perfect town of Bedford Falls paraded gorgeously across the screen and gave way to a supernatural conversation about a citizen who is so happy there he's planning to kill himself. Mike knew that these things were happening, because he knew the film by heart. He watched Tina's dark lashes mesh together to block out the silvery light.

Her breathing slowed and the movement of her chest became a predictable event. Mike watched for it. He was perfectly still. He couldn't feel his own lungs working. Nothing was real but the pale curves in the video-glare. His skin burned like a star in the spotlight. His jeans felt tight. A half-hour passed before he even glanced at the film. The left corner of Tina's mouth crept towards him in a smile, and he felt self-conscious. On the screen, the wet courtship scene from the still played itself out. A snide chuckle escaped her throat when Jimmy Stewart offered Donna Reed the moon to swallow. It was one of Mike's favorite lines, but now he gagged on it.

Tina didn't make a sound for the remainder of the movie. And Mike never looked away again. She moved and some hair fell across her round nose. He wanted to brush it away and touch the soft, fleshy button. He folded his arms behind the chair.

The "Auld Lang Syne" finale filtered into Mike's consciousness. Priscilla hopped off the bed and turned the lights on. "I loved it Mike!" she chirped. "I wasn't expecting to, but I really did!"

"That's great," he rubbed his eyes.

Tina stretched and said: "Did they ever get married?"

Priscilla sighed: "About an hour ago!"

"Oh," Tina shrugged and spooned at the melted ice cream.

"Well," Mike straightened up slowly, "I'd better go now…"

"What?" Priscilla pouted. "Why? I thought you were a night-owl."

"I am. But I have to rest up for the holidays. It's a draining time…"

"I guess," she accompanied him to the door. "Well, I hope we can do something soon."

"I'll call you."

Priscilla watched him slip into his coat and offered her veiny cheeks to his lips. He grazed them with a couple of pecks and looked at Tina over her shoulder.

"Seeya Mike," she called from the bed.

CHAPTER 11

▼

"I wish I could be more poetic, but I can't. I'm really crazy about her," Mike crushed a handful of snow into a ball.

"You're horny," Eric shrugged. He pointed his chin at the projectile: "What are you gonna do with that?"

"I'm gonna hit the 'P' on that sign."

They were standing at the 211 bus stop, twenty feet from a billboard that welcomed motorists to Pointe-Claire. They had been waiting for almost an hour. The Christmas pancakes and coffee had given way to rum and tears. Mike had called Eric and they had agreed to meet at eight. Diane had warned them that the bus wouldn't pass until nine. Mike imagined she was finally lacing up her boots, saying goodnight, and getting ready for the ten minute walk down to Lakeshore road. He wound up and launched the snowball high over the sign. It crashed into a blinking pine several lawns away, extinguishing the lights.

"Oops," he reached down for another handful of snow.

Eric grabbed his arm. "What the fuck are you doing Mike?"

"I'm *going* to hit that 'P'."

He wound up and fired again. This time he hit his mark. Hard. The sign rattled and echoed through the empty holiday air.

"Are you done now?" Eric asked.

Mike rubbed his hands together to warm them: "Uh-huh."

"Good. I *really* want to meet this girl."

"What girl?" Diane appeared behind them.

"Di!" Mike started. "It must be midnight."

"Just about," she nodded. "*What girl?*"

"Her name's Tina," Mike answered proudly.

"Tina what?"

"I don't know."

"How did you meet her?"

"Oh," Mike hesitated, "I just kind of ran into her."

"What?"

"Guys," Eric interrupted, "the bus is coming."

Diane crossed her arms, signaling that she wasn't through. The 211 roared to a halt a few steps away. A sign above the windshield flashed: "JOYEUSE FÊTES". Transportation was free on Christmas Day, but each of them had monthly passes, so it didn't matter. Diane, Mike and Eric filed onto the bus.

The driver, a middle-aged lady with a perm and tanning-salon skin, smiled at the group and said: "Joyeux Noël." The only other passengers were a couple of teenaged girls with too much white powder on their faces. Diane surged ahead and sat down in the back row of seats. Mike and Eric joined her. At the next stop, a woman wearing two layers of jogging suits and a belligerent scowl got on. Her left eye was purple and swollen shut. She clutched a white leather purse tightly against her puffy pink chest. She mumbled something to the driver and stumbled toward the back of the bus.

"Oh Jesus," Diane whispered. Eric stared out of his window. Mike whistled 'Who?'. The one-eyed lady was a celebrity amongst West Island youth. An encounter with her was sure to be harrowing, but immensely entertaining. The girls near the front of the bus giggled and pointed. Mike had always been as respectful of her feelings as possible. Yet he invariably drew her ire. Diane patted his arm protectively.

The one-eyed lady scanned the bus furtively. She silenced the gigglers with a sour look. Then she glared at Mike, forcing him to squint.

She held her purse like it was a newborn child and whispered: "You took my fuckin' money."

Mike kept whistling and looked at his shoelace. He bent down to re-tie it. Diane's grip tightened on his arm.

The one-eyed lady's left arm rose slowly into the air. She repeated, in a conversational tone: "You *took* my *fuckin'* money."

Mike shook his head. He raised his hands and pantomimed his innocence.

The one-eyed lady extended her index finger toward Mike and leaned forward. She shrieked: "*You took my fuckin' money!*"

Diane rose to refute the accusation. Mike pulled gently at her sleeve and cleared his throat. She sat back down. He focused squarely upon the one-eyed lady and said, in a deep, authoritative voice: "No. I did *not* take your money."

The irate woman stared back him. Her tongue probed the depths of her cheek for an appropriate reply. The bus stopped and the driver announced: "Boulevard Saint-Jean." The one-eyed lady jerked her head around, jumped up, and scurried off, taking special care of her purse.

"Man," Mike grinned, "I've been wanting to tell her that for years."

"That woman bothers me," Eric muttered, watching her through his window as the bus pulled away from the stop. "What's the use of being crazy if you can't forget money? There really *is* no escape from capitalist modes of thought."

"Whatever," Diane's upper lip curled disapprovingly.

"I'm serious."

"I know you are. Everything's got to be about proving a point with you…"

"You're wrong Eric," Mike beamed. "There is a way."

"What is this? A seminar?" Diane asked.

"Mike's in love," Eric sighed. "With a real person."

"Oh yes, Tina X."

"If I tell you how I met her, do you promise not to freak out?" Mike hesitated.

"What *is* she? A hooker?"

"No!" he blanched. "I met her—in a round-about way—through 'Dial-A-M8'…"

"Jesus! That's even worse…Is that why those silly girls have been calling our house Michael?"

"Uh-huh," he looked sheepish. He had told Diane that they all needed his help buying Christmas gifts for Eric. And she had believed him.

"God! And now one of them's sucked you in?"

"Not exactly."

"All in good time," Eric predicted.

"I don't want to hear another word from you until I understand what's going on," Diane barked at Eric. She put her hand on Mike's shoulder and cooed: "Just tell me what happened Michael…"

CHAPTER 12

▼

When they got home, Mike left Diane muttering to herself in the living room and called Priscilla. He didn't mind when her answering machine picked up. He hummed through the dull message and said, after the tone: "Hey Scilla! Guess you're not home. Or asleep. Anyway. I called to invite you to 'The Bell Jar' tomorrow. I go there every Boxing Night with my friend Eric—starting this year. It's a fun place. We'll be there around ten. So, I'll see you then—if you can make it. Oh yeah—why don't you bring Tina along? Bye!" Mike hung up the phone and crawled under the covers. He slept well. He didn't even dream.

The next day, he woke up at four and dressed in a hurry for video shopping. He surprised himself by leaving most of January's rent in the bank machine. He only took twenty dollars, just to keep a Boxing Day tradition alive. The store was boiling over with bargain-hunters. He stalked up and down the classics aisle. Finally, he settled on *Till the Clouds Roll By.*

"What's in the bag?" Eric asked, when they met on the corner of St. Catherine and Atwater at six.

"It's Jerome Kern's biography," Mike smiled. "Well, his life got squeezed out by his music, and some pretty cheesy scripting. But it's great music."

"You've seen it before?"

"Oh yeah. I watched Judy Garland sing 'Look For the Silver Lining' and 'Who?' every morning that summer I worked at the factory. The tape finally broke in August. I quit the next day."

"Maybe you should watch the whole thing from now on."

"I guess. But it's a dull story. *Imagine* becoming internationally famous at twenty-nine and marrying the first girl you fall in love with."

"I think you *are* imagining it."

"Well, maybe. I'm in no hurry to suffer."

"Hmm. I hope Tina comes tonight."

"She will!"

"Of course."

They started walking. It was a mild December. There were pools of sleet on the sidewalk. Mike crushed grains of road salt with each step. A woman in platform heels skidded into him, but he held steady. Her purchases wound up in the gutter.

"If you *really* want to see materialism," Mike mused, after she moved on, "you ought to focus on Boxing Day. There's not an ounce of redeeming spirituality about it. It's just a frenzy of people trying to get as much for their Christmas cash as they possibly can."

"Fascinating," Eric seemed a little distracted.

"It is!" Mike chirped. "You wouldn't believe how nasty people get around a '33% off' sign. Especially when the merchandise is running low. I actually considered goosing the woman who got the last copy of *Mogambo* and making off with it in the confusion. And I, as you know, am a man of peace."

"You *sound* like a man on crack," Eric muttered.

"I've never felt this way before!" Mike grabbed his friend's shoulder at the corner of Crescent street and said: "See that guy? The bald one, standing in front of the neon d-cups?"

"Uh-huh."

"I want you to go ahead, by yourself, and look directly at him as you pass. I'll follow a few seconds later and we'll compare notes on the next corner."

"Alri-ight," Eric shrugged.

At the rendez-vous point, Mike whispered: "So. What happened?"

"Nothing. He just stared back at me. I felt pretty stupid."

"He just stared back at me too! I *knew* he would! This is amazing!"

"What are you *talking* about?"

"Look!" Mike pointed at a fortyish man in a gray suit about to cross Crescent. A leather briefcase swung jauntily at his side. "Watch!" The man's professional veneer melted off his face as he neared the burly barker. His eyes flitted nervously from sight to sight, before coming guiltily to rest upon the fleshy snapshots plastered all over the flashing red alcove. The doorman spoke first. Then the man in the gray suit walked past him into the club.

"Ever since I moved downtown," Mike explained, "I've been walking by that strip-club and getting the same spiel from the doorman: 'Sexiest girls in the city, free buffet, special dances, et cetera.' Now. You know me pretty well. Nude dancers aren't my thing. What has always bothered me is: why doesn't the bald guy know it? After all, a doorman has to be something of a psychologist. He saw that briefcase coming and licked his chops. Easy pickings. Why did I get lumped into the same category?"

"I give up," Eric's forehead crinkled.

"I think it's because I usually look so lost. Unless I'm on my way to see a really good movie. And a lost look is a lost look. Doormen are trained to recognize it. And offer asylum. That's what a strip-club *is*, Eric. A block-parent for adults."

"So the fact that he ignored us means..."

"We must know where we're going."

"Yeah," Eric started walking, "I'm hungry."

He ordered a Cajun burger and a pint of *Boreal Rousse* before they even sat down at 'The Bell Jar.' Mike pored over the menu and asked for a vegetarian sub and a coffee when the waitress brought the beer. He noticed Pamela serving a table on the other side of the room and waved at her.

"Don't do that," Eric muttered.

"What?"

"She *saw* us Mike. She's not speaking to me. Apparently I'm an asshole."

"Man! Are you okay?"

"What do you mean?"

"I *mean*," Mike worked up a concerned throb in his throat, "it's been a bad week. First Wendy. Especially Wendy. And now this."

"Yeah," Eric let the beer swish between his half-smiling teeth, "I'm not too popular these days...That's what bothers me about your strip-club doorman test."

"You mean *you* feel lost?"

"I'm a little disoriented, at least."

"Some people always seem sure of themselves," Mike shrugged.

"And you think *I'm* one of these people?"

"Eric. Of course you are."

"But I'm always telling you how confused I am."

"Sure. And I always try to believe you. Listen Eric. For a change, I know how you feel. I *want* Tina. That's my plan, and I'm sticking to it. *That's* certainty, my friend. A goal. *You've* got it on a cosmic level."

"The *cosmos* makes sense. It's the Wendys and Pamelas I don't understand."

"You're just fretting over the casualties. I'm glad you *do* worry about these things. I wouldn't be your friend if you *didn't*. But I doubt you'll ever worry yourself into a stupor. That's *my* department."

"But not since you met Tina, right?"

Mike's coffee arrived. He took a long gulp and declared: "I *feel* different."

"Hmm. What's Diane's final verdict on this feeling?"

"It's not in yet. She's kind of torn. She's always nagging me to grow up. But not *this* way. Her great hope is for me to get a full-time job. She expects me to spend the rest of my time cuddling cats..."

"People have a certain idea of you Mike. Even I do."

"That's fine. Good for them. Good for you."

"Hey! I'm *glad* to see you behaving erratically for a change. But Diane's not as flexible as I am."

"You're not as flexible as you *think* you are."

"Wow. You're quite a sage son-of-a-bitch all of a sudden. I wish *my* boners were this enlightening."

Mike matched Eric's five beers with five coffees. Pamela never came to see them. They had just asked the waitress for a chess board when Priscilla walked in, wearing a purple body-suit that coated her bones.

"Hey Mike!" Priscilla yodeled nervously. "This is my friend Helen."

"Hello Helen," Mike shook the newcomer's hand. He nodded toward his dinner companion: "This is Eric. I *think* we're still friends…"

The two women sat down. Helen had long black hair, bright dark eyes and pursed lips. Her white blouse contrasted sharply with her tan flesh and the shadowy ravine of her cleavage. Mike asked: "Where's Tina?"

"Oh," Priscilla shrugged, "she's in Florida with her parents."

"Christmas in Florida?" Mike snickered. "That sucks." Then he smiled: "So. How was *your* Christmas Scilla?"

"Oh," she blushed and watched her jagged fingernails scratch at a green coaster, "it was fine. My dad gave me five hundred bucks!"

"That's pretty cool."

"No it's not," Helen protested, "he mailed it to her. He lives in B.C."

"It's not *his* fault," Priscilla exclaimed defensively. "My mom divorced him and got custody of me. He *had* to start a new life…"

"Oh sure. He *had* to move three thousand miles away and see his daughter once a year…Your dad irks me!"

Eric fought back a burp and finally gave into it. He shifted uncomfortably in his chair and smiled weakly.

The disgusted look in Helen's eyes matched her petulant mouth. Mike patted his friend's back and said: "Perhaps that was Eric's suave way of suggesting the *Boreal Rousse*."

Helen's lips straightened out and edged toward a smile. "I don't know if I *feel* for that…"

Priscilla giggled: "I do!"

The Cranberries' 'How' slashed through the stagnant air. The waitress appeared. Helen asked for a Bloody Caesar, Priscilla chose draft beer, and Mike signaled that his mug was empty. Eric ordered water, rose with a grimace, gave Priscilla a wobbly thumbs-up, and excused himself.

"Is he okay?" Helen asked.

"Sure, he'll be fine," Mike replied confidently.

"I love this song," Helen stated.

Mike thought for a moment and nodded: "Yeah. It's good."

Priscilla disagreed: "Oh, it's weird. The Cranberries are so morbid. I like Bryan Adams."

"I don't find it morbid," Mike scratched his chin. "It's visceral."

Their drinks arrived. Eric returned after about half-an-hour, looking relieved but exhausted. Mike's eyelids were jacked up by the caffeine. Both women seemed uncomfortable when he focused on them. He imagined his intense green gaze burrowing into Tina's eye sockets. Priscilla became incoherent about halfway through her second pint of beer. Helen's lips loosened to the point of an occasional grin. Mike spent the rest of the evening getting to know her. Her last name was Dawley. She was enrolled in Social Studies at CEGEP, but she rarely attended. She worked as a barmaid most nights of the week and thought she might like to become a lawyer.

Eric clasped his hands on the table and buried his face in them. He drifted in and out of consciousness. He smiled every time he heard Mike say something funny—which was quite often. He winced whenever Mike asked an unsubtle question about Tina—which was also quite often. A few minutes after three, the lights went on. Helen went to find Priscilla, who had wandered off around two-thirty. Eric yawned and stood up. Mike bounced out of his chair.

"What a night!" he exclaimed.

"Yeah," Eric yawned again, "let's go."

Helen met them in front of the pub. Priscilla, wearing a Jack-O-Lantern grin and a fragrant orange smear across the front of her body suit, leaned heavily against her friend's shoulder. "Wanna kiss me Mike?" she giggled.

"Uh," he blushed.

"Don't worry," Helen reassured him, "she doesn't know what she's saying."

"Nope," Priscilla grinned on, "I don't. Wanna have sex with me Mike?"

Helen shrugged and waved Priscilla's rag-doll wrist at Mike and Eric. "*Goodnight* everyone."

Eric waved back. Mike smiled: "I had a lot of fun! It was really nice to meet you Helen. We should do it again."

"Sure. You could stop by my bar any night. Or," she smirked, "we could all go out in a couple of weeks—when Tina gets back..."

"That's a great idea!"

"Uh-huh."

She waved her own hand and dragged Priscilla into a cab.

Mike coasted through the interim on a tideless body of confidence. He arrived on time for all four of his days at 'MarcoSport', without a trace of his customary martyred look. He threw himself into the conversation at lunch, although his claim that the plot of a *90210* episode had been stolen from an *Andy Hardy* movie drew blank stares. He hit many posts and signs (and a few windows and cars, by accident) with snowballs. He declined a couple of invitations to New Year's Eve brawls. He worked hard on his screenplay. He cancelled his ad on 'Dial-A-M8'.

In mid-January, Helen called with a detailed plan. Tina would be arriving on the following Saturday. They would meet at around ten o'clock the next night at BJ's, a Crescent street dance club. Mike winced at the thought, but his good mood held. He didn't care where they were going.

At nine-thirty on Sunday night, Mike sat whistling on the blue couch, stroking Marbles and finishing a crossword. He heard a click in the door and looked up at Diane and Vito.

"It's cold out there! Minus twenty for sure!" Diane exclaimed, reluctantly unbuttoning her black coat.

"That sucks," Mike grimaced, writing Deborah Kerr's name in the blank spaces of 57-Across.

"He don't care babe. Right Mike?" Vito winked. Diane whacked him on the arm and took his coat.

"Uh, sure Vito," Mike nodded.

"Just be *careful* Michael," Diane warned. She brushed snowflakes off the coats and hung them up in the closet.

"Yeah Mike. Don't say anything stupid and screw things up."

Diane wound up to swat him again, but he was out of range. She mouthed something menacing at Vito and turned sweetly toward Mike. "Where are you going?"

"Oh," he sighed, "BJ's. It's on Crescent."

"That's a great place!" Vito cheered. "Lotta hot chicks there!" He looked apologetically at Diane: "Of course, that don't mean anything when you've already got your first pick." Diane's eyes smiled at him.

Mike grinned: "*My* first pick will be there."

"Well," Diane's voice softened, "I hope I get to meet her soon." Her jaw dropped: "Michael! Is that what you're wearing?"

Mike stood up, rotated slowly and looked down at his plaid shirt and gray jeans. "Uh huh," he nodded, "this is what I always wear."

"*Exactly*. If you're *really* crazy about this girl, do something special with your clothes…"

"I will. I'll take them off as soon as possible!" Mike grabbed his coat.

"Michael!"

Vito put his arms around Diane and patted her head. He soothed: "Take it easy, babe." He raised his voice and called over his shoulder: "Good luck Mike!"

"Thanks. Good night Di! Love ya!" He locked the door and made a bee-line for the elevator.

A few blocks away, Mike joined a long line of people outside BJ's. He didn't see any of his new friends among them. Eric had decided not to come, explaining that he had a new semester to deal with. Also, it wasn't his kind of place. Mike had never been to a dance club, but he had heard enough of the obnoxious dance-mixes on Montreal radio to know that it wouldn't be *his* kind of place either. Gradually, he edged toward the entrance in a leathery swarm that reeked of cologne. He heard snippets of conversations that revolved around "getting really wasted" and "scoring."

Inevitably, Mike found himself face-to-face with a stocky, bald doorman who looked like he had an extra skull's worth of bone wrapped around his brain. He shot Mike an unimpressed glare and said: "ID?" Mike fumbled for his wallet and pulled out his Medicare card. "Okay," the doorman mumbled and opened his manicured fist, "twelve bucks."

"Twelve!?"

The doorman resorted to a slow drawl: "Twe-el-ve. It's Sun-day. All—you—can—drink."

"But, I'm not going to drink anything…"

"Do I care? No. *Me*, I take your twelve bucks. *You*, you decide from there. You wanna go home kid?"

"Here's the money."

"Don't forget to coat-check. That's two more dollars. Better get used to spending if you want to pick up in here," the doorman called after him. Mike followed instructions and left his coat with a woman in a black outfit that was stretched beyond the point of blackness. Errant rainbows of light cut through the darkness. A drum-and-bass heart pumped blood into pale limbs that flailed and fanned the smoky air. Mike improvised a dance of his own; wobbling on tip-toes, peering over the tangles of hair-sprayed heads. Finally, he spied Helen laughing and talking with the barmaid. She grabbed two glasses filled with dark liquid and stepped into the crowd. Mike followed her.

He caught up to her just as she reached a high table with six stools crowded up against it. He tapped her on the shoulder.

"Mike! You made it!"

She gave him a hug.

"It was close. You didn't tell me it was *twelve* dollars."

"Aw," she grinned, "you'll have a good time."

She turned to the group at the table—which included Priscilla, Tina, and three people he hadn't met—and screeched: "Mike's here!"

Mike waved his hand through the air and mouthed "hi's" at everyone. Priscilla spilled her drink and smiled. A glaze of bewilderment covered her eyes and teeth. A girl with long brown hair and a dignified mouth tried to clean up the mess and keep Priscilla from dropping her face into it. A blonde girl and a curly-haired guy, deep in conversation, occupied the stools closest to the wall. Tina watched the spectacle with interest. Her dark eyes were amused.

Helen put the new drinks down and crossed her arms. "Oh Pris. I don't think you need another one…"

Priscilla propped her head up and yelled: "I do!" She took a sip and wagged her finger: "Call me Scilla! Right Mike?"

"Sure," he nodded, then turned toward Tina. She looked very comfortable in a woolly beige sweater. The Florida sun had added a few freckles to her round nose. His fingers spun in his pockets, itching to connect the dots.

"So," she leaned toward him, "this was your idea?"

"Going *out* was my idea," he smiled and rolled his eyes across the room, "*this* wasn't."

"What other ideas have you got?"

"You'd be surprised."

"I doubt it." She slid off her stool and announced: "We're going for a little walk. Mike's ears hurt." She grabbed his hand and led him out onto the street. They strolled around the block. Tina didn't say anything. Neither did Mike. She swung his arm slowly through the frigid air. Her thumb traced a path up and down the veins in his wrist. They arrived back at the door to BJ's and showed the green ink on their hands. Mike smirked at the doorman. They walked back to the table. The mess had been cleaned up. And Priscilla was gone.

"Ears feeling better?" Helen asked.

"Now they're frostbitten."

"Really?" Tina said. She put her lips close to his right ear, then closed them on the lobe. Mike's circulation revived. He tilted his head back, let her work her way down to his chin, then snapped forward and caught her mouth in his. Something brushed against the inside of his cheek. Mike wondered if he still had gum in his mouth; a sugar-and-salt taste took him by surprise. He opened his eyes. They reflected back at him in pupils that widened and widened and withdrew behind pale flesh. Mike kissed her eyelids and her nose and she ran her hands up and down his spine.

Suddenly, she pulled back and said: "I'd better find Pris."

Mike grinned at the small group at the table. He had their undivided attention. The girl with long brown hair finished her drink and asked: "What's up with you Mike? I thought you were Priscilla's friend."

Mike opened his mouth, but it hadn't readjusted itself to speaking. Helen answered for him: "He is."

"Don't get me wrong," the brown-haired girl said, "I think you made the right choice." She extended her hand. "I'm Donna."

Mike shook her hand and hopped onto the stool next to her. "It wasn't exactly a choice." He looked at the couple at the far end of the table. "And you are?"

"Laura," the blonde girl waved.

"I'm Rob," the curly-haired guy blustered, slapping Mike on the back. His face was beat-red with laughter. "I like you already Mike."

"I like everyone tonight," Mike beamed. "Where do you guys think Priscilla went?"

"That's no mystery," Donna smirked, "she's sick." She picked up her glass and looked at it critically. "Although I don't understand how *anyone* could get sick on this booze-flavored water."

"She wasn't feeling well all day," Helen explained.

"What else is new?" Laura spoke up. "She doesn't eat any vegetables. I just wanna pin her down and force roughage down her throat."

"It's psychosomatic," Rob cupped her left hand between his palms. "You know: anemic mind, anemic body."

"None of you seem to like her very much."

"Are you kidding?" Helen laughed. "We *love* Pris. But it's hard to take someone seriously when you've been picking them up off the floor since the first grade-eight house party."

"You all grew up together?"

"Uh-huh," Donna nodded, "in the country. Near the US border."

"Except for Tina, of course," Laura added. "She's from the city. Pris just met her this year. At school."

Donna smirked: "Pris makes friends easily. Everyone wants to join her private nursing squad. You watch," she pointed at Mike, "you'll be doing it soon."

"I'd make a bad nurse."

"Oh I don't know," Tina's fingers gripped his shoulders. "You couldn't be worse than me. I can't do a *thing* with Priscilla. She's crying because you like me."

"That's awful," he grumbled. U2's 'Sunday, Bloody Sunday' pulsed through the room. "You know," he mused, "this is the first decent song they've played." He brushed Tina's auburn bangs out of the way and parted her rosy lips.

The kiss lasted until a waitress approached the table and cleared her throat: "Excuse me. But your little blonde friend is throwing up on the bathroom floor and telling everyone she's got mono. We'd like her to leave…"

Helen and Laura went to fetch the casualty. The little group reconstituted itself on the sidewalk in the cold night air. It was just past midnight. Soon, Priscilla emerged, balanced awkwardly on grudging shoulders. She had plastic Japanimation eyes and teeth.

"Great," Donna crossed her arms, "now I know what a million bucks looks like."

Everyone laughed—including Priscilla. Everyone felt bad for laughing—except Priscilla.

"I feel like this is kinda my fault," Tina said. "I'll take her home."

"I'll help you," Mike volunteered.

They piled into a taxi and Tina gave Priscilla's address to the driver. By the time they reached the apartment building, Priscilla was a snoring corpse. They fished through her purse for the keys and brought her up to the seventh floor. Mike dropped his charge on the waterbed and she sank into it like an anchor. Tina started washing dishes.

"I'm hungry," she said.

"Me too," he walked up behind her and kissed her neck.

"Kraft dinner?" she giggled.

He ignored her and pulled off her sweater. He ran his tongue along her shoulder-blade. "We'll order something. Later."

She turned to face him and he unfastened her bra. His fingers traced whirlpools around her taut nipples. "You know, we're kind of lucky tonight," Tina smiled. "My mom doesn't allow me to sleep at guys' houses."

"You're kidding!"

"I'll never kid you Mike. Remember that."

CHAPTER 13

▼

Tina's last name was Heyde. It was the one thing Mike was sure of after dating her for six months. They had met each other's parents. Tina's mother was a short blonde woman with a sharp nose who spent most of her life in power-suits and aerobics-wear. Her father—who had his own apartment—was a thin, balding man who tried very hard to keep a tough DeNiro scowl on his face at all times. He was an insurance-claims investigator. Of course, she had a step-father: a thirty-something mechanic named Hugues with a loud voice and an anabolic physique. Tina and he didn't get along very well.

Tina's visit to the West Island went off without a hitch. Everyone stayed sober and barely a word was spoken. And Diane made an effort to overcome her suspicions. One day, she and Tina went to the hair salon together. They returned with identical jet-black dye-jobs. Mike told Tina he liked the new colour, but she believed his eyes, which begged to differ. She had only asked for his opinion out of politeness.

Tina was eighteen. Like a lot of young Quebecois who didn't know what they wanted to do with their lives, she had registered in Social Studies at CEGEP. Her favorite class was German, which she had attended three times, in all. She had learned one phrase—"*Ein* frush-tuck, *bitte*"—which, she proudly declared, meant: "Could I have a breakfast, please?" (Mike pointed out that this left far too much of the matter up to the cook's discretion.)

Homeopathy and the Tarot fascinated Tina. She slept with a velvety bag full of cards under her pillow and haunted every New Age seminar in the city. She gave up on CEGEP and decided to study California massage at CHB—the Canadian Holistics Bureau—starting in the fall of 1994. In the meantime, she needed a job. Shortly after the hair-dye incident, Diane offered her one at the cafe. The reports on her work were very good.

Mike liked to watch Tina's face as she scrutinized the cards for answers to his questions. There were tiny ripples in the smooth surfaces of her eyes when she sat amongst her mystical artifacts. He spent most of the readings trying to read her. He wasn't very good at it.

To celebrate their semi-anniversary, Mike and Tina went to see a romantic-comedy: *It Could Happen to You.* It was Mike's choice. Tina liked going to the theatre, but she never seemed to care what they saw. At dinner before the movie, he gave her a present: a set of 'Inner-Child' cards. He had no idea what they were good for, but he liked the drawings.

"They're beautiful Mike," she smiled. Her lips stood out even more than usual. She was wearing a rather complicated white dress that her mother had given her. She looked uncomfortable. He picked up the bill, took her hand, and kissed her in the aisle of the restaurant.

"I'm glad you like them. Can we look for *my* Inner Child later?"

"Sure."

They paid the bill and walked out into the street. It was hot and very humid. Thunderstorms rumbled in the back of everyone's minds. The movie was playing at the Faubourg, a shopping centre that wanted desperately to be "European." Mike liked the Faubourg theatre. It was small and dimly lit and rarely played action films.

They bought popcorn with topping and settled into their seats. The room was about half full. The movie was based on a true story: a New York cop promises a hard-bitten waitress half of his lottery ticket instead of a tip, and sticks to the bargain after he wins four million dollars, amazing everyone. Especially his wife. She—and many other evil-minded people—imagines that the two-million dollar tip is for services *other* than those normally provided by a waitress. As in most Capra films, the characters stumble out of a fairy tale onto the front page of a scandal-sheet. However, the movie ends optimistically: affirming that eccentricity trumps greed, in the battle for the big pulsing heart of the community.

Mike took a few mental notes for his great academic study of romantic-comedy, and he managed to keep his eyes on the screen, but he paid more attention to the buzzing in his left hand, pressed up against Tina's stomach. It shook every time she laughed. Mike smiled and told himself that the evening was a success. They rose with the crescendo of the score and made their way out of the theatre. Outside, they found it had rained, and the air felt relaxed, like an athlete's muscles after a big win.

Mike swung Tina's arm gently and said: "Let's walk."

"Sure."

On Pierce street, they met a woman with a worried face sitting on the front steps of a comic book store. "Can you help me?" she pleaded. "I lost my job last week and my U.I. cheque won't be in until *next* week. My kids have nothing to eat..."

Mike pulled a five dollar bill out of his pocket and handed it to her. Tina did likewise. The woman took the money from them and lines melted off her face.

"Thank you. Thank you so much."

"No problem," Mike continued swinging Tina's arm. They walked up to Sherbrooke and headed toward N.D.G. The stroll lasted about an hour. The conversation was entirely tactile. Little rubs and taps with fingers and thumbs.

It was eleven o'clock when they reached Tina's house. Inside, it was dark and cool and quiet, except for the barking of the dogs penned up in the living room. Tina opened the gate and rubbed noses with them as they burst into the hallway. Then she grabbed Mike's hand and pulled him into her bedroom.

With her other hand she turned on the stereo—loud. The buzzing in Mike's fingers spread through his whole body. They fell backwards onto the bed and she cleared an assortment of stuffed animals onto the floor. After six months, he was quite familiar with her buttons and snaps and zippers; and the skin beneath them. He still didn't know if he knew what he was doing. But he knew he was doing the only thing he wanted to be doing.

He heard vague little moans that seemed to come from out of nowhere. For Mike, intimacy was a silent movie. She had once asked him why he never made a sound during sex. He really didn't know. It felt like a lobotomy. He was a pulsing flatline until her body jarred against his.

Mike pulled out of a pink limbo to get a better view of things. Tina jerked her chin toward the bedroom door. A black title-card flashed in front of his eyes: "OH NO!" Then he heard loud knocking and Mildred, Tina's mother, calling: "Boo-bear! I'm home!"

They hurried into their clothes. Mike looked in the mirror and laughed. As usual, he would wander out of Tina's room with rose-red cheeks and eyes like spears of mint and try to look virginal. And succeed handsomely. He didn't understand Mildred's Victorian attitude toward her daughter's sexuality. She was so hard-nosed about everything else. Tina took the interruption in stride, as always. She ran a paw through her tousled hair, licked a bit of sweat off her upper lip, and reached for a thick packet of weeds lying next to her bed. She lit it with a match, then blew on it until the tip smoldered. The room smelled like a sweet sunset.

"I have to purify you," she said.

"I thought we already did *that*."

"Ha-*ha*." The smoky wand was made of sage. It was supposed to cleanse auras. Tina called it her 'smudging stick'. She circled his body with it. He submitted to the rite because he liked the scent; and the feeling of being allowed into a secret world—even one he didn't believe in.

Tina put the stick back where she had taken it from, turned off the stereo, and grabbed Mike's arm. "Alright, let's go."

She led him into the living room, where Mildred and Hugues were curled up, watching CNN. Tina let her mother hug her and Mike felt a goofy smile on his face.

"*So* Boo," Mildred's voice had an insinuating tone, "what did you two do tonight?"

Tina shrugged and Mike jumped in with a synopsis of *It Could Happen To You*. Hugues stopped him with a yawn and asked: "You know if the Expos won, Mike?"

"No," Mike shook his head, "I don't care anymore. The season's just about over."

"Yeah, the fuckin' strike! Great timing huh?"

Tina sighed and said: "Well, it's past my bedtime."

Mike looked at the VCR clock. It was two in the morning. He coughed. His throat felt raw.

Mildred jumped up. "Are you sick Mike?"

"Looks like something's starting…"

"Give him some echinacea Boo," Mildred smiled benevolently. "You've got to try it Mike. It boosts your immune system."

"Uh, sure. Sounds good."

Tina brought him into the kitchen. She presented him with a brown paper bag full of herbs. "Boil the leaves for about twenty minutes and let it steep for another half-hour." She led Mike to the door, after a round of good-byes, and kissed him on the porch. "Will you get home alright?"

"No problem. It's not that far…"

"Great! Drink the echinacea. Call me tomorrow?"

"Uh-huh," he nodded. "I love you."

"I love you too."

She closed the door.

CHAPTER 14

▼

Mike had to work the next day. He spent the morning planning to sing the praises of echinacea, when he spoke to Tina. He *did* feel much better. But he got her machine at lunch and when she answered her cordless at six o'clock, he could feel her fingers on the 'end' button. He didn't have much time.

"So. We doing anything tonight?"

"Oh…I don't think so Mike. I have to do laundry."

"Laundry again? How many clothes can three people go through?"

"It's got to be done."

"Sure, I know. Well, I could come help you and then we could go eat."

"Oh, I don't know Mike. I'm feeling kind of tired…"

"How about a massage? I don't care how good you are. You can't do yourself."

"Not yet. I can't wait 'til I learn reflexology. It's all pressure points in your hand…"

"You don't want a massage?"

"No thanks. I'll be fine."

"Hey! What do think about this O.J. Simpson thing?"

"I guess he killed her…"

"I don't mean *that*. I mean, don't you find it interesting? As an event? There's nothing else on the news."

"Not really." She paused for so long that he wondered whether she was still there. "Listen Mike. There are wet clothes in the washer. I can't leave them. I'll call you back later, okay?"

"Sure."

Mike dropped the phone on the hook. *What the Hell*, he thought. He had done his best. He decided that—in the final analysis—it didn't really matter whether he saw her or not. He would always be himself. And she would always be what he wanted. He had reached the pinnacle of desire and found it frozen and windswept. Oh, the cold was bracing, sometimes. But there was no place to sit and enjoy it. There was no choice but to push on, drawing deep exhilarated breaths that scorched his lungs and kept the black ice in his chest well chilled. And all the while, gangrene was setting in.

Mike switched off the TV and threw himself onto the blue couch. He was still there when Diane walked in twenty minutes later with an armful of groceries. He got up and offered to take them to the fridge.

"Since when are you thoughtful?" she smirked, but there was relief in her voice. Her gray t-shirt had small stains under the arms and her hair was frizzing.

He shrugged and took the bags into the kitchen. When he got back to the livingroom, Diane was tied to an anchorman. Her hair looked perfect again.

"Do we have to have the TV?"

"No," she pressed 'power', "we don't."

"Good." He sat next to her.

"What's up?"

"I feel like talking."

"So talk."

"I don't know what to talk about."

"Vito's right," she smiled. "You *are* funny…Why don't you tell me about one of your dreams?"

"I haven't had one lately."

"Really? That's too bad. I liked them, you know."

He sank back into the couch and curled his knees into his stomach. "I always thought you were humouring me."

"Sure. I was."

He shook his head. "Where's Vito?"

"'Nother business trip. Where's Tina?"

"Doing laundry."

"Oh."

"Yeah."

She rubbed his arm. "She's just like that, Michael. I give her all the boring jobs at work. She just slips into a Zen state. She never screws up. But she hates being at cash. She hates dealing with people...If she says she's doing laundry, believe me, she's doing laundry..."

Mike sat up. "I don't think she's *lying*. I wish she *was*. At least then I wouldn't know where I stood..."

"That's weird Michael."

"Sorry. That's how I feel."

"But you seem to have a great time with her."

"Sure. But she's like one of those McDonald's promotions. Available for a limited time only..."

"That's mostly because of her mother's rules, isn't it? That's what you told me..."

"Yeah, but isn't it funny how people turn their prisons into fortresses?"

"Have you talked to her about this?"

"We don't talk about *anything*. We just snuggle, and so-forth..."

Diane blushed for him. "She seems so innocent..."

"She is. There's no contradiction there."

"No offense Michael, but I wonder why she picked you."

"I wonder too. I guess I look good in desire..."

"How can you be happy in a relationship like that? You've never even seemed interested in sex."

"Surprise. But, honestly, I don't know if I'm happy. I just can't stop thinking about seeing her again."

"That's not a *good* thing. Love shouldn't be that stressful."

"How do *you* deal with not seeing Vito."

"I don't really think about it much. I know how he feels about me. And I know I'll see him again. So I just get on with my day…"

"How's the café?"

"We just got the dieffenbachias I asked for. They look great! And I think Mr. Gochnaur is going to approve my plan to turn the place into a Middle Eastern oasis. Customers love cheesy stuff like that. And it'll be fun to design."

"Sounds good."

"Mm-hmm. I thought I'd be seeing more of you there…"

"Yeah, well, I don't know if Tina would like that."

"God!" she jumped up. "Let's go see a movie. Your choice. What's playing at the rep theaters?"

"But," he mumbled, "she's supposed to call back…"

"Why? To tell you her socks are dry?"

"I don't know why…"

Diane disappeared into her room and returned in a fresh green blouse. She threw a copy of *The Mirror* at him and said: "Come on! Choose!"

Mike flipped through the paper. His mood brightened as his fingers blackened. "Hey! There's a Mickey-and-Judy musical playing at 8 o'clock! *Strike Up the Band*! You'll *love* it Di!"

"*God*," she sighed. "Wash your hands Michael…"

CHAPTER 15

▼

Wind slashed through Mike's window and bled summer sweat out of his room. The night air promised clean September rain. He rummaged deep in his dresser drawer, looking for his favorite gray sweater. The phone rang. He grabbed it and heard Eric's voice.

"What's up Mike?"

"I'm glad you called back. How do you feel about being the fourth on a double-date?"

"Who with?"

"One of the country girls. Her name's Dawn. I haven't met her. She went straight to university in Nova Scotia after high school. But she had some kind of breakdown out there, so she's starting back at square one closer to home. She just moved in with Helen. From what I hear, she's a little crazy. Writes wild stories and has several imaginary friends that she talks to. She's supposed to be quite pretty…"

"And what led to this idea?"

"I don't know. Tina says Dawn wants to meet one of my friends. Just based on Helen's description of me."

"That's interesting…"

"Is it?"

"What's going on with you and those girls?"

"Well…I feel really comfortable around them. Even Scilla. It's just Tina I can't figure out."

"She's too aloof for you."

"Hey! What happened to: 'Stop whining and enjoy the sex'?"

"I guess I feel differently today. I'm in love today."

"What?"

"Yeah. She was in my summer polisci course. Her name's Sandra. We went dancing last night and it went really well. She's still here actually. She's in the shower."

"That's great!"

"Yeah. It is. She's really cool Mike. I want you to meet her. She teaches me things. I think that's what I love most about her. That and her ass."

"Lovely."

They made a plan to see each other later in the week. Mike reached under the coffee table for his phonebook and wondered who to call. He was flattered that a girl he had never met trusted him so completely. He didn't want to fail her. But he didn't have many male friends.

The last name on a short list was Graham Blair. He volunteered immediately. Then he wasted ten minutes asking questions about Dawn. Finally, Mike whistled and said: "Okay Graham! We're gonna be late. Meet me in front of the Egyptian. Leave now!"

Mrs. Parker and the Vicious Circle was playing at eight. All Mike knew was that it was about Dorothy Parker and Dawn was eager to see it. He had no idea what to expect, but he hadn't contested the choice, because he didn't have a better suggestion.

Mike and Graham rushed into the theater just as the previews ended. Mike grumbled about "missing the best part" as they stumbled down the aisle. In the darkness, a hand clutched his sleeve and pulled him into a seat. Graham squeezed past crouched knees and disappeared behind Tina's hair. Mike ran his fingers through it and said: "Hello."

"Why did you bring *him*?" she whispered.

He shrugged and kissed her.

The silver Alliance pyramid spun against a purple screen. Soft sad saxophones did something to his ears, and he found himself, for the first time in months, caring more about what he was seeing than whose hand he held. The first shot was a slow study of a beautiful lock-jawed mouth spilling corrosive lyrics; poised between a savage bite and a crying jag. The scene shifted to a Hollywood soundstage, introducing Robert Benchley in peak bumbling-suburbanite form. On the sun-pocked lot, Benchley runs into Mrs. Parker. The two share an elegiac hug and a few words that were like salt in Mike's eye: "Visiting hours are *over*, Mr. Benchley."

In just a few minutes, the film established a mood of amiably bleeding regret that stung Mike. The bulk of the movie was a twenties flashback montage of murderous quips and suicidal introspection. The old vague suspicion that he was a cripple revived in Mike's mind. The problem, as he saw it, was how much weight other shoulders could bear. The characters in the film never made up their minds. Benchley and Parker slashed each other with love and laughed tears into the wounds, but their tongues never touched. Mike liked to believe that no one could stand on their own. But if Tina was a cripple, she had damned good wooden legs.

The scenes washed over Mike and sealed his numb past behind him. He foresaw himself ransacking Tina's body for needs she didn't have. It occurred to him that he was the kind of person who might spend his life feeling under women's wrists for a brand of authenticity...

The lights went on and he got up to stretch. He glanced at the girl sitting next to Tina. Her eyes were mosaics of blue, green, and gold crystals. She noticed Mike looking at her and reached for his hand.

"Hi. I'm Dawn Paris."

"It's nice to meet you."

"Why?" she smirked. Her front teeth pushed off each other at odd angles and every word that passed through them was slightly distorted.

"You've got great taste in movies."

"Thanks."

Graham rocked in his seat like a boy confined to his room on a hobbyhorse.

Mike jutted his chin at him. "This is my friend Graham."

Dawn shrugged and said: "I thought we were going drinking."

Tina yawned: "Yeah yeah. We'll go to Helen's bar. It's just around the corner."

They left the theatre. Dawn raced ahead and had a pitcher on her table when the others walked in. Everything about The Pub was stale. They played dusty seventies guitar-rock and constant reruns of sports events on the television monitors. The walls were orange and brown and singed by cigarette smoke. It was two flights deep in the ground, under a bank, and there were no windows. Most of the customers were students: afraid to go home to their books and afraid to think about the consequences. So they drank the cheap beer. And even that was rumored to be recycled.

The only bright thing in the place was Helen. She loved being there and it showed. She walked toward her friends' table, humming Weezer's 'Say it Ain't So'.

"What do you guys feel for?"

Graham ordered shots for himself and Dawn. Tina ordered a rum-and-coke. Mike asked for a coffee. Helen reminded him that it wasn't very good. He assured her that he didn't care. She smiled: "I love this! I wish you guys came every night!"

"I might *do* that," Dawn mused. "Can you bring me some lemons, Hellie?"

"What for?"

"I need them."

"O-kay…"

"Good. Good."

Helen left them. Dawn looked at Mike. "You're not drinking?"

"No."

"Like in the movie. Like Mr. Benchley." (Benchley had not taken a drink until the age of thirty-one. He died twenty years later of cirrhosis of the liver.)

"Hopefully not too much like him…"

"Oh, I think you are, Mr. Borden."

Mike avoided her eyes. He had reached the same conclusion, but he had almost forgotten.

"What a boring movie," Tina said. "All those babies, whining over nothing…"

Dawn's head swiveled. Blood rushed into her pale cheeks. Her lip curled upward but her teeth remained sheathed. One eyebrow crawled contemptuously under her long red hair. The other hung close to a blue-green universe of mischief, pity, and dread. "It's the best movie I've ever seen."

"Psh."

Dawn turned to Graham. "What did *you* think?"

He was rocking again. "I-I loved it."

"Mm," she mumbled.

"So—uh—Dawn," Graham coughed, "what brought you to Montreal."

"Well," she rested her soft chin on her hand, "I'm studying lit at Marianopolis. But I'll tell you something," the slight lisp in her voice took over as she lowered it, "my first love is explosives. Bombs and metro stations. That's what I dream of. I'm scouting around, looking for the perfect target. Right now I'm leaning toward Lionel-Groulx. It needs a new name anyway."

Graham smiled dutifully. Mike's insides hemorrhaged with laughter. Tina whispered in his ear: "She's been drinking all day."

Dawn's face grew serious as she fished through her beer for a strand of hair that had fallen in. She pulled it out and flicked the moisture on her fingers at Graham.

"Hey!" he tried to protect himself.

Helen returned with the drinks. And the lemons. Dawn grabbed one and bit into it. She focused on a table full of linebacker-types ten feet away. A freckly piece of beef with a brown crew-cut leered back. Dawn's face was a mask of disdain as the acid seeped into her tongue.

The scrum conceded their impotence. Five pairs of eyes slunk into their beer mugs.

"What're you doing?" Helen demanded.

"I'm sucking a lemon."

Helen walked off shaking her head and the serious drinking began. Between rounds, Dawn spoke in non sequiturs, harassed the neighboring tables, and made the occasional brilliant observation. She wondered aloud whether Graham was ticklish and proceeded to find out. He was. She asked Mike for a list of movies to avoid, gravely took notes during his lecture, then made plans to rent each one. ("Now that I understand what you hate about Stanley Kubrick," she explained, "I'm sure I'll appreciate him all the more.") Graham kept buying her drinks, but he never gained control of the situation he was trying to create.

Tina sat back in her chair like a cat on a window-sill watching a traffic jam. Dawn kept spinning her wheels. She floored Mike. For a minute, he got lost in her wildness. It was his wildness too. Then he leaned across the table to kiss Tina's lips.

Dawn giggled and grabbed Graham's arm. "C'mon! They need privacy!"

Graham followed her with a dull smile.

When Mike's mouth slipped off Tina's, they were alone at the table. He looked around, but saw no sign of Dawn or Graham. He felt relieved. But there was no comforting reason why he should have. They walked over to the bar and asked Helen what had happened.

"They said goodnight," she shrugged. "They're gone."

"I guess she *did* like Graham," Tina said.

"Guess so," Mike nodded.

CHAPTER 16

▼

Mike parted brown macramé curtains and stared out of the Canadian Holistics Bureau. Behind him, he heard Tina and a group of fortyish housewives dancing in circles and chanting: "We are *one* in the infinite *sun*." There was sage in the air. Too much sage. The room smelled like the prairie equivalent of an old widow's boudoir. A foot struck Mike's left calf and he spun around. It was Julian, a middle-aged man with a green saucepan on his head.

After a month and a half at her new school, Tina had invited Mike to experience it for himself. Of course he had accepted. They had spent the afternoon in Tina's living room, slithering amorously between the couch and the carpet. Around four-thirty, they had jumped into their clothes and rushed off to the school. She had introduced him to her classmates and they had all crept into the sagy room, where the instructor—a gaunt six-foot woman with frizzy brown hair—whispered orders like a New Age drill sergeant.

Mike watched Tina strut clockwise and counter-clockwise, mouthing the lyrics of the song. As usual, her cheeks had a healthy freshness that fades off most faces before the first morning yawn. But he had never seen her look so *awake*. Some of the ladies had cloudy, moved eyes, but Tina's glinted like beetles' wings under a flashlight. Julian started to cry and the group closed in on him for a hug. Tina hung back. She gawked at them. Like a tourist watching a geyser at Yellowstone.

Mike limped away before the hour was up. He waited outside the building. Soon, Tina joined him and asked: "What did you think?"

"Guess."

"I don't know," she shrugged.

"I found it embarrassing."

"Yeah, they're a bunch of drama-queens. The class is almost over too. That made it worse tonight."

She hitched her arm to his and they started to walk.

"I don't understand what *you* get out of it. You're *not* a drama-queen."

"No. But I've never felt more like myself than at school. No one pries. No one tries to *understand* me. Maybe it's because the criers keep them busy. Whatever. It works for me."

Mike swallowed hard and tried to smile.

"One of your pals said I've got a 'beautiful aura'."

"Mm? Which one?"

"I can't tell them apart."

She let go of his arm and hailed a cab.

"Well, I think I'll go home now. I'm kinda tired."

"Really? You don't want to get something to eat first?"

"No. I'll be fine. Goodnight." She kissed him and got into the car.

Mike turned his back on the exhaust and crossed Sherbrooke street. He walked a few blocks to a junk-shop that he loved. A 'closed' sign stopped him at the door. Twenty-five cent novels and the wind-blown mess of his hair played in the dark glass. He shrugged and followed brown leaves to a pay-phone. A bright blue 7:01 blinked on the display. He stared at it until his fingers remembered Helen and Dawn's number. Half a ring later, he heard a click, a quick breath, and a "Hello."

"Hi, uh, Dawn, it's Mike."

"Hey! How are you?"

"I'm all right. I was just wondering what you guys were up to."

"Not much. Why don't you come over?"

"Really?"

"Sure," she lisped. There was a smile in her voice. "I'll make some popcorn and rent *2001*."

"Funny."

"Mm-hmm."

"See you soon." He hung up the phone and walked to the metro. There was no one on the street and no moon in the sky. It was early but it felt late.

He buzzed the apartment around seven-thirty. Helen had lived there for four months, but the ghost of the previous tenant still haunted the name-plate next to her number.

"Yes?" Dawn giggled through static.

"Abacassis please," Mike asked formally.

"Abacassis is dead."

"Where do I send flowers?"

The lock clicked and he took the elevator to the fifth floor. He knocked at door #501 and Dawn wrenched it open. Her body was spastic with laughter and balanced on one foot. She coddled the other one in her hands. There was a black phone sprawled off its hook on the living room floor. Dawn hopped to a gray couch and fell on it.

"Are you okay?" Mike yelped.

"Uh-huh. It's just my baby-toe…"

"What happened?"

"I walked into the wall. It's broken."

"Are you sure?"

"Uh-huh." She stretched her foot toward him and shook it. "Look how it wiggles."

"Jesus! Should we go to the hospital?"

"They wouldn't be able to do anything. I'll just immobilize it. Could you get me the masking tape in the kitchen drawer, next to the stove?"

Mike fetched the tape-roll and handed it to her.

"Thanks."

She stared at the dangling toe. She pressed it tight against its neighbor and unraveled some tape with her teeth. Determined gasps slipped through them and steamed up her eyes. She blinked and the gold flecks in the blue burned the fog away.

"Could you hold my foot steady while I tape it up?"

"Okay," he nodded. He knelt in front of her and grabbed hold of her heel and calf. The taut bulge in her leg surprised him. The warm, pinkish skin over it had gaping pores. She had taken a bath recently. She took a deep breath and wrapped several layers of tape around the toes.

"There." She pulled her foot out of his hands and limped around the boomerang-shaped coffee table.

"Will it be okay?"

She grinned: "If it doesn't heal, I'll just chop it off."

"You can find another assistant for that one…"

"Squeamish Mike?"

"Uh-huh."

"Too squeamish to watch me finish a mickey of vodka?"

"That's your business."

"Good. It's in the kitchen. There's some iced coffee in the fridge for you."

"Iced coffee in October? Why?"

"It's better that way."

Mike wandered into the kitchen and found a large tortoise-shell lapping from a water-dish. She had wide ears, a healthy pink tongue, black gums and a distinguished stomach-pouch. Her yellow eyes brimmed with accusations.

"Hey!" he called into the living room. "Where'd this cat come from?"

"That's Inez," Dawn called back. There was a tenderness in her voice he'd never heard before.

"Inez?"

"Uh huh. We've been friends since I was thirteen."

"Is she nice?"

"Pick her up," she giggled.

He heard her hobbling toward the kitchen.

"O-ka-ay." Mike approached the cat and spread his arms.

"No don't!" Dawn put her hand on his shoulder. "She'll come see you later."

"Why'd you stop me?"

Her eyes were Chinese boxes of color: "I-I didn't want her to hurt you."

He handed her the vodka and helped himself to the coffee. They walked back to the living room and sat down. Dawn took a long swig from the bottle and smiled at him. It was a quiet smile: unencumbered by a giggle or a crack. She looked comfortable in blue-checked flannel and Levis that followed the arcs of her hips. She put the vodka on the table.

"So. Where's Tina?"

"Oh. We spent the day together. She went home. She was tired. Of me I guess."

"Come on!"

"Well..."

"What happened out here!?" Helen burst into the room in a beacht-owel-turban, trailing clouds of steam from the bathroom.

"I walked into the wall. See!" Dawn kicked her foot in the air.

"Does it hurt?"

"Uh huh."

"So I guess you're not coming out with me."

"No. Mike and I are having too much fun with Dial-A-M8. Right Mike?"

He repeated Dawn's words to himself until they made sense. Then he said "Right," and picked the phone off the floor.

Dawn took it from him and pressed it against her ear.

"Ooh! They waited for me! I have five new messages!"

She reached for an Italian phrasebook on the coffee-table and punched a series of numbers.

"Hi Tony. This is Peaches. I'm so glad you wanted to speak to me…" Dawn caricatured her lisp. It still gave Mike goose bumps.

"Oh, I understand. Of *course* you need variety…"

"Ooh, I can *imagine* how big it is…"

"I just *love* Italian studs…"

"Oh that's *so* cool! I'm trying to learn…"

"Okay," she flipped through the pages, giggling on low, "uh, *prendere la pillola?*…"

"No no. I didn't make a mistake. That's what I wanted to ask you…"

"Okay. How about this one: *il…tuo madre…è…una…puttane.* Did I say that right?…"

"Tony, don't get mad. No one's going to commit adultery with a sourpuss…"

The voice on the line rose and she dismissed it. She looked at Mike, pressed some buttons, and threw him the phone: "Your turn!"

Oil oozed from the receiver: "I can't bear the thought of you sitting there by yourself…Why don't I come over and finish what you started?"

Mike put gravel in his deep voice and cooed: "I'd love it, big guy."

"Who's this?! Where's Peaches?"

"This *is* Peaches."

"Mother*fucker*!!!"

Mike hung up the phone. He beamed at Dawn: "What does your ad *say?*"

"Guess," she laughed wildly. He joined her.

Helen's pursed lips said: "I didn't think you were this silly, Mike."

She left the room to get dressed.

"See what you've done," Mike gasped melodramatically, "*you* are the enabler!"

"Good!"

"Are you ever serious?"

"Not often."

"Not even when you're writing?"

"Especially not then."

"I've heard about your stories."

"Have you?"

"Do I have to beg to see one?"

"No," she took another long swig of vodka, "but you'll have to wait until Helen leaves. She treats them like puzzles."

"So?" Mike asked.

"So...they're not...And why should they be?"

Mike tried to think of something to add. Then Helen marched through the room, announced: "Bye guys! —Bye? —*Bye!*" and hurried off. She wasn't gentle with the door.

"Okay," Dawn said, "I'll read you a story."

She rummaged through a black hassock in the corner of the room that doubled as a TV stand. She pulled out a red folder and hopped back to the couch. The quiet smile returned: "Ready?"

"Uh huh," Mike nodded. He leaned back, closed his eyes, and listened.

"Dorothea would not go quietly. That much was certain. Which was odd because she had never said a word until then. But she woke up that morning with a headache and a mission. Her brain was aboil in the juices of truth. At long last, she had a message to communicate. It was this: '*I have nothing intelligible to say to any of you! Do you understand me!*'

"She was prepared to scream it from the rafters. If only her knee would heel. But not in English. That would undermine her purpose. She breakfasted on the skins of five egg rolls and limped down to the river. Her friends were frolicking there. It was a dark morning. The sun was pale and silvery. She put on her snorkel and gnashed the air with it like a mad elephant. She made elephantine noises too. The frolicking ceased.

"'Good one Dorothea,' yelled the boy with the good stubble. 'Can you do a bison?' *What do you think I was just doing?* she wondered. She decided his stubble wasn't so good. If he thought she was playing charades, he should have told her not to make a sound. *And what about those sounds?* she thought. *Didn't they curdle your marrow?* She went home to rethink her strategy. Actually, she went home to eat more batter. She knew she'd never have a strategy.

"'Dorothea talks now,' the whole town was saying. 'It's true she ain't any too interestin', but giv'er time.' *Time*, she agreed, *that's what I need. Time to perfect my technique as an arsonist. Time to think my way out of this fog of clarity. Time to remember how to be quiet.*"

Mike's body seized up in the grip of inexpressible laughter.

Inez jumped onto the sofa.

"She's beautiful," he said.

"Yes."

Dawn reached for a black hair-pick on the table and held it near the cat's face. Inez purred instantly and rubbed her whiskery cheeks against the plastic.

"She loves her pick."

"How old is she?"

"Seven."

"She was born on the farm?"

"No. We got her when she was a couple months old…"

"Do you have any pictures?"

Dawn started to get up.

"Rest your toe," Mike said. "Where's the album?"

"In my bedroom. On top of the bookshelf."

Mike went to get it. He turned on the light and looked at Dawn's room. It had clean hardwood floors. There were a few paintings on the walls. Strange, fuzzy-lettered words and question marks caught in dark color-webs. A single mattress covered by a horse-blanket lay in the far right corner of the room. Across from it, on the other side of a small window, was a rickety desk. It could barely support her typewriter.

There was a short black bookcase next to the desk. Its shelves were crowded with cracked volumes and cassette tapes. Mike glanced at the selection. Some of it he liked (*Wuthering Heights, Poems of Edna St. Vincent Millay*), some of it he hated (*Works of Sir Walter Scott, Greatest Hits of the Eagles*), most of it he was indifferent to.

Mike took the album and inspected an old dresser next to the door. He wondered if it had been passed down to her through the family, or bought at the Salvation Army. The wood was the color of a deep bruise. A framed picture of Inez, one bottle of perfume, and a neatly folded pair of pyjamas rested on it. Mike switched off the light.

He returned to his spot on the couch. Dawn opened the old book and blew dust off the plastic that covered the photos. There were no people in the first ten pages. Every shot was of a cherished farm animal. A huge gray quarter horse figured prominently. "That's Moon-shadow," Dawn explained. Finally, a scrawny version of Dawn appeared, holding a black and orange bundle close to her undeveloped chest. She stared directly at the camera, and she already had a woman's eyes. Her lip was curled up in defiant tenderness.

Mike touched the picture. "You have blonde hair."

"Sure. This is just dye. See."

She leaned toward him.

He nodded: "Uh huh."

They talked for hours, using the album as their text. Helen never came home. They didn't notice. They noticed the sun.

"God I'm tired," she yawned. "Aren't you?"

"Yeah, kind of."

"Why don't you stay? You can sleep in my bed. I'll use Helen's. She wouldn't like it, but she never stays mad for long."

"No. I'd better go home. The cats must be starving."

"Yeah," she sighed.

She led him to the door.

"Well, I'll see ya," she lisped. She brushed her hand across his arm. Bees stung him from the inside.

"Goodnight."

CHAPTER 17

▼

Mike stood at his window and watched tinsel bounce off the pavement. The street wore November mirror-puddles and brown-leaf mulch. He had spent the day choking on dry heat at MarcoSport, looking forward to a dip in the mist. He had rushed home to call Tina, to ask her to join him. She hadn't answered. He had eaten and finished two coffees. Then he had watched *Singin' In The Rain*. He was almost ready to leave. Almost.

The telephone rang.

"Who *is* this girl Mike?" a peevish voice yelped.

"Graham?"

"I mean: *what* is she? What the *Hell* is she?"

"Why don't you just tell me what she did?"

"Oh I will Mike. I will. Just let me catch my breath."

"Good idea," Mike mumbled. He kept watching the rain.

"Okay. Well, you know I've been dating Dawn for about two months."

"Uh-huh."

"And today was my birthday."

"Happy Birthday."

"Yeah, thanks. Anyway. My parents took me out for dinner. Chinese buffet."

"Uh-huh."

"So I asked Dawn to come with me. Because she's my *girlfriend*. And it's the kind of thing you're *supposed* to do with your girlfriend."

"So what happened? She didn't come?"

"Oh she came Mike. She came."

"But she upset you?"

"She upset *everyone*. Especially my grandmother...I mean she started off okay. She wasn't very talkative, but I didn't mind that. I just wanted her to smile a bit, enjoy the free meal, and show them I've grown up."

"Uh-huh."

"Instead, she picked at one plate of food all night. I mean she *dissected* this spring roll. All she ate was the crust and a few bits of mushroom she found inside. And she kept making sour faces at our meat. She gets this *look* sometimes Mike. Like a hanging judge..."

"Yeah, I've seen it."

"Anyway. That was bad. But dessert was a whole lot worse."

Mike chuckled in anticipation.

"Don't laugh. Please don't laugh. It wasn't funny...Dawn got up and said she wanted something sweet. She actually excused herself from the table. She even smiled. My grandmother nodded at her. I started to think everything would be okay. I watched Dawn walk to the buffet. She had a black skirt on. It looked pretty good. I mean, her body's not *great*, but she's good-looking, don't you think?"

"I do."

"I was so *proud*. You must know what I mean. When you have to wait as long as *we* did, you spend every minute between dates worrying that it isn't real. That it's all a practical joke. Half the time that I *am* with her, she isn't very reassuring. I mean, she's always disappearing on me or playing some kind of trick. But for a second there, I felt great. I sat with my mom and my dad and my grandmother, and I watched Dawn. *My* Dawn. Then everything went to shit.

"She poked through the cakes and pies, but didn't take any. She walked right by the ice cream. Then she saw the fortune cookies. A big silver salad-bowl full of them. She stood in front of it, with her back to me, for about a minute. Then she just grabbed the whole fuckin' thing and carried it back to the table. She had the same polite smile. She sat down and started cracking open cookies. Mike, she didn't eat *any* of them! Not one! She tossed the cookies on her greasy plate. But she made a neat little pile out of the fortunes as she read them. She whispered the words. To *herself.* My grandmother poked me with a chopstick: 'What's she doing Graham? What's she saying?' I-I shrugged. I froze. And then Dawn started cackling! *Cackling* Mike! Really loud! Everyone in the restaurant was watching! It was horrible. Horrible! She made me look like an idiot!"

"I'm sorry Graham. But I don't know why you're surprised…"

"Yeah I know. She's crazy. She's fuckin' crazy!" He screeched. Then he added, under his breath: "She's crazy everywhere but in bed…"

"Spare me."

"I'm serious Mike. You'd think she'd be wild and kinky. But she's actually kind of inhibited. She won't even…"

The call-waiting beep interrupted. Mike switched lines. Dawn's lisp greeted him. He switched back.

"I've gotta go Graham. It's long-distance. For my sister. I'll call you back…"

He returned to Dawn with a scolding tone: "What have you done?"

"Aw! Who spoiled my surprise?"

"Graham."

"That dork! He didn't even laugh!"

"I guess he thought the timing was off."

"It was perfect! I waited a whole hour. I gave them a chance. But I couldn't stand his dad's stupid jokes and his mom's stupid advice and his grandmother's…uh…well, just his grandmother. Who cares about Graham's *grandmother?*"

"Well, you *are* dating him."

"So?"

"Don't you like him?"

"Sure I do. He's goofy. He makes me laugh. I even thought I loved him for a while. That's the thing about me, Mike: I can make myself love *anyone*. But I've never taken him seriously."

"That's obvious."

"Well, he can take it or leave it."

"I guess so."

"Come on Mike," she sounded worried, "I'll read your fortune. We'll keep going 'till we find one you like."

"Cute."

"Hey, it was a buffet. Why should we be allowed fifty egg rolls but only one stupid proverb? I was completely within my rights. Which is good. I'll bend the rules when I have to, but I prefer to slip *through* them, if I can."

"I see. You were exploiting a cosmic loophole. Standing up to fate."

"Exactly. Also, I wanted to get the Blairs moving. I was tired of them. Is that so wrong?"

"I guess not."

"You should have seen them Mike. They didn't believe it was happening. I could see all of their tonsils!" She broke into a giggle. "And then grandma started begging the owner to forgive me. I would've grabbed the almond cookies if it had gone on much longer..."

Mike laughed helplessly.

Dawn's voice glowed: "It was good."

"Sure," Mike regained his composure, "but I feel bad for Graham. You treat him like a prop. Or maybe I just feel bad for myself, because Tina treats me the same way..."

"She couldn't."

"Why not?"

"Because you've got integrity."

"Have you discussed this with her?"

"Of course not. Tina doesn't do that. But I've seen you together. The way you touch each other. It makes me sick, but I'm happy for you too. I don't know how the Hell you managed that."

Mike was startled. "I don't know what to say…"

"Just stop worrying, that's all."

"I'll try…What are you doing tonight?"

"My dad's driving me back to the country for the weekend."

"When's he getting there?"

"Oh, he's been here the whole time. I told him I had to make a phone call…"

"You're crazy."

"Thanks."

"Have a good weekend."

"You too. Good night."

Mike hung up the phone. Dawn's words whistled through his brain. He carved a new image of himself out of her breath.

He had never called Tina twice in one night before. He had never dared. She always got back to him when she was ready to feed him a cue. But he told himself the script needed rewriting. He dialed her number.

"Hello?" Tina answered.

"Hey."

"Hi Mike. I got your message before…"

"Uh huh. And you didn't feel like answering it?"

"Well, I've been reading. Anyway, I figured you'd be out by now."

"I wanted to be."

"So why aren't you?"

"Because you didn't call me back."

"Don't try to *guilt-trip* me Mike. We didn't have plans tonight."

"I'm n—I'm not *guilt-tripping* you Tina! I just want to see you. It's been four days…"

"What's the difference?"

"Is that really what you think?"

"Stop whining Mike."

"I'm *not* whining," Mike whined.

"So. You're not whining and you're not guilt-tripping me. Okay. I guess I'm pretty dumb tonight."

"Why are you doing this?"

"Because this is not cool Mike. I thought you understood me. There's a lot going on in my life. You know that."

"I know you *say* that. But I don't know what could possibly be…"

"What could possibly be what? More important than you? Is that what you were going to say?"

"Maybe."

"Well I'm sorry. But *I'm* more important to me right now."

"Oh yeah. The great Spiritual Quest."

"Where's this sarcasm coming from?"

"From the pit of my stomach. Where it's been since I met you. Tina I love you! I want to see you. I want to be on your mind when I'm not around…"

"You're making me the *center* of your life!"

"No kidding! That's what love's all about!"

"No it isn't! Not for me. I can't believe I'm hearing this from you!"

"*I* can't believe you're so surprised. Did you think I'd just take this forever?"

"I didn't think about *this* at all!"

"No," Mike choked, "I guess…you didn't…"

"I'm sorry Mike. I don't want to hurt you. I don't want to hurt anyone. But I can't spend my life worrying about whether I'm neglecting you."

"No. It's not—it's not…"

"I feel *really* uncomfortable right now Mike. I don't think we should see each other for a while."

"You're—you're breaking up with me?"

"How can you even *want* to be with me? This is obviously killing you. You sound hysterical."

"Be-because I love you."

"And why's that?"

"Because…"

"Let's talk in a few days Mike."

"Okay…I love you…"

"I love you too."

Mike dropped the phone. He felt like a *pinata*. Like he'd been hand-crafted for the beating he'd just received. His lips had been cracking for months. And then he had handed Tina the bat. But she didn't want the candy inside him.

Mike sank into the couch. The front door clicked and he heard Diane and Vito laughing in the hallway. He grabbed a pen and started rifling through the Gazette for the crossword. He drew a mental picture of himself smiling and tried to color it in with his lips.

"I don' know babe. I think maybe I'm gonna haveta getchoo one of those electronic agendas…"

"Look who's talking!" Diane tapped Vito's arm gently.

"Hey! Me I don't pretend that I'm little-miss-organized!"

"I'd like to see you pretend to be little-miss-anything…"

"Oh you would hunh?" Vito smiled. He looked at Mike. "Hey Mike! What's up?"

"Not much."

"We won' be here long. Your sister forgot our free passes to the movie…"

"It's no big deal," Diane shrugged and hustled toward her room.

"Naw," Vito raised his voice so that she could hear him, "it's no big deal Mike. But maybe you should ask Tina about a *herb* for memory problems. Y'know, in case it gets worse…"

Diane returned with the papers. She smirked at Vito: "Gee, I *hope* it doesn't get *much* worse. I might forget your number."

"Ha. What movie we going to see babe?"

"I'm not telling you."

Their comfortable banter made Mike wince.

Diane sat on the couch next to him and looked into his eyes. "Are you okay Mike?"

"Yeah," he pressed his palm to his forehead, "just got a headache."

"Did you take some aspirin?"

"Uh-huh, about twenty minutes ago. I'm sure I'll be fine soon."

"You want me to make you some tea before we go?"

"No thanks, Di. I think I'll take a nap…"

"Okay," she kissed his cheek. "I'll see you on Sunday."

"Good night."

Vito opened the door for her and waved: "G'night Mike. Don't forget about those herbs."

"I won't."

Diane shot him a final glance.

Mike threw the Gazette back on the coffee table and turned out the lights. The conversation with Tina ran in loops through his mind. He never told anyone anything he was thinking until he had processed it. Other voices in his head just clogged up the works.

Mike hated kind words of advice. He hated Tina for pushing him toward the gauzy floodlight of sympathy. He saw himself exposed: to Diane's mothering throb, to Eric's philosophical chimes. He imagined their voices blending into a murderous dirge. His only escape was a swift appraisal of the situation, before the news got out. Then he could smile hermetically as the compassion rained down.

But he couldn't decide how he felt. He had goaded Tina into breaking up with him. Was he happy then? Happy about what? That he had understood the logic of their relationship better than she had? Was that even true? Tina was as clever as she was absent-minded, and maybe he had only reminded her of something that she already knew. Something she would have put off indefinitely. Meanwhile, he would have had continued access to her body. He had never had access to her mind.

Mike looked at the VCR clock and realized how much he wanted to call Dawn. He whispered the phone number to himself. He tried to imitate the voice that had given it to him. It wasn't a musical voice. She couldn't sing at all. It wasn't cultured—although she had a good vocabulary. It wasn't even feminine, in any traditional sense. It was kind of husky. And she had a pronounced lisp. But every sound her palate brushed meant something to him.

Were her huge tonsils were responsible? (Mike had seen them because—whenever she had a cold—she would open her mouth wide, stick out her tongue, and say: "I have phlegm. What color is it?"). Did the triangular space between her front teeth put the edge on what she said? It didn't matter. Her words sank into him. Entered his bloodstream.

Dawn had called around 8:30. Mike dialed her number at ten o'clock.

"Hello," a male voice answered.

"Hi, could I speak to Dawn please?"

"Sure. I'll pass you to her."

"Hello?" she asked tentatively.

"Hi."

"Mike! Uh, let me switch to the phone in my room okay?"

"Sure."

He waited until her voice returned.

"Okay. What's wrong?"

"What do you mean?"

"Come on."

"Well…"

"Did Tina's cards tell her you're the wrong sign?"

"No, but I guess I am."

"What?" her voice quavered.

"She—she broke up with me…"

Dawn started to cry. He couldn't really hear it. But he felt it. And he wondered why he hadn't thought of that. He touched his face. His eyelashes were slick. He wiped the moisture on his shirt and smiled.

Dawn sniffed: "She's crazy…"

"Oh I don't know…"

"Are you going to be okay?"

"Yeah."

"Good," she brightened. "Don't do any laundry this weekend!"

"What?"

"I'll be back Sunday night. There's this laundromat-cafe that just opened near my place. It's called Sudz. Look it up in the phonebook. Meet me there at eight o'clock. I'll buy you a coffee!"

"Okay."

"Goodnight Mike."

"Goodnight."

CHAPTER 18

▼

At five o'clock the next day, Mike sat eyeing his king's pawn. Eventually, he reached out and pushed the piece forward two squares.

"Do you want the whites?" Eric asked him.

Mike stared at him.

"Do you want to go first?"

"Oh," Mike mumbled, "uh, no, that's okay."

"Alright," Eric moved his own king's pawn.

Mike sipped his coffee and tried to focus on the game. It soon got out of hand. Knights and bishops blitzed from all sides and all he wanted to do was castle. He didn't get the chance. Eric wouldn't let him.

"So, she just said 'I love you too' and hung up?"

"That's all."

"What a fuckin' crock!"

"No, I think she meant it."

"You think the two of you will stay friends?"

"Yeah. I do."

"I don't know Mike. Don't pin your hopes on it."

"I won't. No more pins *or* needles."

"Well, she's right about one thing. You *did* make her the center of your life."

"Not quite. She never let me..."

"You almost sound happy."

"Well," Mike shook his head, "I'm not. That's check-mate, isn't it?"

"Uh-huh."

Mike eased back into the couch and watched Eric put the pieces away. Eric opened the last bottle of his six-pack and folded his arms over his chest.

"Mike, I've been here for three hours, and I still don't have a clue how you're feeling."

"What do you mean?"

"Let's put it this way: when you told me about all this, I was worried you might kill yourself. I'm still worried."

"Come on! You think I'm that much of a drama-queen?"

"I guess I do. Have you forgotten the stuff you've said about love over the years?"

"No. But maybe I was wrong. Or maybe I was never in love with Tina at all. Not the way I wanted to be."

"Hey. You *told* me about her. Sounded like love to me."

"Well, that's the thing. I'm starting to think that true love *can't* be described. You wouldn't even try…"

"Whatever."

"Besides, the love I'm talking about can't just *end*. On the phone like that. It *can't*. If it does, it wasn't love at all. It was something else."

"That's convenient."

"It is. I also think it's true."

"Well," Eric shrugged, "this is ridiculous. I keep expecting things to humanize you. But nothing does. You just keep finding new base emotions to build your pedestal on."

"Eric…"

"I won't bother telling you about Deborah. I *feel* like I love her, but it's probably not *true* love. It might end! We can't have that! Not in Mike's perfect romantic sphere!"

"I'd love to hear about her."

"Some other time," Eric pulled his coat out of the closet. "Looks like you're gonna be fine. That's all I wanted to know." He paused at the door. "Except that was the worst game of chess you ever played. *Something's* bothering you..."

"Yeah, you're getting too good."

Eric smiled: "I'll see you later."

"Bye."

Mike closed his eyes. There *was* something. A harp-string garrote caught his throat. His fingers grasped a melody as he choked.

⁂

Mike got to Sudz early on Sunday night. He had expected to get lost, but he hadn't. He tossed a bag of mixed clothes into a lime-green washer and sat down. Only one other table was taken. The room was small and dim, but large windows let in headlights and lamplight from the street. The air smelled like fabric softener and coffee perking. The machines hummed together and Mike almost fell asleep.

Dawn showed up at eight. A small bell tinkled when she walked through the door. She glared maliciously at the apparatus.

"I wanted to surprise you. Your eyes were closed."

Mike unzipped his lashes with his knuckles.

"You surprise me when they're open."

Dawn smiled her quiet smile.

She stood facing him, rolling a black hockey-bag from side to side across her back. He had never noticed how tall she was. About five-eight, he guessed. Since he had last seen her, the rusty dross had been rinsed from her long hair. She wore blue jeans and a red chain-link wool sweater. Her cheeks were spiced by the cold and the red made her blue-green eyes heat up.

"Aren't you going to put your clothes in the washer?" he asked.

"Uh-huh," she nodded.

She lugged her bag to the machines and claimed two of them. The clothes were pre-separated into lights and darks. Mike couldn't be bothered with such things, but he admired her meticulousness.

Dawn poured in the soap and set the dynamos whirring. She bought two coffees at the counter and brought them to the table. Mike took one from her and said: "Thanks."

"No problem," she smiled and sat down. "So how was your week-end?"

"I thought a lot. I barely moved."

"Yeah? I did a lot of walking. There'll be snow on the ground soon."

"The fall is so short."

"It is. But, I mean, that's the point, isn't it? I mean, autumn is just a dying gasp. And how long does that take? The rest is a wake."

"That's pretty morbid."

"Sure. We're morbid people Mike."

"Are we?"

"Hadn't you noticed?"

"I guess I'm not as self-aware as you. I thought I was too happy."

She sipped her coffee and her lips recoiled. "Damn! Still too hot!"

"Okay," Mike conceded, "maybe I'm *not* happy. But I *want* to be."

"Yeah. That's what things with Tina were all about, right? Wanting to be happy?"

Mike stared at her: "What else?"

Dawn kept a disapproving eye on her steaming mug. "I guess you're right. What else could there be?"

"I wish you'd just drink your coffee."

"Me too."

Mike watched his feet dangle. He didn't know what to say next. He thought Dawn might walk out on him and their clothing. But she didn't. She said: "I broke up with Graham."

"What?" Mike looked up.

"Yeah. I told him it wasn't working out."

"When?"

"Yesterday. On the phone."

"Oh man."

"I know. But what the Hell? I really didn't feel like seeing him."

"So what happened?"

"He asked me what he did wrong. I said: 'Nothing. But I only call you when I think of a new way to torture you.'"

Mike laughed.

Dawn laughed too.

"So we're both single," Mike said.

"*Everyone's* single."

"Maybe. But we've been singled out."

"What does that mean?"

"Oh. Did you want to have a conversation that makes sense?"

"Not particularly."

"I didn't think so."

When the rinsing and drying and folding was done, they looked at each other, wondering whether the evening had ended. Finally, Mike asked: "Wanna come over? We could watch a movie."

"Sure."

They left stained mugs on the table and a smile on the face of an old man who had been trying to read the paper all night. It was a chilling thirty minute walk, but they didn't pool their warmth.

Mike was relieved to find Diane and Vito on the couch when he opened the door. He had expected them to be in bed. It was after eleven o'clock on a Sunday night.

Diane muted the television and said: "Are you okay Michael? Eric told me what happened." Then she noticed Dawn. "Who's this?"

Mike performed the introductions. He had told his sister a few superficial details about Dawn, but they hadn't stuck in her head. She judged the newcomer by her demure appearance and looked at her trustingly: "*Is* he alright Dawn?"

"Well," Dawn thought for a moment, "he's given up that silly idea about the river, if that's what you mean."

"What?!"

"She's kidding," Mike hugged Diane. "I'm fine Di. Really."

"What have you been doing?"

"Laundry."

"Oh."

Vito cleared his throat: "Me and your sister thought it would be fun to play a board-game. Scrabble or something."

"Really?" Mike looked at Diane.

Her smile was almost convincing. "Uh-huh."

"Great!" he turned to Dawn. "You up for that?"

"Sure," she nodded. Her smile was *very* convincing. But it wasn't the kind that marketing execs put on boxes.

"Alright!" Mike got the game out of the closet and Diane pulled two chairs up to the coffee table.

Diane drew an A and went first. She placed a conservative CAT on the board for ten points. Dawn played next. She scowled at her tray for a few minutes. Then her eyes lit up. She put down all of her letters—spelling the word BATERING—and yelled: "Yahtzee!"

Diane muttered: "Batering…batering…that's not a word!"

"Yes it is," Dawn looked deadly serious.

Mike chuckled: "Use it in a sentence."

"Ummm…umm…"

"Do I have to get a dictionary?" Diane threatened.

Mike put a finger to his lips: "Shh! She's thinking."

"She can't think a word into the English language! Some of us have to work tomorrow…"

"Oh alright," Dawn gave up and rearranged the letters to spell BERATING. "But it was more fun the other way…"

"Jesus!" Diane shook her head.

Vito got up to get himself a beer.

The game plodded along for an hour and a half. Mike couldn't concentrate at all. Diane's questions about his emotional state and Dawn's acrostics kept him busy. Vito passed half of his turns. He looked exhausted. He didn't say a word to Dawn the whole night.

The game ended at twelve-thirty with Dawn in the lead. Diane kissed Mike's cheek and said: "We'll talk some more tomorrow Michael."

"Okay."

She waved weakly at Dawn and dragged Vito off to bed.

Mike whispered with a smirk: "Di's not a night-person. It was sweet of her to stay up and annoy me…"

"Yeah, well, looks like *I* annoyed *her*."

"Di likes to stick to the rules. Even when she's playing a *game*."

"She doesn't like games?"

"She hates them. What do they produce?"

"No wonder she was so cranky."

"Well, you didn't help."

"Thanks a lot!"

"Come on," Mike smiled, "you think I'm looking for my sister's approval?"

"Approval of what?"

"Of…my friends."

"Oh," Dawn grabbed her bag.

"Hey! You're leaving?"

"I'm tired."

"But the metros aren't running. Why don't you stay?"

"Well, I *do* have most of my wardrobe with me…"

"That's right," Mike nodded.

"Okay. I'll change into my pyjamas."

"You can use my room."

"Thanks."

She went in and closed the door behind her. Mike brushed his teeth and stretched out on the couch. Soon, Dawn emerged wearing plaid flannel.

"I'll just stay here," he yawned. "You can sleep in my bed."

"Are you sure?"

"Uh-huh."

"Thanks."

"Don't thank me 'till you've tried out my bed."

Dawn smiled: "Goodnight Mike."

"Goodnight."

CHAPTER 19

▼

At nine the next morning, Dawn touched Mike's forehead. Then quickly withdrew her hand. She said she had to go. She said she had a class. Mike drawled a good-bye and crawled to his room. The bed sheets smelled like her perfume. He wrapped himself in them and stayed there all day.

Tuesday threatened to be a re-run. Until Helen called with news of a big outing the girls were planning for Friday night. It was the last weekend before exams and everyone needed to stockpile some fun.

Mike passed the invitation on to Eric and asked him to bring Deborah. Then he got up and circled November 25th on his calendar. Everything beyond that date seemed like part of someone else's life. Someone who had made up his mind. He wanted to speak to that person. Ask him how he'd regained his bearings.

Gradually, "Dawn" had replaced "woman" in Mike's vocabulary. Infinite possibility collapsed into dreadful certainty. And the pressure was intense. He floated back to bed, trying not to think. He might as well have tried not to breathe.

🐦🐦🐦

The Showbar was a big brown barn on St-Jacques street. It took Mike an hour to walk there, but he still managed to be early. The doorman's watch flashed 10:02 when Mike handed him the $2 cover. The plans were for ten-thirty. It was cold outside, so he went in anyway. But he wished he'd brought a book.

It wasn't crowded inside, but every face he saw seemed to be expecting someone. The place looked like a western dance-hall, with a few disco-balls tacked onto the ceiling at the last minute. The specks of silver just made everything look browner. Pearl Jam's *State of Love and Trust* was playing.

In the far corner of the room, he saw Dawn sitting with a pitcher. He walked toward her. She smiled when she saw him:"Hey!"

"Hi," Mike sat down.

"How was your week?"

"Okay. Yours?"

"Busy...um...we're both early..."

"Yeah, it always takes me less time to walk than I think it will."

"Hmm. I always need a few drinks before I see a crowd."

"I know. You're shy."

A waitress passed by. Dawn ordered two orgasms. Mike ordered a coffee. They sat looking at each other while they waited. Dawn swallowed her shots. Mike sipped his coffee. Hole's "Gutless" came on.

"I found a way to use batering!" Dawn blurted. "Wanna hear?"

"Of course."

"It's a poem. A short one."

"Cool."

She cleared her throat:

"Batering, batering
Through the town
Catering, catering
To my frown.
Baleful eyeballs
Roll and reel
On long black stalks
With ev'ry squeal
Batering, batering

Under water
Catering, catering
To the grouper
Frying pan, skillet-man
Watch the worm
Dismiss the fish and
Stop the squirm."

Mike dropped his chin on the table and tried to channel his thoughts. A hand pressed his shoulder and Helen said: "Hey guys!"

Donna, Priscilla, and Laura were with her. They all sat down. They talked mainly about school. Deadlines, exams, and thoughts of dropping out. No one talked about going back to the country.

"But you came here to study, right?" Mike asked Helen.

"I came here to *be here*," Helen answered.

"What about you Dawn?"

"Mike loves small towns," she addressed the group. "But, you know, people there aren't any worse than anywhere else. It's just that here, when some fucker ruins your day, you don't know their name and their cousin and their dog. That's why I like Montreal."

"A very Dawn answer," Laura said. "You should know better by now Mike."

"I guess."

Dawn spoke up: "Why don't you see for yourself Mike? Come back to the country with me next time I go."

"Okay."

"Maybe we'll meet some hunters," she snickered.

The conversation went on. Only Laura expressed any interest in leaving the city. Once she'd made enough money to settle down. She was in her second year of graphic design, and seemed more motivated than the others. Priscilla, Donna, and Helen were on the verge of failing. Non-attendance was the main problem. Mike identified with them. About five weeks into his CEGEP career, he had started hanging out at the park when he was supposed to be in class. His mother found out about it when a report-card full of zeroes came in the mail.

Dawn was doing well at Marianopolis, a private CEGEP that was run more like a University, but her parents were having trouble paying the bills. She acted like she didn't care about school. But she acted that way about everything.

Around eleven-thirty, Eric showed up with Deborah. She was tall and thin with long frizzy black hair and smart brown eyes. They listened to the defeatism for a while and then withdrew into a conversation about Nietzsche. Mike watched them. They seemed more like people trying to do a crossword than people in love. He wasn't impressed. But then, he had never *wanted* to do a crossword with anyone.

A band began belting out Offspring covers at midnight. By one o'clock, nothing made sense to Mike. Every once in a while, Laura would say something practical, like: "How are we gonna get Pris home?" And Dawn would blink lucidly across the table. Eric and Deborah had dropped Nietzsche in favour of the dance-floor. Donna and Helen had picked up tall guys with long hair. And Priscilla had passed out in her chair.

Mike got up to use the washroom. But it was so disgusting that he decided to wait. He pushed back through the crowd. About halfway, he ran into Dawn. She was incredibly drunk, but it only showed in the way she looked at him. Dead on target.

The band screeched:
"By the time you hear the siren
It's already too late
One goes to the morgue and the other to jail
One guy's wasted and the other's a waste."
Mike laughed.
Dawn stared: "What?"
The band added: "Keep 'em separated."
They walked back to the table.

At three o'clock, blinking neons pushed them onto the street. There was a lot of snow on the ground and more in the sky. Everyone decided to go back to Mike's house. They poured into cabs. When they got there, Mike checked Diane's room (to make sure she was staying at Vito's) and put the kettle on. Then Eric found Mike's old toboggan and everyone rushed off to Mount Royal.

Except for Dawn. She stretched on the blue couch and let Marbles chew her hair. Mike brought her a coffee and sat next to her toes.

"What should we do?"

"Watch a movie?" she shrugged.

"Which one?"

"Do you have *When Harry Met Sally*?"

"Actually, I do."

"Let's watch that."

"Okay."

He went to get the cassette. He put it in the VCR and turned out the lights. Dawn sat up when he joined her. They shared the couch like it was a raft sledding through rapids. Mike saw the Castle Rock lighthouse cut words into orange black dusk. But that was all. The mellow jazzy scenes didn't belong in his living room.

He heard Dawn's skin twinkling under blue jeans, through blue flannel, behind blonde hair. The blonde also hid crackling blue eyes. He tried to catch them.

Their tuning-fork silence threatened to go on forever. But it didn't. Mike dug his fingers into her hair and struck eye-contact.

"Are you tired?" he asked.

She leaned into him: "A little."

His fingers slid down her back.

"Me too."

"Good night?"

"No."

Her lips brushed his chin and their tongues touched through the wedge in her teeth.

At six-thirty, they went for breakfast at Pierrette's. Mike was out of coffee and they weren't tired anymore. It was only a couple of blocks away, but the walk took twenty minutes. There had been a real blizzard. Snow crews marauded the streets like an occupying army. Mike wondered if the trek was worth it. Dawn tackled him and sucked snowflakes off his lashes.

The diner was empty, except for a couple of low-rent hookers in jogging suits eating grease-fries and crooning along with Whitney Houston. Pierrette's was the last refuge of yesterday's throwaway ballads. It was smoky but no one was smoking. It smelled like beer-breath but they didn't sell alcohol. Mike and Dawn sat in a bright-orange window-booth and looked at the menus.

A veiny waitress sagged into their table and said: "What can I getcha dearie?"

"I'll have a cheese omelette," Dawn answered. "And coffee."

"Of course," the waitress nodded. "And you honey?"

"Uh," Mike thought, "same for me please."

"Two number threes," she wrote on her pad. "I'll getcher coffee."

Dawn smiled: "What a nice waitress."

Mike laughed.

Dawn said: "What?"

"This is gonna take getting used to."

"What?"

"You."

She touched his hand. Her quiet smile deafened him.

BOOK THREE

CHAPTER 20

▼

"This is ridiculous," Diane muttered.

"Well, it's pretty crazy," Eric nodded back.

Mike smirked up at his sister, standing cross-eyed and cross-armed on the landing above. He said: "You're gonna make him drop the couch. On me."

Eric yanked his end higher.

"Don't worry."

Mike took a final cautious step back and put his end down.

"Alright."

Diane followed them down the steps, coddling a plastic carrier filled with blankets and fear. She opened the glass door.

"Let's go."

Vito stood outside, rubbing his hands together. He had finished loading Mike's boxes into the van.

"I'm glad the snow melted."

Mike smiled at him: "Me too."

They slid the couch in and closed up the hatch. Mike and Eric knelt in back. Diane sat in the passenger seat and Vito took the wheel. They drove off.

Diane stroked fur inside the blue cage on her lap.

"You're going to have *three* cats," she worried.

Mike nodded: "To start with."

She looked back sternly. "It's ridiculous Michael! You don't even have enough stuff to fill a small van! What kind of home will it be?"

"One with lots of room for cats..."

Vito laughed: "He's got it all figured out, babe." They stopped at a red light and he touched her arm: "Diane's just worried 'cause she thinks you'll get married before we do."

"No, I'm not."

Mike said: "I feel like I'm already married."

Eric shook his head: "Marriage is a public event. It defines your status in the community. You guys are moving in together."

"That's right. And no one invited 'the community'."

They pulled up in front of an old brick box. Bright crimson doors and a throbbing neon sign bit into the drab material of the building. The windows had stained glass in them. Mike still couldn't make out the designs. They looked like someone's idea of a family crest. Purple shields and green mushrooms.

"Welcome to Verdun!" he announced.

Dawn stood on the curb, with a green cat carrier between her legs. She jutted her chin at door 554. Her eyes flickered playfully, homicidally.

"It's locked. I knocked, but no one answered. Then I leaned over the railing and looked in through the window. They haven't moved yet."

Eric's jaw dropped: "What?!"

Mike kissed Dawn: "Where's your stuff?"

She laughed: "In that van on the corner. My dad had to leave. He was already late for work."

"That sucks. But it was nice of him to help. It was nice of all of you."

Diane slammed her door shut.

"Michael! What are you going to do?"

"I don't know. Knock louder. Kick the door in. Dawn could do it."

She giggled: "I'll try..."

They climbed a rusted-slinky staircase to the balcony. There were five flats in the building: one on the ground floor, two on the second and two on the third. Mike and Dawn's place was in the middle, on the left. Eric, Vito, and Diane took turns pounding on the door. Bits of paint flaked off on their knuckles. Meanwhile, Dawn smacked the window with a stick she had picked up. Mike watched and laughed. He nearly fell down when a shaggy, bloodshot face peaked out from the bunker.

"What's goin' on man?" asked a pair of chapped lips.

Dawn pointed her stick at him. "It's December first 'man'. We're the new tenants!"

"Oh Jesus," the man muttered. He kneaded brown clumps on his face and turned to yell: "Hey Donnie! It's December first man! We gotta leave!"

He swung the door open and welcomed them in. He introduced himself as Doug. Meaningless guitar-sounds drifted out of the back room. Doug tried again: "Hey Donnie, man!". It had no effect. He motioned for them to wait and went to silence the guitar player.

Mike looked the place over. The front-room was double-sized. The hardwood floors were discoloured but basically intact. There were four or five little craters. He didn't see any bugs. There was a stained brown couch next to the window. It was missing a cushion, but the two that were still there looked comfortable. The coffee-table was a piece of plywood balanced on two boxes full of Ramen noodles. The other half of the room contained stacks of seventies-coloured albums and a record-player that wasn't plugged in.

Dawn went to inspect the stained glass. She smiled at Mike: "You were right. They *are* mushrooms."

He smiled back: "This is gonna be great!"

Diane sighed: "How many places did you look at?"

Dawn walked back toward Mike and grabbed his hand. "Just this one," she answered.

"God!"

"What's the matter?" Mike asked.

Diane stared at him: "Michael, it's a hole."

Eric and Vito stood silent.

"Well, sure," Mike nodded, "but it's only three hundred a month."

"Yeah, and it's got oil heating," Dawn added. "It's cheaper than electricity."

"I guess you know what you're doing," Diane muttered.

"C'mon Di! What'd you expect?"

"This. Unfortunately."

"I hadn't noticed the molding on the walls," Dawn whispered. "It's good." She stared at Diane: "We'll clean it up. And I'm going to paint. We're not Doug and Donnie."

Mike squeezed her gently. "Shh!"

Doug and Donnie stood in the hallway, squinting apologetically. They each wore tangled beards, black rock-fan T-shirts, and ripped jeans. Thick blue veins strangled their thin arms. Donnie's hair was going gray, and he was a couple of inches taller. Doug did all the talking.

"I don't know how," he scratched his head, "but we just forgot, man. Anyhow, we don't have much stuff, so it won't take us long. But we'd really appreciate it if you could give us a bit of a hand."

Eric and Vito pounced on the couch and pushed it through the doorway. Doug grabbed a bunch of records and followed them out. They ran into problems on the winding staircase, and Mike heard Doug stammer: "Just, uh, just throw it over the railing man. It doesn't matter."

Mike and Dawn walked through the dirty blue kitchen to inspect the back room.

"Aren't you going to carry me over the threshold?" she giggled.

"How about a piggyback?"

She climbed on his back and they stepped into the room. She hopped down and curled up in the far-right corner, after moving Donnie's guitar out of the way. "Here's where we'll sleep."

Mike joined her on the floor. There were no chips in it, but it felt rough and chalky. It had never been varnished. He reached under her shirt and ran his hands over her back-muscles. Then he kissed her. Their room had white walls and a white globular lamp dangling about two feet below the ceiling. It had a large closet and a glass-paned door that opened onto the back balcony. Dawn pointed toward it and said: "There's a great spot out there for a bird-feeder."

"Cool," Mike kissed her neck, "the cats'll love that." His hands reached the skin under her jeans and he wished that he had closed the dark brown door.

Dawn ground her zipper into his and her thighs were rockets. Her eyes leapt at him. She whispered: "Let's get this move over with."

⁂

At eleven-thirty, Mike, Dawn, Eric, Diane and Vito were eating pizza in the living room. Inez, Marbles, and Pandora were hiding under appliances. Doug and Donnie had driven off, with their records and their busted couch, in an old red pick-up, in search of a home. But not before they had mentioned that the oil heater didn't work properly. It breathed a choking hot smog into every corner of the house. Dawn had thanked them for the information and called the landlady. A maid had told her that Mrs. Sacoransky would be away for the winter. So she had gone to Canadian Tire to buy a couple of space heaters.

"This heater's great," Mike said. He and Dawn were lying next to it, on her horse-blanket.

"Uh-huh," Diane sighed. She rested her head in Vito's lap, on the blue couch. He massaged her temples.

Dawn looked at the clock, hanging uncomfortably on a new wall. She yawned and said: "It's getting late."

Eric finished his slice and nodded in agreement. Then he cleared his throat and said: "You guys are dealing with this well. I mean, it's been a pretty crazy day."

"Hey," Mike shrugged, "it's just one day."

"Yeah," Diane sat up, "and it's just one winter."

"Okay babe," Vito suggested, "we better go."

"Whatever."

"You wan' a lift Eric?"

"That'd be really cool."

"C'mon," Vito smiled. "Enjoy the new place guys."

"Seeya," Eric waved and followed him out.

Diane blinked confidentially at Mike until Dawn left the room. He hugged her. She gave him a hundred dollars for the space heaters and whispered: "If you get too cold, or *she* starts acting really crazy, you know you can come back."

"Yes Di."

"Don't be over-confident! You've been dating her, what, a week?"

"Yeah."

"Do you know how many things can go wrong?"

"I know."

"Well, I'm happy for you," she kissed his cheek. "I wish I liked her."

"Me too. Good night Di."

"Good night."

He watched from the balcony as the van drove off. Dawn joined him. She put an arm around his waist and pressed her palm into his waving hand.

CHAPTER 21

▼

Mike woke up early the next morning. They had placed the mattress directly facing the balcony-door. It was black and wet outside. The glass was black and wet too, with a glossy finish of light from the street-corner lamp. He watched Dawn's transparent hand brush his cheek. Raindrops slithered down the pane and distorted the canvass. But did not spoil it.

Dawn's nose twitched against Mike's neck. She rolled onto her back. Her skin was branded red by their closeness. Her long hair spilled crazily over the bed. He felt some in his mouth. She smacked her lips on the morning and he kissed them. Then he laid his head on her breast and waited for her eyes to open. When they did, they focused on the balcony and she whispered: "Listen to those fat little birds!"

Mike turned and saw a crowd of starlings, gathered at the green plastic feeder. They had been there all along.

Dawn kissed the back of his neck and asked: "When do you work next?"

"Not until Thursday."

"Hmm. I think I'll take the next three days off."

He sat up. "I thought this week was important. The exam reviews and stuff..."

"Uh-huh," she smiled.

"Okay," he smiled back. "What should we do today?"

"Get donuts!"

"Now?"

"Yeah!" She pressed her face into his chest. "Must...have...*dough*-nuts," she whispered.

"Okay," he laughed.

They dressed and hurried out. It was six in the morning. It was a twenty minute walk to the Dunkin' Donuts on Wellington street, the commercial heart of Verdun, a working-class suburb of Montreal. Delivery trucks sped over pot-hole puddles, spritzing the concrete. The last round of a conjugal bout rang through a half-open window. Wet cats peered out of garbage bag piles.

Dawn improvised a song about donuts. Mike read business-signs aloud. They stopped in front of a thrift-store window. He pointed at a wooden rooster. She liked a tall jade lamp. They passed a twenty-four hour video store called "Boom". There was a self-serve computer at the check-out desk. Several pairs of running shoes dragged worn laces in circles behind a flimsy partition labeled "XXX". Mike and Dawn looked at each other and laughed.

The large pink Dunkin' Donuts was packed. Elbows and chins rested on coats and toques, piled onto tables next to sticky wrappers and mugs. The muzak was loud and the voices were louder. A group of boys scrambled for the attention of a girl with a tough mouth. Old men spat hockey clichés at each other. Random loners exploded and fell silent. Mike's tongue felt sooty. Visibility was low. Behind the counter, sugarry glazes danced in the neon.

"What should we get?" Mike asked.

"It's so hard to choose."

"I know."

Dawn eyed the specials. "It's only eleven-ninety-nine for forty-eight!"

"What!?"

Dawn's eyebrows moved like storm-clouds.

"We'll have lots," she lisped.

"Okay," he nudged her up to the cash, pressing his chest into her back, cupping her ribs in his hands, "you pick."

His knuckles grazed her small breasts and her voice cracked. She ordered six custard, six maple, six chocolate, six cherry, six old-fashioneds, six coconut, six double-chocolate, and six Bavarian cream. The countergirl tucked the donuts into boxes and Dawn handed her twelve dollars.

They ate donuts in bed and showered together. They passed the soap back and forth under the hot spray. He rubbed shampoo into her hair. It took a long time to wash. He sat cross-legged on the bathtub floor and she eased onto his lap. He massaged her head and the perfumed rinse oozed down the drain.

They jumped into the cold and rushed to the bedroom. They turned the space-heater up to maximum and camped in its red shadow. When the chill left their bones, they got ready to leave. They had decided to make a grand tour of the metro system. Mike had mentioned it on a whim. Dawn saw the trip as research for a project: "An Encyclopedia of Metro Freaks". She packed a camera, a notepad, and twelve donuts in her schoolbag and slung it over her shoulder.

They started with Verdun metro. It was a deep cement hole, painted white, purple, and orange. There was a small store that sold snacks and bad coffee to commuters. The clerk looked up from a tabloid when they passed him.

At eight-thirty in the morning, Jehovah's Witnesses guarded the turnstiles. They had zealous eyes and fists full of information.

"Exhibit A," Dawn whispered.

She took a copy of *The Watchtower* from a woman with a gray perm and struck up a conversation. Mike sneaked his buspass through the slot and leaned against the transfer-machine.

He watched. He couldn't hear what was said but Dawn's lips were tart. She crossed her arms and listened. Then the permed woman nodded and touched her hand. Blonde hair fell across Dawn's cheek and she brushed it away. She waved good-bye to the woman.

When Dawn came through the turnstile, her eyes gurgled softly.

"What happened?" Mike asked.

"She told me how happy she is."

She threw *The Watchtower* into the garbage.

They walked down to the platform. Men in suits waited next to kids dressed for panhandling. A pregnant woman and a guy with long hair screamed at each other. Someone had left the keys at home. A man in a jogging suit gave the play-by-play of a game that took place in his head. Dawn snapped photos.

The long-haired guy patted the woman's arm and approached Dawn. She tensed for an argument.

He said: "Hey, uh, I was just wondering: could I get some copies of those pictures offa you, sometime?"

"Um."

"My wife's in labour, and we're going to the hospital. I wanna remember how she looked."

Dawn nodded: "What's your number?"

He gave it to her and she wrote it down. The man went back to sit with his wife.

The metro roared out of the tunnel and stopped. Everyone poured in. Mike and Dawn wrapped their bodies around the schoolbag, to protect it from the crush. Mike realized he had forgotten to shave and tried to turn his head to check his face in the glass. Dawn distracted him by whispering: "Get ready to push. No one gets *off* at these stops."

They spent the day on the green line, taking notes and eating donuts. They hardly spoke. They watched each other watching the world. They paid special attention to beggars and buskers, the constants in a fluid system. Their favorite was a portly old man at Peel metro. He stared gravely at a songbook on a music-stand and delivered *a cappella* Christmas carols. His voice was impossibly off-key and he changed all the verb-tenses.

The stations at the east end of the line were unfamiliar. They explored the neighborhood around Honoré-Beaugrand, the last stop. It combined the worst features of suburb and slum. The streets were sterile and poorly lit. And the houses were run-on blocks of cement. The parks weren't landscaped or run-down. Just ruthlessly mowed. The terminal itself was quite empty, even at rush-hour. On the way home, they stopped at McGill: Dawn liked the Eaton Center's fake poinsettias and she wanted to steal one.

They devoted Tuesday to the orange line and Wednesday to the blue line. The donuts ran out early Thursday morning and Mike had to bring a sandwich to work. He really hadn't slept all week. The easy-listening station played Christmas music and he coasted through the day. When he got home, Dawn threw her book aside and led him to the fried zucchinis she had made. She invited him to spend the weekend in the country and they fell asleep in their clothes.

***

They caught the ten-forty-five bus on Saturday morning. It had puffy red seats and a washroom. Dawn seemed to know everyone. She glared at them and muttered "Country people," under her breath.

"So what're we gonna do?" Mike asked.

"We'll see the woods. There might even be bottlecap berries left."

"Bottlecap berries?"

"They're the best."

"Okay."

"Then we'll go to the haunted house."

"What makes it haunted?"

"No one lives there."

"That's all?"

"Well, maybe enchanted's a better word."

"Enchanted?"

"I can ask questions too."

"I'm more determined."

"Okay," she smiled, "storytime…When Dawn was a little girl, she liked to go walking in the woods at night. She always hoped that something would scare her. Once she saw a bear, but the bear didn't see her, and there wasn't much of a thrill in that. A few times she saw hunters and threw rocks at them, but her aim wasn't very good. She imagined monsters behind every tree, but they were never there when she looked.

"One day, while she was out walking. A drooling fox came into her backyard. The fox bit her dog and three of her cats. Her father had to shoot all of the animals. After that, Dawn's parents wouldn't let her walk in the woods anymore. It was too dangerous, they said. But she plotted and plotted, and the first chance she got, she ran off, looking for the ghost of the murderous fox.

"Instead, she found a house that nobody lived in. The door was unlocked and she went inside. The last people had taken all of their furniture, except for an old bed in a room on the second floor. Vicious coils sprouted from the mattress, but Dawn squeezed her small body between them. It started to rain and there wasn't any moonlight. But that didn't scare her. She lay there thinking and she thought that she could think there forever. Then she heard her father calling for her and she crawled under the bed. When the voice got really close, she crawled back out and went to wait for him under a pine tree, because she didn't want him to find her in that house. She never told him about the house. She never wanted to tell anyone. And the not-wanting-to scared her to death."

Mike put his arm around her. He said: "We'll go."

The bus pulled into Ormstown at 11:55 and they got off. Dawn's father was waiting for them in his car. Mike shook his hand and introduced himself. The man had a strong grip but a soft voice. He didn't hug his daughter but it was obvious that he wanted to. Dawn tossed their bags into the trunk and said: "Let's go! I'm hungry."

It was a ten minute drive to the Paris's home, in a tiny village called Lincoln. Dawn asked questions about the family pets and chuckled at her father's mild anecdotes.

("Shadow's getting fat," he said.

"How come?"

"The cats have stopped chasing him.")

They turned off the highway and rolled up a driveway to the house. It was a long white rectangle, a converted trailer, camouflaged by shrubs and a sun-deck.

Shadow, a huge German shepherd, waited at the door, barking maniacally. Dawn kissed his muzzle and he relaxed. Mr. Paris rubbed the dog's shoulder and said: "We missed her, hunh boy?" Mrs. Paris emerged from the kitchen, pulled off her oven mitts, and stroked Shadow's ears. She smiled at Mike: "He gets so excited when Dawn comes home."

Mike said: "He's beautiful." He knelt down to look the dog in the eye. Shadow licked his face.

"Careful," Mr. Paris warned, "he might like the way you taste."

"Don't be stupid Johnathan!" his wife laughed. Then she snapped her fingers. "Wait 'till you see what's in the kitchen Michael!"

She showed him into a small spotless room crammed full of appliances. There was a hot pumpkin pie on the *faux*-marble counter.

"Mm," Mike reacted.

"*Someone* told me it's your favourite."

"It is!"

Dawn took a granola bar from the cupboard and said: "We're going for a walk in the woods."

"Oh Dawn! Not yet! It's lunchtime. I just have to put it in the microwave."

"Oh, well, okay. Just call us when it's ready."

Dawn led Mike into her room and closed the door. It was empty except for some old clothes in the closet and the word "Inez" grafittied on the walls in big red letters. She giggled and said: "Aren't they funny?"

"They're so nice."

"Yeah, I guess they are."

"You're lucky Dawn."

She took his hand.

"I'm blessed."

A few minutes later, they sat down at the table and Mr. Paris attempted to say grace. His wife and daughter snickered until he stopped. (They allowed him to keep Jesus as his personal saviour, provided he didn't go on about it.) Mike watched heavy snowflakes dropping like leaves from the sky. Lunch was a thick stew made from lentils, kidney beans, turnips, potatoes and parsnips. Dawn hardly touched hers, but Mike had two helpings. He also had two slices of pie. The nutmeg stung his tongue without paralyzing it and the filling was smooth. The crust was a little burnt and tasted like ashes from a sweet bonfire.

When Mike put his plate in the sink, the kitchen window was spackled over by whiteness and the wind shoved the trees like a schoolyard bully.

Dawn came up behind him and said: "We're still going, right?"

"Sure."

"Are you two crazy?" Mrs. Paris asked. "You didn't even wear boots!"

She started washing the dishes.

"That's true," Mike nodded.

Dawn bit her lip.

"So we'll fall. So what?"

"It's so cozy in here. I saw some games in the living room."

"You want to play a game?"

"I think it makes more sense."

"I guess you're right."

They went into the living room and Mike scanned the shelf.

"What's Balderdash?"

"It's pretty fun. You make up definitions for obscure words and try to fool each other."

"Sounds great!"

"Yeah."

Mike opened the box and started setting up the game. Dawn sat next to him on the couch. Mrs. Paris brought them two steaming mugs full of hot chocolate. Mike took a thick sip and touched Dawn's cheek.

"We'll go next time."

"Okay."

CHAPTER 22

▼

Mike gave a dollar to the Salvation Army Santa and looked for Tina. There was a crowd in front of the Ogilvy's window and he dove into it. The display had been up for a month, but it always looked better on Christmas Eve. The rabbits hopped less mechanically; the chickens swayed in time. He wondered if they knew their days were numbered. He didn't see Tina. He pictured her in line somewhere, weighed down by gifts, not caring whether she showed up or not. Rekindling the friendship was his idea. He kicked at a patch of ice on the sidewalk.

A hand touched his shoulder.

"I'm sorry I'm late."

He stopped kicking and turned around. Tina's hand stayed on his shoulder.

"That's alright. What's a few minutes? I've been waiting a month."

Tina smirked: "Don't tell me you noticed. You've been busy."

"I guess I have."

"Should we go in? I'm freezing!"

"Of course."

She took his arm. They walked through rotating doors into another crowd. Mike strained to hear "The First Noël". Silver, green, and red decorations spun gently in shopper's-breath turbulence. Tina pulled off her hat and scarf. Her long auburn hair fell across her face. Mike brushed it aside and looked at her. The last summer-freckles had gone from her cheeks. Chapstick glazed her lips. Her brown eyes were a little red.

"I missed you Mike."

"Me too."

"I was afraid you hated me."

"Why didn't you call?"

"I thought I'd leave it up to you."

Mike shook his head. He had called on a whim, on the anniversary of their first meeting. He was superstitious about dates. He said: "I'm glad I called."

"Me too."

"What are we looking for?"

"Well, I need perfume for my mom and a toy for my cousin. You?"

"Oh nothing."

"You don't have any shopping to do?"

"I'm getting books for Dawn. But not here. At a used book-store."

"Why did you suggest *this*?"

"I like the decorations."

"You're weird Mike."

He shrugged.

"Alright," she took his arm, "let's get the perfume first."

"Sounds good."

She led him to a mountain of fragrance, on the second floor. It was a circular glass counter, buried under bottles of all colours and shapes. A mirrored pillar at the center of the circle exaggerated the selection. Three ladies prowled the perimeter, placating the hordes. Tina picked up a green sampler and sprayed her wrist. She asked: "What do you think?"

Mike brought her hand to his nose.

"Not bad."

She sprayed her other wrist from a blue bottle.

"How about this one?"

"Better."

She smirked.

"Really?"

He shrugged.

"I don't know."

She asked for a blue box, labeled *Sun, Moon, Stars.*

"I think you're right."

"Great."

"You're a big help."

"I try."

"Now the toys."

They squeezed onto the escalator. Impatient climbers jostled them together. Her body made him feel his skin. But not his nerves. Touching her was a gratuitous pleasure. He had no urge to plunge; he was content on the surface; and he noticed ripples that he hadn't felt before. She looked at him.

"You haven't said a thing about Dawn."

"No."

"I wasn't surprised, you know. I was always jealous of her."

Mike looked dubious.

"Jealous?"

They got onto the next escalator.

"Well, okay then, I noticed things."

"Like what?"

"The way she seemed more like a woman, whenever you were around…The way you seemed to be looking through the same kaleidoscope, when you looked at each other."

They got off on the fourth floor.

Mike said: "You know. You're right. That's what it's like—I think."

Tina laughed: "I think you're both insane."

"Yeah."

Mike pointed at a shelf full of games. They walked past it down an aisle of stuffed toys. Tina picked up a yellow creature in blue-striped pyjamas.

"This is cute."

The toy erupted into song:

"Bananas

In pyjamas

Are bouncing down the stairs!

Bananas

In Pyjamas..."

She put it down, but the song continued.

Mike muttered: "That's ridiculous."

"It starts when you press their hands," she mused.

"So?"

She touched off a whole row of them. The lyrics spilled out in anarchic waves. A crowd gathered in the aisle. She smiled at Mike and said: "I think I'll get a book too."

Tina paid for the perfume and they walked down St-Catherine street to "Café Books". The sun had gone and white lights in the bare trees replaced it. They hovered against the black sky and the brick, competing with the neon.

"Café Books" was dimly lit. It was undecorated, except for a sprig of mistletoe that hovered over the cash. A temporary shelf had been set up, near the entrance, as a display for Christmas anthologies. Mike picked up *Murder For Christmas*. Tina went straight for the religion section. The owner, a pink man with a long white beard and a blue beret, cleared his throat and poured out two cups of coffee. They each took one from the counter.

"Merry Christmas," the owner smiled.

"Merry Christmas," Tina replied.

Mike nodded.

"Do you have a children's section?" Tina asked.

"Against the back wall, to the right."

"Thanks."

"No problem."

The man's eyes followed Tina to the back of the store. Mike sipped his coffee under the mistletoe. When he had finished, he scanned the fiction shelves.

Mike saw reflections of Dawn in the women on the covers of Penguin Classics: storms laced with lucidity. Her self-image was closer to Dorothy Parker and Janis Joplin: leaning towers of self-destruction. Parents and friends worried about her, but Mike never did. She was the only person he had ever taken seriously. He picked out a few novels: *Wives and Daughters, Great Expectations, Middlemarch*; and balanced them off with *The Portable Curmudgeon* and a cat-photo hardcover.

Tina bought a Dr. Seuss book: *I Wish That I Had Duck Feet.* Mike joined her at the cash and paid for his items. The owner wished them a merry Christmas again and locked the door after them. It was cold outside. Tina took Mike's arm and they walked toward the metro.

"Dr. Seuss is okay for a three-year old, right?" she asked.

"I think so."

"Good."

At the corner of Guy and St-Catherine, Tina hailed a cab and opened the door.

"Gotta get home. Lots of presents to wrap."

"Oh. Yeah."

She smirked: "Didn't you get wrapping paper?"

"I'm sure Dawn's got extra."

"I hope so."

She hugged him.

Mike came home to a smoky apartment. He wondered if Dawn had tried the furnace. But he could still see his breath in the air. He called her name, but she didn't answer. Marbles and Pandora joined him at the door. Inez was stretched out on the couch, next to a smoldering pile of plastic in a pie tin on the coffee table. Mike poked through the remains with a pen and turned over a blackened Polaroid. He could just make out a pinkish corner of Tina's smile.

He put down the pen and walked to the bedroom. No one was there. He doubled back down the hallway and stopped at the bathroom door. He heard water trickling and knocked.

"Come in," Dawn lisped.

He found her curled up tightly in the scalding tub. Blood gushed through her muscular body, close under the skin. The air was thick with steam. Sweatlike beads covered every surface. Dawn's hair was slick with shampoo and she massaged it listlessly. Mike knelt on the bathmat and touched her back. She shivered, but kept staring straight ahead, at the tap.

"I know. I shouldn't have done it," she said.

"What's wrong?"

"Let's pretend it never happened."

"How can I do that?"

She turned to face Mike. Tears hovered over her irises, refracting their meaning into a million holograms that danced around and inside him.

"Why can't you?"

"Because...because you're upset."

"I'll get over it."

"I don't ever want to hurt you."

"Too late for that."

"But...but...what—?"

"Let's not talk about it."

"We have to."

"No. We don't."

"We do, or I'll never forget it."

She dropped her face into her soapy hands.

"You never will anyway."

"They weren't *that* important."

She looked up.

"Really?"

He nodded and tried to smile.

"It...it isn't *that* at all. It's..."

A few tears escaped down her cheek.

"Oh."

"You see what I mean, don't you?"

"I guess so."

"Why did you do it?"

"I don't want to talk about it."

"I mean...what were you thinking?"

"You know."

"I do?"

She raised her voice: "Yes!"

He pressed his fingers to her temples.

"Dawn..."

She massaged his wrist and stared at him with feral eyes.

"Don't make me."

"I...I want to know everything about you."

"I don't believe you anymore."

Mike drew his fingers back as if they'd been stung.

"I see."

Dawn grabbed his arm and cried: "I was afraid you weren't over it! Okay?"

"I didn't know I had to be."

"What!?"

"Whatever *it* was, it's part of what I feel now. For you. For everything. Don't you see?"

"No. I don't. I thought I was enough."

"Enough? You made it happen. No one else could have. Isn't *that* enough?"

"Enough!" she almost screamed. "You sound like you don't even need *me* anymore!" She calmed herself and whispered: "There are so many things we never did..."

"What does that mean?"

"Figure it out."

"*Tell* me."

"I don't want to come second. Not even to your feelings for me."

"That doesn't even make sense."

She grabbed a towel and ran past him. He mopped up the wet foot-prints in the hallway and knelt on the kitchen floor, listening to her sobs and the rumble of the space-heater.

Hours later, Mike opened the bedroom door. He crawled into bed next to Dawn. She lay quietly on her side, staring out the window. He found her hip under the blanket and kneaded her neck with his lips.

"It's almost midnight."

She shrugged.

"Do you want to watch a Christmas movie?"

She shrugged again.

"I love you Dawn."

She turned over.

"I love you too."

His smile glinted in her wet eyes.

"C'mon."

"Okay."

CHAPTER 23

▼

Mike pressed a hard white buzzer with a black "203" printed on it.

"Yeah?" Eric intercommed.

"You ready?"

"Uh-hunh."

"Don't forget the chess board."

"I won't."

"Okay."

Mike stepped through the glass doors onto the walkway, freshly soaked by the apartment lawn-sprinkler. He leaned against a "No Parking" sign and extended his arms in the air. It was mid-April and he had a T-shirt on.

Eric bounded out of the building, with a beige-knapsack on his back, and said: "So where's this place?"

"Westmount. It's about a forty-five minute walk."

"Cool. It's a nice day."

"Yeah," Mike looked up, "but it's a little too sunny."

"Give me a break! It's not *hot*."

"No. But it will be. Soon."

"Let's go."

They walked west on de Maisonneuve at a relaxed pace. The last ice had melted a week earlier and there weren't even puddles to dodge. The rush-hour smog was half-an-hour away and the air smelled like blossoms and resurfaced dog-droppings.

"So. *Diane* got Dawn this job?"

"Uh-huh."

"Didn't she get Tina a job there too?"

"Yep. They all work together now."

Eric wrinkled his forehead.

"That's bizarre! After what you've told me..."

"It is."

Eric laughed: "Doesn't Diane *hate* Dawn?"

"Well, no. She just thinks she's childish and irresponsible."

"She also thinks *you* are childish and irresponsible."

"Pretty much—so there's hope."

"You're her brother."

"True. But it's more than that...Siblings don't *have* to be close. Especially not in *my* family."

"Hmm...And what about Tina? You told me Dawn can't stand the *idea* of her."

"Well, that's getting better. I mean: they *are* friends. It's just that Dawn doesn't think exes should speak..."

"So we're gonna *hang out* with them all afternoon? You trying to make a scene?"

"I'm just trying to live my life."

"*Sure.*"

They waited for the green light at Atwater and crossed the street into Westmount. Trees sprung up at the border and panhandlers vanished.

"So," Eric continued, "You said Dawn quit school?"

"Yeah," Mike sighed.

"What's the problem? You did it too."

"Yeah, but I'll go back."

"You don't think she will?"

"I know her pretty well."

"Sure."

"And you? Essays done?"

"Yeah. Just have one exam next week."

"Expecting straight *As*?"

"Hopefully *A+s.*"

"Cool."

"I worked hard."

"You've got, what, one year left?"

"Yeah. After that: grad-school!"

"Have you got a thesis in mind?"

"I don't know. Radical movements. Paradigm-shifts. That kind of stuff. I want to study the way *change* is effected."

"That's funny. *I* wish I knew how to stop it."

"I'm talking about *social* change."

"I *know* Eric."

"Well, I don't believe in Providence. I want to know where to push."

Mike shrugged: "At the movie theater."

"*Maybe.*"

"Are you still dating, uh…"

"No. Karla."

"Should I bother trying to remember this one?"

Eric smirked: "Fuck you."

Mike grinned back: "We're here."

They climbed a step onto an empty terrace. Eric pulled up a chair and Mike peeked in through the large window. He caught Dawn's eye under the black visor of her La Paz cap. She was behind a cash register, serving a customer. She cocked her chin in the air and her bottom lip jerked over her crooked front teeth, sending ripples of mouth across her cheeks.

Mike looked back at Eric, noisily setting up the chess pieces on a green plastic table. He shook his head.

"Hey! We're not playing out here!"

"Why not?"

"Because."

Eric laughed.

They walked through the heavy wooden door. The cafe was practically empty. Dawn kissed Mike over the counter. Then she smiled at Eric and said: "Hello."

"Hi."

"What do you guys want?"

"A large coffee," Mike said.

"Me too," Eric nodded.

"Okay."

She got out two large mugs and filled them. She put them on the counter and flourished two customer cards and a hole-puncher.

"You get a free coffee after the purchase of five."

She machine-gunned the cards, leaving three more "free coffee" squares on each.

Mike touched her hand and took his coffee.

"Thanks."

"No problem."

"We're just gonna play some chess over by the window."

"Don't hurt each other."

They set up at the table.

Eric whispered: "Seems like you guys are in it."

"In what?"

"Whatever you said you could never describe."

"Maybe…"

"Move."

"Okay."

Mike tried starting with his king's pawn, for a change. The game slipped through his grasp in the first five turns. He settled his chin on his knuckles to watch the inevitable collapse.

Dawn came up behind him.

"Losing?"

"Yeah."

She closed her hand on his: "Oh well."

"Where's Diane?" Eric asked.

"At the bank, getting change. She'll be back soon."

"What's it like working for her?"

"Oh, not bad. She doesn't ask anyone to do things that she wouldn't do…"

"Yeah," Eric smiled, "she's a kinder, gentler perfectionist."

"Actually," Dawn looked at Mike, "she got some really good news today…"

"Really? What?"

"You'll see."

She slid her fingers over his arm and ran back to serve a customer.

Mike pressed his tongue into his cheek: "I wonder what happened…"

"Check-mate."

"Again?"

"Sure."

They revived the slaughtered pieces. This time, Eric took the whites and opened with his queen's pawn. Mike opted for attrition. At the first sign of danger, he killed the white queen and lost his own.

"What are you doing, man?" Eric asked.

"Adjusting."

"Hmm."

The room began to fill up. Men and women in office-wear filed through the pine door to choose from the waxed pastries and the deep salad-pits. Mike watched Dawn grudgingly take her Janis Joplin CD off and switch on a soft-rock station. Behind her, a man with a stiff mustache beamed on the logo above the chalk-menus. Mike sipped his free coffee and wondered why anyone went to La Paz cafes.

Tina came out of the back room, nodded at Dawn, and dropped a dish-cloth on the back-counter. She snatched a muffin from a glass tray and came out on the floor.

"Hi guys!"

"Hello," Mike smiled."You remember Eric?"

"Uh-hunh."

Eric pulled up a third chair.

"Hey, have a seat."

"Sure."

She peeled the paper off the muffin and took a bite.

"I'm starving."

"Are you on a break?" Mike asked.

"Yeah."

"Cool." He looked at the tense game in progress. "We'll finish this later. Right?"

"You bet we will," Eric smirked.

"*Chess*," she yawned. "Who's winning?"

Mike shook his head: "Do you care?"

"No."

"Then let's change the subject…"

"O-kay."

Her big eyes froze wide and she buckled her lips. Then she turned to Eric and announced: "Did you know that you can boost your immune system by sitting under green light?'

"Ah!" Mike interrupted. "Now *I* don't care…"

Tina squinted at him: "You'll *have* to listen when I get my own info-mercial."

Dawn passed by and said: "Why don't you play duck-duck-goose?"

She went to clear a table.

Mike chuckled: "What are the rules again?"

"I'm *not* getting up."

"Let's talk about *you*, Tina," Eric said firmly. "What's it like serving coffee to spoiled Westmounters?"

"Not too bad lately. Dawn's new, so she doesn't hate people yet. I've been in the back room all week…"

"Oh."

"Some customers are alright." Her pink lips spread. "I have a date with one tonight."

"Really?" Mike leaned toward her.

"Yeah, he's been flirting with me for months. His name's Lance. Diane noticed that he only comes in when I'm working. And he always takes a long time choosing what he wants on his sandwhich."

"You were charmed by his indecision?"

"No. His eyes. They're so calm. But not dull. Maybe it's got something to do with his age. I *like* older men."

"How old is he?"

"Thirty-eight, I think."

"Wow."

"*Anyway.* He came in earlier today and he asked to see me. I came out from the back and he said he wanted to take me out to dinner. I said: 'sure'. It was pretty smooth. But I've been expecting it for weeks. I was starting to wonder about him."

"What do you mean?" Eric asked.

"Tina's face is completely transparent," Mike explained. "It's the best and the worst thing about her..."

"Thanks a lot Mike!"

"See. Now she wants to be angry, but she's not."

"I see what you mean," Eric nodded.

"Should I leave?"

"Don't bother," Mike smirked, "you already know what I think."

Tina crinkled her nose at him.

Mike's eyes leapt over her shoulder toward Dawn, busy making a cappuccino.

"So how's she doing?"

"Dawn? Good. She's an efficient lunatic."

"Uh-huh."

The door opened and Diane marched to the cash with a bagfull of rolled coins. She distributed them into the register, tied her long hair with an elastic, and put on her cap.

She curtseyed before taking a seat at the chess-table.

"*What* an *honour.*"

Mike got up and hugged her.

"Hello Di."

"And you brought Mr. *Concerned* with you. You know Eric, our coffee's not Fair Trade."

"That's okay, I didn't pay for it."

"What?"

Mike said: "*I* did."

"Oh. Not that I think Fair Trade is a bad idea, mind you, but La Paz foams at the thought of it."

"*Westmount*," Eric sneered.

"Are you kidding? Who else has the luxury to be good?"

"What do you mean Di?"

"I'm not crazy about the Westmount honeys that apply here, looking for pocket money. That's why I keep hiring Mike's girlfriends. But believe me, they care more about Colombia than, say, Verduners do."

"You've got a point," Eric nodded. "But *indirectly...*"

"O-*kay*," Mike turned to Tina, "What do *you* think?"

She frowned and said: "I hate coffee."

"Anyway," Diane sighed, "maybe they'll listen to me someday. I just got a promotion."

"You're kidding!" Mike exclaimed.

"Nope. I'm going to help redesign the Montreal-area stores."

"Cool."

"Yeah. *Great*," Eric nodded.

Diane rubbed her hands together. "Like here: I'm visualizing a Hyde-park concept, with Eric up on the counter, next to the muffins, telling people how bad they are..."

Tina finished her snack and said: "He could even throw a few. They'd get the point."

"I *like* the muffins."

"Come on Di, no one's got a tape-recorder..."

"I *do*."

"*Okay*."

Eric crossed his arms and smiled at Diane: "I'd love to do something like that with you."

She shook her head gently. "Who knows?"

"Sounds like you guys are having fun," Dawn observed, resting her chin on Mike's shoulder.

"It's a good mix," he nodded.

"You mean the soup-of-the-day?"

"No."

"Good. 'Cause it's not."

"No respect," Diane sighed.

"None," Dawn smiled.

Mike kissed her. "I *hope* not."

The sky coloured and dripped rain on the terrace. Diane left promptly at five. Eric won the decisive third match and rushed off to meet Karla. Tina's weather-beaten date picked her up at six. Dawn brought Mike another coffee and he traced messages for her in the moisture on the window. They watched each other until the last customer finished his soup at seven-thirty.

Dawn let out a squeal and locked the door behind him.

"Don't you close at eight?" Mike asked.

"Well…"

She counted the cash. Mike listened to the coins rattling and watched the puddles on the street. He looked back to tell her it had stopped raining, but she had gone.

The back door creaked open and Dawn's finger beckoned. He found her in the cold storage room. She had slipped her legs into black leotards and was pulling a black top over her head. At her feet was a bag filled with gardening implements. Mike ran his fingers over her hips and waited for blonde hair to explode through the collar. The sweater had a hood and she quickly brought it down over her forehead. He peered into her blue-green eyes.

"What's going on?"

She flashed a crematory smile and lisped: "The gardens are ripe for the picking."

CHAPTER 24

▼

Dawn giggled: "Uh-oh."

Mike looked up at the balcony. Their neighbour, Madame Tremblay, snored on a lime-green lawn-chair. Her cigarette, velcrowed between two limp fingers, hovered near extinction over an empty can of Pepsi.

"What do we do?" he asked.

"Maybe if you run up quickly…"

"Okay."

Mike sprinted up the steps and pushed his key into the lock. Dawn took a deep breath and hefted four bags of tulips, begonias, and dirt. She tip-toed past him into the apartment. The old woman kept snoring. Mike closed the door.

Dawn dropped the bags and smirked.

"Now you're an accomplice."

"I liked watching you work."

They brought the flowers to the back balcony and Dawn got them settled into pots.

"I love Westmount dirt," she whispered. "*Imagine* the garden we could have…"

"Imagine the *jobs* we'd have to have."

Mike went to the kitchen to make coffee. Dawn finished her chore and put her earthy hands on his shoulders.

"Are you making some for me?"

"Did you want some?"

"Uh-huh."

He turned to face her.

"Of course I am."

She kissed him.

"What should we do after?"

"Go to Mount Royal?"

"Sure."

They drank their coffees and threw on extra sweaters. It was past midnight and the temperature was near zero. They bought a bag of peanuts at the twenty-four hour *dépanneur* and caught the night-bus. With no traffic, it was only a fifteen-minute ride. They got off near the steps on Peel street and climbed together.

Lean squirrels paced on the sidelines. Mike opened the bag and tossed a few nuts into the crowd. Then he offered a handful to Dawn. She ate one and scattered the rest.

On the path to the Chalet, he took her hand and said: "I can't believe we've never been here together."

"I've only been here once."

"Really?"

"Uh-huh."

"When?"

"I was sixteen. I was dating this guy…Jimmy. He was, well, he was an asshole, but he was my first boyfriend. Anyway, he and his friends wanted to go on a spree in the city, so I told my parents I was sleeping at Priscilla's and went. I was the only girl."

"What happened?"

"We got into a few bars and we got pretty drunk…We could have done *that* in the country; but I got to use my fresh fake i.d., and that made it fun. Then one of the guys said he knew where to get some really good coke. I went along with it, but I didn't see why. It cost more than booze and who knew what would happen? The dealers were jerks, but they had a good pit bull that drooled on my sleeve when I patted his tummy. I wanted to steal him away from it all...I stuck to my vodka but all the guys snorted.

"Then someone said: 'Let's go to the mountain.' I was drunk and confused, but I just remember laughing. We bought marshmallows and built a bonfire to roast them. When that was done, I tried thinking deep thoughts about Jimmy, but I couldn't: he was a waste of time and he kept grabbing my ass. He was really shy when we were alone. It was just a show for the boys. They all whooped and smirked. Just teenagers, I guess. I remember their faces, sweating in the firelight. I wasn't scared. I was scared I'd kill them. So I ditched them and took a nap in the woods.

"The next morning, I planned to go straight to the terminal and take the first bus to Ormstown. But then I decided to find Jimmy. So I could break up with him. When I got to the spot where we'd made the bonfire, only one guy was there. A farm kid with crooked yellow teeth and a stupid laugh. I didn't even know his name. But he was dead..."

"What!"

"His throat was slashed. I called the police and they questioned me. I had to testify at the trial. They never really found out what happened, but all of those guys got light sentences. I got grounded."

"Jesus!"

She smiled quietly.

"That's my teen-angst story. What's yours?"

"Just one? You know, suburban kids work hard at this stuff."

She squeezed his hand.

"Just one."

"Okay. Well, let's stick with sixteen then...One summer night, I was out late, playing a role-playing game at Eric's. I used to do anything to get out of the house. But I always had to catch the first bus home in the morning, so I could do my Gazette route. Anyway, this one morning, I did the papers and found my mom still awake, crying on the couch. There were broken things on the living room floor, and I could hear my dad stomping around upstairs. They didn't usually fight that long. But they didn't *usually* finish two bottles of rum either. Actually, they hadn't quite finished it. My mom was trying to fit the last of it into her mouth. I offered to get her a funnel. It didn't matter *what* I said to her when she was that bad.

"She looked up at me and started on a swearing riff laced with bits of stuff from the morning news. (She called me a 'fucking Gorbachev.') I went to my room and put on a movie I had just bought: *Libeled Lady*—a screwball comedy. It was great. I turned up the volume and got really into it. About halfway through the movie, I heard screaming over my laughter and paused the movie. I peeked out of my room and saw my sister on the phone in the kitchen. She was telling someone about my mom swallowing a whole bottle of pills and frothing at the mouth. She gave them the address and hung up. I closed the door and pressed play."

They stopped at the Chalet. During the daytime, worn shoes and ice cream drops criss-crossed its tiled floors between paintings that commemorated the glories of New France. At night, the doors were locked, and the building turned back into a gray stone fortress. They walked through the courtyard to the observation balcony and admired the city until Dawn's eyes doubled back upon blooming flowers.

"Oh-ho," she murmured.

"Oh no," Mike ran his fingers up and down her back.

"I've filled all my pots…"

"Don't you like the view?"

"It's not important, is it?."

"Not really."

"Neither are the flowers."

"So what is?"

"Nothing?"

"We should lie down for this."

"Yes."

They found a natural gutter behind the Chalet and slid down into it. The ground was cold under Mike's back. Dawn's body rained across his chest. He closed his eyes.

"This is good."

"Yeah it's good."

"But it's hard."

"Sure it is."

"Well, maybe the stars are pasted with spit to the firmament."

"And maybe this dust isn't any more permanent."

"There's no love and no lust."

"No you."

"No me?"

"But everything matters."

"Think we should?"

"We don't have to."

"No, but we could."

"Couldn't hurt…"

"Ow!"

"Should've worn a skirt."

There were no more words. Voices rustled through rotting leaves.

⁂

Mike followed Dawn's eyes through her breath in the air.

"You know, I used to think just having sex would solve all my problems. I wanted a strong guy to spin me and hold me while the world whirred by."

"And now?"

"It's whirring all by itself. Can't you see?"

But Mike heard the whirr in her lisp.

He blinked over her shoulder and whispered: "It's a beautiful world."

She bit her lip.

CHAPTER 25

▼

Mike woke up two years later on a queen-sized bed. It was 7:15 on a bright morning and there were birds at the feeder. He flipped over and projected his day onto a dirty pillowcase:

He would slide his hands under Dawn's pyjamas and rest them there for a while. She would wake up from the dreams his fingers inspired just in time to kiss him goodbye. Then he would wander naked into the kitchen to feed the cats and boil water for instant coffee and instant oatmeal. He would put on the Clash's *Sandinista!* and swallow breakfast, with "The Magnificent Seven" on repeat. Finally, he would take a two-minute shower and rush off to the metro.

He would arrive late at MarcoSport, without offering any explanation. He would type until Celine Dion came on the radio and then go to the lunchroom for a coffee and a phone call. Dawn would whisper until an executive came into the room, forcing Mike to hang up. He would call once more before she left for work at twelve-thirty. Then he would type out the rest of the day and return to *Sandinista!*, putting "Up in Heaven(Not Only Here)" on repeat.

Mike turned on his side to look at the day from another angle. The details of Dawn's body glazed over his eyes. He watched her waving from the bedroom window; making fun of her boss during a commercial; pointing at mushroom fried rice on a menu. He thought about calling in sick. Dawn's lungs pulsed against his chest and he breathed aged perfume off her neck. She yawned and screeching filled his head. Mike turned to stifle the alarm. Dawn exhaled as his hand slipped past.

CHAPTER 26

▼

"Good morning."

Mike put down his book and hugged his sister. She slid into her side of the green booth and picked up a Crayola-bright menu.

"Been waiting long?"

"No. I was in line for about fifteen minutes, but they passed quickly—this place has great chicken statues!"

"I knew you'd like them."

"*You* did this?"

"Uh huh. Freelance job."

"When?"

"Last year."

"That's crazy!"

"Well, you know my tastes are more…austere, but they wanted kitsch, and I kind of got into it."

"I don't mean that. It looks fine. But you've *got* a full-time job…"

"Mi-*chael*," she shook her head and turned a page, "So…I guess you know what you want?"

"I'll know when they ask me."

"Then I'll be quick."

"Don't worry about it. You drove a long way for breakfast."

"Yeah the traffic was pretty bad for a Saturday too. But it's worth it. I never come downtown anymore. And I never see you."

"I was thinking the same thing."

"There's so little time."

"That's what I meant."

"When?"

"Before."

"Oh. Well. You know...sometimes even a little time is too much."

"You mean like waking up ten minutes before the alarm goes off? You lie there and you think about turning it off or setting it ahead or having sex, but you just wind up with your finger on the buzzer, waiting to ambush the noise when it comes."

"Something like that."

"I don't agree."

"With who? Yourself?"

"I think those ten minutes are important. Even if we never do anything with them."

"I think...no one should wake up before their alarm clock. Ruins the surprise..."

A waitress brought them coffee and took their orders.

"So. How's Vito?"

"Oh. You know. Fine."

"Fine?"

"Sure."

"Are you worried Di?"

"'Bout what?"

"About nothing happening."

"Hey. I'm not the one who works three days and sleeps four."

"I'm not saying I'm better."

"Aren't you?"

"No."

"But Dawn..."

"I guess the surprise is ruined."

"I think people should surprise themselves."

"That's not what you said before."

"When?"

"Who's lecturing who?"

"Oh Michael..."

He touched her arm.

"I guess I am worried," she sighed.

"How come?"

"Vito wants to get married. For real this time."

"And?"

"I can't. There's not enough."

"Enough what?"

"I don't know. It's just not *sound*."

"I've got the reverse."

"It's a problem either way—isn't it?"

"Yeah."

The food arrived. Mike poured syrup on his blueberry waffles. Diane ate her omelet plain. They both asked for refills of coffee.

"So what're you going to do?"

"I don't know. I *love* my life Michael. Except for *this*. I don't have *time* for this."

"Did you tell him?"

"Sure. We've been fighting like crazy. He thinks it's *time*. Whatever *that* means."

"I kind of know what he means. At a certain point you get trapped in re-runs and the only way out is to plan for the future, if you can..."

"Are you telling me you're giving up on Dawn?"

"Giving up? No. I look at her and I see her last year and the year before and tomorrow but it's the same as yesterday and I go crazy trying to see her now. I'm hooked. I never get tired of watching her, but I never see anything new..."

"What do you expect Michael? You've been together a long time."

"Maybe. But when I call from work and she picks up the phone, it hits me..."

"What?"

"Whatever it is..."

"Well, you can't have a relationship on the phone."

"I *know* Di."

"Are you saying you're not *attracted* to her anymore?"

"Are you kidding? She looks like Gwendolyn."

"The dream-girl?"

"Yeah. And maybe that's part of the problem. Nothing seems real when I'm *with* her."

"You can't lose sight of reality. I think that's why Vito and I have done so well: he doesn't try to pull me out of my orbit. At least, not until lately."

"Maybe he's just not capable of it."

"Maybe not. But it's starting to get heavy."

"Dawn pulls, but there's no gravity…I thought I felt it—once…"

"You have to make it yourself."

"Maybe you're right."

"Eat your waffles Michael."

CHAPTER 27

▼

Mike settled into a dark corner of "The Bell Jar" and squinted at the yellowing pages of *The Name Above the Title*. He couldn't see very well, so he looked around for Pamela. He didn't recognize any of the waitresses. He hadn't been there in a while, but the place hadn't changed much. It still catered to the same people: university-types who couldn't handle the dance-music and body-suits on Crescent street. But the board-games were gone and the crowd had grown older. There was less flannel and less smoke. The younger kids had graduated to techno and trip-hop, but the "Bell Jar" kept playing alt-rock.

A soothing baseline on the soundsystem caught Mike's attention. The sound bled into a low, lisping female voice:

"Everything is good these days but
All of my friends are dying.
Davy may and Lisa may but
Nobody else really wants to stay.
Nobody else really wants to sta-a-ay."

A buoyant guitar jangled over the last syllable, changing the mood of the song entirely. The voice returned:

"I said:
Open the do-oo-or.
Open the door I can't stay here anymore.
Open the door…".

"What's the book?" Eric asked, taking a seat.

"It's Capra's autobiography. I got it for five bucks!"

"Cool. I wish I had time to read fun stuff."

"Hey, this is serious. I'll be writing papers on it soon."

"What?"

"I got into the Communications department."

"At Concordia?"

"Yeah."

"When did you decide to do this?"

"Oh, it's always been part of the plan. Sort of."

A waitress appeared at the table. Eric ordered a *Boréal Rousse*. Mike asked for a coffee. Sleater-Kinney's "Good Things" erupted from the speakers.

"This is great Mike!"

"Yeah, I'm excited."

"And you're gonna work on Capra?"

"Hollywood romantic comedies."

"What're you gonna do with them?"

"Well, I want to figure out why they make me feel the way they do…I also want to connect them to film noir…But that might be too big for a little honours thesis…"

"Too big? There's no such thing! That's the problem with academia. You'll see. I'm sick of reading about life through a magnifying glass…"

"Is that why you're having trouble finishing the thesis?"

"I don't know. I guess so. I signed up for this degree to rescue Natural Law from relativism. I refuse to leave hard reasoning to the cynics, even though—of course—they're more into it. But now it's all about writing judiciously and doling out footnotes in honour of every stupid thing that's ever been published on the subject. I haven't lost faith, but I really wonder if it's coming across in the writing. Worse—I'm starting to realize that *no one* is going to read the damn thing…"

The waitress brought their drinks. They thanked her and paid her.

"But you're going to finish it, right?" Mike asked.

"Oh, yeah, sure...I'll get a great mark and it will look good on my c.v. I'm just saying: don't expect to do anything earth-shattering at University. The paper-trail goes back three-thousand years and you can't start a fire strong enough to light the beginning..."

"That's fine. I just want to work some things out for myself."

"That's the right attitude. I wish I had it."

"Maybe you didn't ask the right questions."

"The right questions ask themselves. The rest is just a game."

"What's that? Natural Law?"

Eric smiled: "Yeah."

He got up to use the washroom.

Mike tried his book again, but the light still wasn't good enough. He hummed through Weezer's "El Scorcho", Bikini Kill's "Outta Me", and Everclear's "Fire Maple Song". At the next table, a couple started on their third pitcher and a fight. Mike turned and watched a line of drunks throw darts at the wall. It was only twelve-thirty, but the place was clearing out—the office lurked on the horizon. Mike had tried going to bed early, but it didn't help.

New Kingdom's "Suspended in Air" bounced off the walls. Eric returned and picked up his beer.

"I've been thinking," he said, "this could be the best decision you ever made. You'll stop writing under the influence and start exerting some."

"That's the idea."

"I've always believed in the transformative power of art."

Mike smirked: "It's true. You've always been magnanimous about that."

"Give me a break, okay? I write essays."

"Are you going to keep doing it?"

"I don't know. I might take a year off and apply to law school. I want to do something practical."

"Me too. There's nothing else."

CHAPTER 28

▼

Mike got off the metro at Lionel-Groulx and followed a crowd up to the turnstiles. Tina sat cross-legged in front of *L'Arbre de Vie*—a sculpture left over from Expo '67, with "the races of man" carved into a tree-trunk. She was reading *The Tao of Pooh*.

Mike leaned on a wooden nose and said: "Hey."

Tina closed the book and stood. Dust fell from her patchwork skirt. "Hi Mike. What's new?"

"Oh," he shrugged, straightening his body.

She let her nose twitch. "You look good."

"You do too."

"So. We're gonna explore the Concordia library?"

"Yeah. I want to get some Emerson. He keeps coming up."

"Where?"

"Oh. Communications. Philosophy. Lit."

"You like the classes?"

"It's better than working."

"I'll bet."

"You want to walk? Or take the metro?"

"Let's walk."

They climbed another flight up to Atwater. Gusts of October chimney-smoke mixed with rush-hour fumes. The sun had set.

At the intersection of Atwater and Ste-Catherine, Tina smiled: "It's cool. Not like this weekend."

"No. Not like this weekend."

"Didn't you go to the country?"

"Yeah."

Tina inhaled the Westmount air. "We should do this more often."

"We should."

"Let's avoid La Paz okay? I don't want to deal with *that* on my day off."

"Me neither."

"Cool."

"Is it driving you crazy?"

"Oh. You know me. I can curl up and get comfortable in any old shoe. But I have to set limits."

"Makes sense."

They followed a path through Westmount park and stopped at the makeshift lake. Mike watched a German Shepherd chase red leaves across the surface of the water. Tina closed her eyes.

"Do you want to know what happened?"

Tina's eyes remained closed. "Do I?"

"Yeah. I think so."

"Okay then. But let's walk…"

"Sure."

They moved on to Sherbrooke, once they had passed La Paz. Mike took a deep breath.

"Dawn and I broke up."

"No *kidding* Mike. But why?"

"Well, I've been thinking about it, and I don't know."

"So just tell me how."

"That's easier—I think. It, uh, well, I was kind of excited about the whole thing. Dawn's been working weekends for months and we hadn't been to the country in a while. You know I love it. Especially during the fall. We were going to visit the haunted house she liked to play in. I've been hearing about it for years…But I woke up with a sore throat and Dawn had worked sixteen hours the day before…"

"I know. Everyone called in sick."

"Neither of us jumped out of bed. We didn't have time to eat breakfast and we almost missed the bus. We got coffees and chocolate at the station, but that didn't help much…

"The sun was really bright. I couldn't see the cows through my squint and I baked in the window. Dawn passed out and our moist hands slipped apart…"

Tina winced.

"I know, I know: I'm only remembering it this way because of what happened…Anyway, we got to her parents' place and that was kind of depressing. Their old dog—Shadow—had died and the new one was kind of a bust. A runt German Shepherd that probably had Chihuahua blood. Mr. Paris half-seriously asked us to take the dog home with us. When I said we'd think about it, Dawn didn't look happy.

"We took Advil with lunch and went out. I wanted to walk through the forest, but the highway was quicker, so we took that. It was scorching and there were hardly any trees. But we *did* find an apple stand. The people who ran it had known Dawn when she was a girl and they gave us some cider. They all kept talking about her hair and how beautiful she was and it made me feel worse…She *is* though. Not in that perfect model way, but scarier—because it doesn't make sense. I've always thought Venus would have crooked teeth…"

"What are you saying? You broke up because she's beautiful?"

"No. I guess not."

"*Focus* Mike."

"Yeah. Well, we walked a little further and stopped to rest under a big red maple. I sank down against the trunk. Dawn stretched out in front of me, balanced on one hip, facing the road. She brushed her hair away and peeked back over her shoulder. Her cheek was red. I looked at her, tilted my head to let the sweat drain, and looked back again. She never blinked. My T-shirt was a dirty sopping rag glued to my arm-pits. I pulled it off. More hair fell across her face, but she didn't move. Her eye dilated in the shade and her teeth started to show. I

wondered how far we'd have to walk, but I didn't ask. Finally, I
hopped over her and offered her my hand. Her other eye was bright
and sealed against the sun. A tear sizzled on her cheek. She got up and
turned back toward the house. I watched her go. Then I started thinking about sunburn and put on my shirt."

"That doesn't sound like a fight."

"It was enough. I'm glad Mr. Paris talked to himself on the drive
home. As soon as he left, Dawn started packing."

"What are you going to do?"

"Luckily, Eric's lease is up next month. He'll move in. I don't know
where she's going."

"I'm sorry Mike."

They crossed the grounds of Concordia's Loyola campus, passing
red old buildings on the way to the ugly new library. Students littered
the grass—discussing books they could no longer see. There wasn't
much of a moon.

Mike found a collection of Emerson's essays and started reading
"Self-Reliance" in the check-out line. Tina met him there and piled
geology texts on top of his book.

"What are these?"

"I'm getting into rocks."

"You want to get ice cream after? MacDoherty's is close."

"Isn't it kinda cold?"

"We can eat inside. Come on."

"Sure. Why not?"

The librarian stamped the books. Mike put them in his schoolbag
and stopped at the glass door. It had started to drizzle and the trees
were losing leaves.

"Damn," Mike shrugged.

"We can still do it."

"Really?"

Tina mused: "Ice cream on a blustery night…"

"It's perfect."

They half-ran to MacDoherty's, three blocks away. It was an old-fashioned parlour, with a lacquered brown counter and antique signs. The walls were covered with old movie posters. A stained-glass mosaic of a blue and white sundae hung above the sweet altar of buckets. The place was empty, except for a counter-girl, who tossed aside an issue of *Cosmo* and smiled: "Can I help you?"

"Should we split a sundae?" Tina asked Mike.

"Split one? I'm too hungry…"

Tina smiled: "I guess you're right. This *is* a celebration, after all…"

Mike got a strawberry sundae. Tina got caramel and pecan. They took a table near the back of the store, beneath a framed ad for *It's A Wonderful Life*. Their spoons clinked against glass bowls.

"You think this is a celebration?"

"Sure. This is a very good thing Mike. You guys have done nothing for three years. And now look, already, you're going to university—and who knows what Dawn will do?"

"Yeah. Who *knows*."

"Don't be like that Mike."

"Like what?"

"Whiny."

"I'm almost done."

"Good."

"Yeah. It could be good."

BOOK FOUR

CHAPTER 29

▼

A roaring black storm-shroud dropped. Green alarm-digits and street-lamps swirled down the drain. Mike felt his way along silk-muscled legs to the foot of the bed. He walked to the balcony door. Moisture licked his palms through the windowpane. He stood in the dark, trying to hear through the rain. A stray headlight flashed on the glass. Cold starlings flew through an empty bed reflection. Mike burst through the door. Black wing-beats bled into the roar.

"There is no life, my darling, until you have loved and been loved. And then there is no death…"

Mike squinted at the high white ceiling. He had fallen asleep on a mattress in his new room, watching *Portrait of Jennie*. A soft-focus wave smashed into a lighthouse, drowning the romantic speaker in a Debussy theme. Mike stopped the tape. He plugged in a shadeless brown lamp and reached for the phone. He punched in the number for Dial-A-M8.

Mike wrote his new box number and access code on the back of an old notebook. He traced circles around them and said:

"Hi. This is Mike. I'm twenty-three. I'm about five-foot-five and weigh about one-thirty-five. I have dark hair and green eyes. I'm a down-to-earth, easy-going guy just looking to talk to someone interesting…"

He pressed * for another attempt.

"Hello. My name is Mike. I'm a twenty-three year old student. I like music, movies, coffee, walks on Mount Royal...Same as everyone else..."

He pressed * again.

"Uh. Hello, this is Mike. I'm a student. I'm twenty-three. I'm hoping to meet a woman I can have a good time with. Preferably someone who's also a student and a good conversationalist. I..."

*   *   *   *

"Hi. This is Mike. I'm twenty-three and I just started a bachelor's in communications at Concordia. I'm still recovering from a pretty serious break-up and I'm not sure what I'm looking for. I guess I'm hoping to meet some new people, talk and see what ha...pens..."

*   *   *   *

"Hey. This is Mike. I'm a little worried. I'm just spewing clichés here...I don't really know *what* I'm like. It depends who I'm w—...Well, if you like my voice, send me a message okay? It's box 18750."

Mike heard footsteps in the hall. He pressed # and got up to investigate. There was a twelve-pack of Sleeman's on the coffee table. Mike sprawled on the couch, listening to laughter on the balcony. The footsteps came back toward the living room. Eric gestured toward Mike.

"...and this is my roommate."

A pair of cigarettes waved through the air—one held by a slouching blonde with scraggly hair, pasty cheeks and child-star blue eyes; the other by an older man with short, dyed-platinum hair, veiny arms and a scar-shaped smile. Mike sat up.

"These are my friends: Paula and Alex," Eric announced.

"Hello," Mike waved back.

Everyone pulled up chairs and sat down, placing their bottles in a crescent-moon formation on the coffee table.

Mike yawned: "What's going on?"

"We were hoping you'd play hearts."

"Do we have a working deck?"

"I'm not sure."

Eric jumped up and started going through every drawer in the house.

"No. We don't," he yelled from the kitchen.

Mike stood up.

"I'll get some at the dépanneur. I need coffee and cat food anyway."

Paula finished her beer.

"I'll go with you. I'm out of cigarettes."

She pronounced the last word "tsi-garet-th."

Alex blinked at her.

"Could you get me a May West?"

Paula slipped into her coat.

"Could you give me some money?"

Alex fumbled through his pockets and pulled out a ten-dollar ball. He handed it to her.

"You want anything Eric?" she called.

"I'm fine."

"Alright, let's go."

She raced down the stairs. The wind blew red leaves through a cold black sky and ironed out her hair. Mike took slow short steps. Paula slackened her pace.

"You know Eric from university?" Mike asked.

"The university *bar*," she smiled.

"Ah. What do you study?"

"I write."

"Creative writing?"

"Mm-hmm."

They walked into the dépanneur. Patrique, the talkative karate-champ clerk, flashed his long black fingernails at them. Mike nodded and kept his head down. He picked up a box of Cat Chow and a jar of instant Nescafe. The cards hung from a rack near the stationary at the back of the store. Mike reached for a ninety-nine cent happy-face deck. Paula poked his shoulder.

"Come on Mike. You're not paying. Get a pack of Bees."

"Okay," he smiled.

They paid and walked back to the apartment.

Mike dropped the cards on the table and went to make coffee. Eric put on Rage Against the Machine's *Evil Empire*.

"What do you think of this?" he asked, when Mike returned with a steaming mug.

"I like the sound. But the lyrics are kind of…naive…"

"Man! I'm exactly the opposite!"

"Eric," Paula sighed, "do you really think the world is controlled by faceless corporate *demons?*"

"Well…no…but it's the right spirit…"

"Did you get my May West?" Alex asked Paula.

"Oh, uh, sorry sweetie. I forgot. Maybe Eric and Mike have bread?"

"Want a bagel Alex?" Mike asked.

"Poppy or sesame?"

"Poppy."

"Um, maybe I'll order pizza."

Paula smacked his arm.

"You're supposed to thank people when they offer you food."

"Yeah-yeah. Thanks Mike. But no thanks. You got any menus?"

"In the kitchen. Next to the phone."

"Thanks," Alex smirked. "I'll be back."

"He's such a bastard," Paula lit a cigarette.

Eric opened the new box of cards, took the jokers out, and started shuffling.

"I'll deal," he said.

"Alex! We're starting!" Paula yelled.

"Will you fuck off please?" he yelled back. "The bitch put me on hold!"

Mike turned to Paula.

"What does Alex do?"

"He teaches lit."

Mike chuckled: "Charles Bukowski?"

"Chaucer and Spenser mainly."

Eric dealt the cards.

Alex returned, muttering: "Never again…"

He picked up his hand.

"Aw, what the fuck?!"

"Shut up Alex."

"Yeah-yeah."

Paula passed three cards to Eric and touched his bright sleeve: "That's a nice shirt."

"Thanks," Eric smiled.

The speakers blared "Riding Down Rodeo With A Shot-gun".

"I can't deal with this. It's too aggressive…"

"Are you kidding?" Mike asked. "It's just right."

"You want the CD? I was going to return it…"

"Sure."

"Fine. It's yours. But I'm going for the Bob Marley."

"Whatever…"

"Did you pass yet?" Alex demanded.

"Uh…here," Eric shoved three cards toward him and dashed for the stop button.

"Do you have any Tragically Hip?" Paula asked.

"No," Mike snickered.

"You don't like the Hip?"

"They're a beer-commercial band…"

Her blue eyes widened.

"I like that."

Eric clattered through the pile of CDS.

"We can all agree on *London Calling*, right?"

No one complained.

"Good."

Paula led the two of clubs and everyone concentrated. Alex took the Queen of Spades, but he squirmed out of further danger by playing a low heart. Mike's ace and king of hearts stuck him with eight points. He retrieved the notepad from his room, tore out a fresh sheet of paper, and wrote:

Paula	Mike	Eric	Alex
1	8	4	13

Alex dealt the next hand. They arranged their cards and passed them quietly. Eric led the two of clubs. Alex took the trick with the queen of clubs and led the king. Mike tossed the six of hearts into the mix. Alex reeled in the cards with a smile and led the ace of clubs.

"Did you see that?" Paula pointed a lit cigarette.

"No table-talk!" Alex snarled.

"He always does this! He's going for control!"

"You fuckin' *cunt*!"

"Jesus…Relax," Mike played the four of diamonds.

Alex stood up and glared at Paula.

"Forget about cards—I don't even want to *live* with this bitch anymore!"

"There's only one bitch at this table," Paula replied.

Mike touched her arm.

"You wouldn't have got it anyway Alex."

"No?"

"No," Mike shook his head.

"We'll never know, will we?"

Mike spread his hand on the table. There were seven hearts in it.

"Let's see yours."

Alex showed a good control hand. All the high spades and five hearts—but he was missing the jack.

"See," Mike smiled.

"Yeah-yeah."

"Deal them again," Eric sighed. "And *no* table-talk," he wagged his finger at Paula.

"Fine," she crossed her arms. "I only said it 'cause it was obvious…"

"Maybe. But it's still wrong."

Alex grabbed the cards and shuffled them.

"Aw don't patronize me!"

Mike watched the cards slide across the table.

"So. Alex. You teach English?"

"I *said*: don't fuckin' patronize me!"

"I'm just asking a question…"

"Pick up your cards and play!"

The doorbell rang. Alex went to answer it.

Mike turned to Paula.

"Is he okay?"

"This is what he's like."

Alex returned with a ham-and-pineapple pizza.

"I *said*: no table-talk," he smiled.

"Good one," Mike nodded weakly.

"Anyone want some?"

"Me," Eric stood up. "I'll get plates and forks."

"Anyone else?" Alex asked pleasantly.

Mike and Paula shook their heads.

"You *know* I'm trying to go vegetarian," Paula added.

"Yeah-yeah."

Mike looked at Paula.

"Really?"

"Uh-huh," she nodded. "But it's hard. I'm going to a Concordia Animal Rights Association party next week. They're giving out recipe-books."

"Sounds cool."

"You should come."

"I will."

"Okay!" Alex picked up his cards with greasy fingers. "Aw, who passed me this *shit*?!"

CHAPTER 30

▼

Mike knocked on an orange melamine door.

"Come in."

He walked into a small room made smaller by wall-to-wall bookshelves. A man with white skin and whiter hair sat at a desk near the window, humming to Mozart. A solitaire game on his laptop screen reflected in his thick glasses.

"Hi, uh, Professor Snell. I'm Mike Borden. I'm in your genres class?"

"Yes of course. Sit down Mike."

"Thanks."

The professor pushed his computer aside and took a sip of espresso from a cream-coloured mug with a large "N" on it.

"Did you have questions about your essay Mike? I thought it was excellent…"

"Oh, uh, thanks, but, actually, I wanted to speak to you about my honours thesis."

"Honours thesis? Isn't this your first semester?"

"Yes," Mike shifted in his chair, "but I'm gonna do full-time summers. I'm twenty-three. I want to get this done."

Professor Snell smiled: "What's your idea?"

"Well, I've always been fascinated by romantic comedy. I think the form gets a bad rap. I've only been in school for a month, but it's obvious that most professors are preaching the gospel of European ci-ne-mah. Naturally, oddball romance seems trite after Eisenstein. But it works both ways. Eisenstein can seem dry and pompous after Capra…"

"Your devotion is touching Mike. And maybe I agree with you. But where's the thesis?"

"Sorry. It's coming. I guess I'm kind of defensive about this…"

"Kind of."

"Well, I just read Stanley Cavell's *Pursuits of Happiness* and…"

"Good book."

"You've read it?"

"It's a classic."

"Oh. Cool. Well, I like his focus on remarriage in screwball comedies. He argues that the genre takes the spotlight off the male—who, in classical comedy, tries to 'win' a bride—and places it on the female—who pauses to consider whether the marriage helps or hinders her development."

"That's the main argument."

"Yes. Cavell shows that the couples in these movies make a new future for themselves by coming to an agreement about the meaning of their checkered past together. So that, even in a case like *Bringing Up Baby*, where the man and woman don't know each other before the film starts, the couple must create a 'shared childhood'—usually by wreaking havoc in some pastoral retreat—before they can truly begin a life together as equals."

"That sounds like Cavell to me. But where do *you* come in?"

"Right here: I think Cavell is too optimistic about the possibility of mutuality in human relationships. I don't believe two minds can achieve that kind of synchronicity. Of course, we can fool ourselves into thinking that it's happened—and that's what I think romantic comedy is about. The genre features imaginative protagonists who create ideal playmates for themselves and then force each other into the roles. To that extent, it *is* mutual—but there's no reciprocity. Cavell's seven movies all lend themselves to my reinterpretation, but I think the purest examplar is a movie he scrupulously avoids—*Holiday*."

"How so?"

"Well, it's about a man who returns from a vacation in Lake Placid engaged to a woman he knows nothing about—except that she wants 'the life I want and the fun I want'. He's an engaging character, and seems fairly bright, except that it takes him the running-time of the movie to notice that Katharine Hepburn tallies much more closely with his description of 'The Girl' than his original choice, her sister. The role of 'perfect playmate' remains static, but there's a last-minute casting-change—for the better, of course.

"Cavell says that the kiss between Cary Grant and Hepburn at the end feels 'unearned', and that, therefore, *Holiday* does not belong with the films he's describing, which are expressly *about* 'earning' a happy future together. I would argue that the kiss is *supposed* to feel 'unearned', that we are *meant* to feel uncomfortable about it, and that, finally, it is exhilarating anyway, because it hits upon a fundamental truth that Cavell, for his own reasons, wants to obscure."

"Which is?"

"That our reach exceeds our grasp. That we embrace our illusions—of each other, and ourselves."

"Wow. Have you written the whole thing already?"

"No," Mike smiled, "only what I've told you."

"It's fascinating—but kind of grim."

"That depends on how you look at it."

"Well, no one will ever accuse you of taking comedy lightly."

"I guess not."

"You'll have a hard time convincing me. But if you're looking for someone to approve your topic, it's done."

Mike jumped up.

"Thanks!"

"Of course, you shouldn't be working on it yet—officially. But anytime you want to talk, just drop by…"

"I will!"

"There's just one thing Mike."

Mike sat back down.

"Yes?"

"I won't like your religious tone on paper. Scholarship—in order to *be* scholarship—must reflect an open mind. It's fine to have a vision. But a vision is not a thesis."

"Are you sure?"

"No. But I'm sure of my grading habits."

Mike laughed: "I'll keep that in mind."

"I'm not worried."

They shook hands.

CHAPTER 31

▼

Mike jumped out of the shower and stopped a whistling kettle. He put on jeans and a black sweater while the instant Folgers melted in an art deco rooster mug. He stirred a drop of skim milk into the coffee and brought it with him to the hall mirror. He fixed his hair in the steam-clouded glass and took a smiling sip. He went into the living room, put on New Kingdom's *Paradise Don't Come Cheap*, and settled into a brown armchair. Eric drifted in with a glass of ice-water and a fresh copy of Fritjof Capra's *Turning Point*. He sat on the sofa and beamed at speakers hanging from the ceiling.

"Sounds good eh?"

Mike smiled: "Sure."

"You don't care. It might just as well be a ghetto blaster."

"True."

"What's up for tonight?"

"I'm going to that animal rights thing with Paula."

"Right, right."

"Wanna come?"

"For some new recipes? I want to finish this."

He waved his book.

"More Gaia-theory stuff?"

"It's a primer for holistic thought."

"You're kidding right?"

"Why? Because I'd rather find out what they're doing to the rain forests than party with a bunch of animal-fanciers."

"Christ!"

"What?"

"You've got that 'Sacred Balance' tone in your voice…"

"That's common sense."

"No it's not."

"What's wrong with balance?"

"Nothing, I guess, until you fetishize it."

"How do I do that?"

"Well, you eat meat."

"So? The food chain is here to stay."

"There you go."

"There I go what?"

"Fetishizing."

"You're insane Mike…"

"I'm not crazy enough to accept anything just because it's 'natural'."

"Okay," Eric waved the book again, "so we're both serious…You don't think *Paula* is, do you?"

"About vegetarianism?"

"About anything."

"I don't know. She's ferocious."

"She's just backed into a corner."

"But she's not like that with me."

"I'm telling you Mike, she'll bring you down. She's floundering."

Mike nodded: "Maybe she is."

"Maybe you don't mind that?"

"Maybe not."

"But what about the first part? You think you're immune?"

"If Dawn couldn't do it, no one can."

"Maybe she did."

"I'm still here."

"You're still talking about her."

"Only because of Paula."

Eric opened his book.

"Oh."

Mike strolled down Verdun avenue and stopped at a white-brick pizzeria. He climbed a gray staircase to the second-floor balcony and rang Paula's doorbell.

After a few minutes, Alex opened the door and said: "She's still getting ready."

Mike followed him into a spotless livingroom tittering with CBC sketch comedy. Alex retreated to a depression in a stiff-looking blue couch, in front of the television. He put his feet up on a triangular coffee-table, next to a large glass of coke and a busted solitaire game.

Alex shook his head.

"Sit down Mike. I don't know what she's doing."

Mike tried settling into a matching blue love-seat, under a Magritte poster.

Alex smiled: "We should play hearts again soon. That was fun."

"Yeah."

"Listen. This could take a while. You know how to play crib?"

"Sure."

Alex hopped up and grabbed a cribbage board from a book shelf.

"Let's play then."

"Alright."

Alex shuffled the cards and dealt six each.

Mike pretended to look at his hand and dropped two red cards, face down.

There were footsteps in the hallway.

Alex quickly laid down his crib and whispered: "Okay. Cut."

Mike hoisted a layer of the deck.

Paula walked in and faced them. Her fingers strummed curls off her cheeks. Blonde swirls fell on her black sweater. Her blue eyes overshadowed the shadows beneath them. She coughed and smiled: "I'm ready."

"We just started a game," Alex replied.

"So?"

"So I want to finish. Don't you Mike?"

Mike shrugged.

"Sure."

Paula sighed and sat next to Mike.

"Alright…"

Alex rearranged his hand.

"Go Mike."

Mike sat up straight and showed his cards to Paula. She pointed at the ace of spades and he played it.

"You don't lead an ace! It's stupid!"

"I guess so…"

"Aw forget it!"

Mike stood up.

"Okay."

Paula bent over the table to see Alex's cards.

"You had a lot of points there."

He looked up at her.

"I'll see you later?"

"Sure."

Mike waved: "Goodnight."

Alex shuffled the cards.

"Yeah-yeah."

Mike and Paula followed bright squiggly signs to the crowded basement of the Liberal Arts annex. They signed petitions, gave a smiling demonstration-coordinator their numbers, and pushed toward the back of the room, where they collected free cookbooks, samosas and plastic cups full of wine. Then they retreated to the damp concrete steps outside the building. Mike scanned the recipes. Paula finished both cups of wine and lit a cigarette.

"You think it'll rain?" she asked.

"I hope not."

"Why?"

"We'll be stuck here."

"It's not so bad here," she smiled. Then she handed him her cigarette. "Hold this for a minute? I'm going back in."

"Sure."

"You want anything?"

"No thanks."

Mike shoved the cookbook in his coat pocket and watched the cigarette burn the moist air.

Paula came back with another cup of wine and sat close to him on the step.

She took a long sip and said:

"I wonder who's paying for all this?"

"You are. If you paid your tuition."

"I haven't yet."

"Me neither."

"I'm aways behind. I'm gonna have to get one of those books with green pages and lines and make myself a budget..."

"We should do it together."

"That's a good idea. Alex doesn't understand—he's been earning a professor's salary for twenty years..."

Mike looked at her.

"He's a lot older than you."

"Yeah, like thirty years..."

"Wow. He's in good shape."

"Only on the outside. You should see him try to play the 'nineties guy' with me, every time he catches himself making a sexist comment about one of his students..."

"Oh man."

"He's lucky I don't care. Or I didn't. But he overcompensates and pisses me off. He wanted to have a big sensitive conversation about whether he was satisfying my needs—at, like, nine o'clock in the morning! I told him to shut up. He yelled: 'I've been fucked by the women's movement!' and stomped off to work."

Mike laughed.

Paula lit another cigarette.

"It's almost over."

"I'm really sorry."

She shrugged.

"It was a bender."

"Does he know that?"

"He should."

"Well, I guess there won't be any problems then."

"Oh, there'll be problems…"

Mike smiled.

"But not serious ones."

"That'll depend."

She stood and shook the cup.

"Let's get more."

"Alright."

Paula downed two more cups of wine. Mike listened to a girl with freckles and a pierced tongue tell her friend about tortured dogs in Korea. A guy in a muscle shirt brought up the treatment of pigs in North America. Someone mentioned hunting and wondered whether anyone had the right to do it. A pale woman in overalls explained that for some people it had a religious meaning. Che Guevara came up often. Mike turned and said to Paula: "Let's leave."

"Okay."

They walked through a bit of drizzle to the "Casse Croûte du Coin" and grabbed a booth. A waitress brought them coffee and menus. Paula lit a cigarette. Mike leaned back against a hard plastic cushion.

"I hate those conversations. Bunch of kids…"

"Excuse me? *You* look about twelve!"

"Maybe to you. You live with a senior citizen."

Paula gasped. Blue pinned back her eyelids.

"Hey be nice."

"I *am* nice."

"Yeah," she sipped her coffee, "you are. So where's all this cynicism coming from?"

"From the heart. I don't believe in idealizing anyone but myself."

"Wow. I didn't drink enough to be *that* honest."

"You don't have to be."

The waitress took their orders and Paula excused herself. Mike put a quarter in the jukebox and picked Everclear's "Amphetamine". Paula returned halfway through the song with a torn copy of *The Mirror*.

"Look what I found."

"Any new movies?"

"I don't know. I'm looking for the 'Rant Line'…"

She flipped through the pages.

"Ah-ha!"

She laughed.

"This is great! Here's one from someone who says they saw Gwen Stefani giving a drunk head outside the 'Foufounes Electriques'."

"What?"

"I'm not kidding!"

Paula pushed the paper toward the center of the table.

"Listen."

She put on a Valley-girl accent and read: "And I, for one, was *not* surprised! We all know that No Doubt are a bunch of fuckin' whores and debasers of Ska! Ska used to mean something! It was a fusion of the most radical European and Caribean music! *Now* it's been turned into Top Forty bitching about break-ups! No *wonder* Gwen's husband left her—she sucks cock in alleyways! And she doesn't even need the money anymore!"

Paula laughed through a deep breath and resumed:

"By the way, if you want to see a *real* ska band, which remains com-mitted to world revolution and world peace, go see Coral Reefer this weekend at the Ska Dome. They fuckin' rule!"

Mike shook his head: "Jesus."

"You just know she plays keyboards for Coral Reefer."

"Probably."

"Here's another one. It's nicer."

This time she read with a mock-Italian accent: "Hey I met dis gor-geous blonde girl at Club Crescent last Friday. It was fuckin' ama-zing. We danced for about halfenhour and den her boyfriend showed up. She blew me a kiss over his shoul-der and I stared at her all night. I'm goin' back man! I hope she does too!"

"That's sweet. Sort of."

Paula nodded.

"You see. People aren't all bad."

"I never said they were. But they're pretty disappointing…"

"No one disappoints *me* more than myself. Did you notice I ordered a club sandwhich? *Plus* I told myself I wasn't going to drink tonight!"

Mike laughed.

"*I'm* not disappointed."

"Yeah but you only care about yourself. You said so."

"No. I care about lots of people. But I don't expect anything from them."

"Or judge them?"

"I try not to."

The food arrived. Paula shook her head and bit into her Club. Mike smiled and poured pepper on his lettuce-and-tomato-on-rye. They ate without talking and paid at the counter. Outside, Paula lit a cigarette and led Mike to a taxi stand. She took a few quick puffs and knocked on the window of an old blue Camry. The driver put his book down and Paula opened the door. They slid into the back seat.

"Verdun," she told the driver.

"Okay," he nodded.

Paula blew smoke out the window.

"You want to come up when we get there?"

Mike smiled: "Okay."

"I've got a fresh Harper's double acrostic."

"Sounds good."

The car pulled up in front of Paula's building and they split the eight-forty-five plus tip. They climbed the stairs and tiptoed through the door into the living room. Paula found the magazine and spread it on the coffee table, next to a couple of pencils, a straw, and a neat column of white powder. She picked up the straw and looked at Mike.

"You can start."

He nodded slowly.

"Uh. Alright."

He grabbed a pencil and scanned the clues.

Paula leaned forward, put the straw to her left nostril, and breathed in. She coughed and wiped her nose with the back of her hand.

"You want anything?"

"No. I'm fine."

She clasped her hands together and moved close to him on the couch.

"Okay! You get anything yet?"

They worked at the puzzle for hours, exchanging hunches and bits of certainty. Mike slumped back against the cushion, watching Paula write and re-write. She moved quickly and drew short constant breaths that inflated her eyes.

An alarm clock went off in the bedroom. Mike touched Paula's shoulder. She turned and stopped breathing.

"I'd better go," he said.

She nodded.

"I think you're right."

She hugged him at the door. He walked down the stairs and onto the street. Seagulls screamed from dripping power lines. The moon was gone but the sun hadn't risen.

CHAPTER 32

▼

Mike put on The Smashing Pumpkins' *Adore* and dragged the Christmas tree box from the cupboard. He screwed the trunk into the base and set it down. Billy Corgan yelped: "I will pull your crooked teeth. You'll be perfect just like me." Mike laid out the color-coded branches in neat piles on the sofa. Then he hooked each piece into its slot and sat down, putting his feet up on the box.

Mike dialed a number, waited through a message, and said: "Hey. It's four o'clock. It's all set. But could you bring some ornaments when you come? Mine're all wrecked. Except for the angel. You know, every year, that tree gets easier to assemble. And every year, I feel less like decorating it...I love you."

He put down the phone and watched the cats chew the fake pine needles. He patted a cushion and said: "Come on guys. Stop it."

Marbles and Pandora joined him on the couch. Mike closed his eyes and stroked their ears. A gothic piano drenched funhouse guitars and a voice trailed off: "You are the ghost of my indecision..."

The phone rang.

"Hello," Mike answered.

"Hi," Eric replied.

"How's the conference?"

"Lame. They just let me talk. No one asked me anything interesting. But New York is awesome! You should've come Mike."

"No money."

"I know."

"No time either."

"You busy now?"

"Just waiting for Paula to show up."

"You've seen her a lot lately hunh?"

"Actually, she's been staying here. I didn't think you'd mind. Things really went sour with Alex."

"Christ! Well, that was a pretty fucked up situation…You don't mean she's moving in?"

"No. No. Just until Alex gets a new place."

"Oh. Well. That's cool—it's going alright?"

"It's going great."

"So you're sleeping together?"

"I'm in love with her."

"You told her *that*?"

"Sure."

"What did *she* say?"

"She was busy saying the same thing."

"Wow."

"You think that's strange?"

"I can't even picture it. What do you guys do together?"

"We hang out, read to each other, try to watch movies—the usual stuff couples do the first few weeks…"

Eric snickered.

"Do you go for long walks to her dealer's?"

"Come on!"

"I see. There's some small-print under the declaration."

"No. I never said anything about it."

"Yeah but it's obvious."

"What is?"

"Everyone's got holes Mike. And hers slip neatly into yours."

"I don't know what that means, but a hole's better than a square-peg, isn't it?"

"Maybe. At least it's a better fit...I should go Mike. Say hi to Paula for me."

"I will."

"See you next week."

"Yep."

Mike hung up and went into the kitchen. He took a blackened metal coffee maker off the stovetop, emptied a rock of grounds into the garbage, and rinsed the pieces in the sink. Then he filled the base with water, poured fresh arabica into the filter, and turned on the heat.

He flipped through Dickens' *Christmas Carol* while the coffee brewed. He kept reading, back on the sofa, once it was done. At the end of each paragraph, he looked at the VCR clock.

At 5:27 he opened a new notebook and christened it "Romantic Comedy Thesis #2". He titled the first subdivider "Dickensian Roots" and scrawled:

> ...they sought to interfere, for good, in human matters and had lost the power forever (*A Christmas Carol*, 7).

Then:

> Scrooge's development from wounded recluse to universal benefactor provides a perfect blueprint (minus the sex) for what would become the Hollywood romantic comedy.

The phone rang again.

"Hello."

"Hi Mike."

It was Paula.

"What's going on?" he asked. "Workshop go late?"

"No. I've been at home. I had a big talk with Alex."

"Really?"

"We needed to."

"I guess you're right. But let's talk when you get here..."

"I think I'm gonna go to bed."

"You can sleep here."

"Since when?"

He laughed.

"You make me sound like an octopus."

"You are. And it's great. I just need to be alone right now."

"Come on. I hate this 'you have to heal yourself' stuff."

"Really? What exactly do *you* need from me?"

His voice wavered.

"What's that supposed to mean?"

"Nothing Mike. Nothing. I just can't go through with this, that's all. I think it would kill me."

"You'd rather kill yourself another way, is that it?"

"Yeah. I think I would."

"What about my tree?"

"You'll have to do it yourself Mike. I'm sorry..."

She hung up.

Mike muttered: "Fuck."

He went back to his thesis.

CHAPTER 33

▼

Mike knocked on Nathaniel Snell's orange door and peeked into the office. The professor was bobbing his head to an early German recording of *The Threepenny Opera*.

"Hi Mike. Come in."

He turned down the music.

"What's on your mind?"

"I've been thinking about melodrama."

Snell smiled.

"Thinking about it or living it?"

Mike laughed.

"Thinking about it. Mostly."

"Sit down."

"Thanks."

"So?"

Mike took a deep breath.

"Well, I've been thinking that my thesis isn't really *about* romantic comedy. The problems I want to write about are just as fundamental to melodrama. The idea didn't just come to me from out of nowhere. I was, uh, reading Raymond Carney's book on Frank Capra, and I started to think about how silly it would be for me to try and write something about romantic objectification in American film without tackling *Meet John Doe...*"

"*Meet John Doe?* That's a political film isn't it? An anti-fascist film?"

Mike shook his head.

"I wouldn't say so."

"Neither would Ray Carney, right? I haven't read his book, but I know that he treats the political sermonizing in Capra as a cover for a more personal, Transcendentalist-style philosophy."

Mike nodded.

"That's how I've always viewed Capra. I've loved him since I was a kid. And I never gave a damn about politics…"

"That's one thing I like about you Mike. You seem to have skipped the radical phase. But you don't wallow in Gen-X cynicism either. You've got a middle-aged man's perspective."

"Is that supposed to be a compliment?"

"What do you think? Coming from a middle-aged man?"

"I think part of you wonders why I never chained myself to a tree or something…"

"Maybe. *I* did it in the sixties. And I don't even like nature."

"I've had other things on my mind, I guess."

"Like melodrama?"

"Right. You remember my argument that the archetypal romantic comedy charts the development of a protagonist (or two) from lonely visionary to happy participant in a reciprocal delusion?"

"I don't accept that. But I remember it."

"Fine. Well, I think melodrama grows out of the breakdown of that delusion. But the breakdown has nothing to do with the failure of the loved one to "live up to expectations". Rather, it occurs when the visionary subject recognizes the artificiality of those expectations—and if *both* participants in the delusion reach this understanding, there is the potential for catching the truth about human relationships in the crossfire."

"So, basically, melodrama makes manifest certain ideas which romantic comedy merely hints at, and may even obscure…"

"Exactly."

"Well, as usual, you're overstating—but I'm not bored. It's all very general though, isn't it? When I think about melodrama, I don't necessarily think about these problems. You're going to have to convince me that I should."

"Alright. Let's take *Meet John Doe* then—you've seen it?"

Snell nodded: "A long time ago."

"Okay. Well. A female journalist, played by Barbara Stanwyck, gets fired by a streamlining paper, because her column doesn't generate any excitement. As a farewell piece, she writes an inflammatory letter and implies that the imaginary sender, a jobless hobo, will commit suicide on Christmas Eve, as a protest against the 'state of the world'. All of New York rushes to 'his' aid; so the paper is obliged to re-hire Stanwyck (with a fat bonus to insure her secrecy), and find a man to play 'John Doe'. This turns out to be easy, because hundreds of transients show up begging for the chance.

"Stanwyck enters into the arrangement cynically, but she quickly recognizes the opportunity to create her ideal man, and takes charge of the screening process. She picks a guy named John Willoughby, played by Gary Cooper; an ex-pitcher looking for money to pay for an operation on his arm. She takes one look and says: 'they'll believe him!'

"There's a lot going on in the movie, including the stuff about the newspaper's owner, D.B. Norton, using the John Doe phenomenon as a springboard from which to launch some grass-roots fascist third party..."

"Yes. I remember."

"But what *I'm* interested in is how Stanwyck remakes Cooper. She works from the blueprint of her revered, self-sacrificing father—carving Doe's speeches out of passages from the dead man's diary. That's standard Hollywood Freud, but what's interesting is the way that Cooper reacts to the treatment. He goes from being a pretty happy-go-lucky guy, to trying desperately to live up to the Doe ideal, to being so concerned with maintaining his individuality that he is *actually* willing to kill himself in order to escape the role she's cast him in…"

"But what does this have to do with that crossfire you were talking about?"

"Well, that's part of the problem. It's tough to shoehorn *two* visionaries into the same work of art. Usually, one character's sense of reality takes the narrative hostage. That's embarrassingly obvious in *Doe*. I mean, there's sort of an attempt to delve into Cooper's mental world, when he tells Stanwyck about a weird dream where he's both her father and the minister at her wedding to another man—and they wind up *spanking* her *together*. But that scene is as lame as it sounds, and Cooper always seems to be reacting to Stanwyck, rather than helping to create her…"

"So it's a failure."

"I don't know. It doesn't generate the 'melodramatic spectacle' I was talking about, but the way it all plays out is fascinating."

"Doesn't it have a happy ending? I *know* he doesn't kill himself."

"No. Stanwyck stops him with an incredible performance. She convinces him that the 'John Doe idea' is alive in him, and that she *needs* him. Then she collapses. He picks her up and steps back from the precipice, resigned to his role."

"That's *one* way to interpret it. But maybe Cooper's a blank slate, leaching off Stanwyck's vision. Or *maybe* that vision actually *transforms* Cooper; after all, he goes from being a useless drifter to the leader of a popular movement. What's so terrible about that?"

"Nothing, except that—by the internal logic of the film—he should've jumped. Cooper's love for Stanwyck gives him the strength to live up to her ideal, but it robs her of the chance to think critically about 'John Doe', or herself. She creates a whole world without noticing and gets trapped in a part of it."

"Interesting."

"Meanwhile, the molten core of personality beneath 'John Doe' goes on seething—with no outlet."

"So you're saying that character is innate; that no amount of contact with the world, or other human beings, can impact upon it."

"I've always said that."

Snell smiled.

"Just checking."

CHAPTER 34

▼

Mike stretched over green bicycle handles and pulled two halves of a bagel out of the toaster. He put them on a Christmas plate and moved through a crowd toward the fridge, holding a butter knife close to his chest. He forced the door open and reached in for the margarine, then knelt down to garnish the bagel. A girl with dark pigtails sat next to him on the dirty tiles and smiled: "You're Mike right?"

Mike nodded.

"I'm Jen. I was in the Master's program with Eric."

"Nice to meet you."

"You too. This is a great party."

"Thanks."

"You don't know where there's an ashtray do you?"

She waved a crumbling cigarette.

"I'm making a mess."

"You can use this plate in a second."

Mike finished the bagel and handed her the dish

"Thanks. Hey what's with all the Christmas stuff anyway? Your tree's still up, I noticed..."

Mike smiled: "I guess I love Christmas, but, really, I don't have anything else."

"Interesting."

"Yeah?"

"Sure."

She stood up.

"Well, I only stopped by to congratulate Eric. I've gotta work tomorrow. See ya."

Mike waved.

"Bye."

Diane walked into the kitchen, clutching a bottle of fruit juice. Mike got up and hugged her. Sleater-Kinney's *Dig Me Out* revved up in the living room.

"Jesus it's loud," she smiled.

Mike nodded: "It's great."

"You like this?"

"I just bought it."

"It sounds like a breakdown."

Mike frowned.

"Where's Vito?"

"Oh, we had dinner, but he was tired. He dropped me off and went home."

"He never comes out anymore."

"He never did, Michael. You only saw him 'cause you lived with me."

"I guess…"

"And you're only saying this 'cause you and Dawn got reclusive. It's not necessarily a problem."

"So you're saying it works for you?"

"Obviously."

"Okay then…"

Diane shrugged toward the hallway.

"Tina's here."

Mike nodded.

"Let's go see her."

"She looks busy."

"No she doesn't."

Tina had her back to the wall, with a wine cooler pressed up close to her lips and her head tilted part of the way toward a tall guy leaning over her. Mike walked over and touched her arm. She turned and smiled.

"Hey Mike."

She hugged him.

"This is," she pointed diagonally upwards, "uh…"

The tall guy wandered off.

Tina shrugged and waved at Diane.

"How are you?"

"Not bad."

"Good. Good. And Vito? Is he here?"

"He's fine. But he was tired."

"Me too."

Mike sighed.

"You just got here."

He took Tina's arm.

"You've got to say hi to the man of honour."

They found Eric sitting on a couch in the living room, arguing with Jen about the qualities of a virtuous citizen. Mike waved at her. She reddened and waved back.

Tina perched on the coffee table and smiled at Eric.

"So. You've Mastered Philosophy?"

Eric smiled: "It was easy. It didn't even struggle."

Mike backed away, avoiding ashtrays and legs stretched out on the floor. Diane watched from the hallway. She shook her head.

"Why'd you do that?"

"I've always thought they should talk more."

"So now you're a matchmaker?"

"Why not?"

"She's too lazy for him."

"Maybe he needs to calm down…Anyway, what about all that 'opposites attract' stuff?"

"What do you mean what about it? Has it ever happened to you?"

"Sure. Always."

"I don't know about *Paula*—it didn't last long enough for me to meet her—but are you saying that you and *Dawn* are opposites?"

Mike smiled.

"Of course."

"How?"

Tina squeezed back into her spot on the wall.

"Yeah Mike. How?"

Diane nodded and moved toward the living room. Mike shrugged and looked at Tina.

"Well, you know, she was wild and unpredictable—and I'm kind of...solid...But I let her see too many cracks. And I pushed her too hard."

"You think she was dependent on you?"

"Well, yeah. Of course she was. And I failed her. She must have talked about this with you..."

Tina shook her head.

"Dawn doesn't talk about you Mike."

He reached for his neck and massaged it.

"Oh."

"I'm sorry."

"Well, uh...did you talk to Eric?"

"Not really Mike. I don't care about his Master's thesis."

"Oh."

"He's a good looking guy. But he thinks too much."

"I thought you'd like that."

"Why?"

"Oh," Mike shook his head, "I don't know..."

"You need some air Mike."

She took his arm. They walked down the stairs to Verdun avenue. Pot smoke drifted out of the alleyways. Beer drinkers and their dogs sat on the balconies. Bright wading pools, crammed into slots of green between little black fences, chilled in the night air.

Mike took a deep breath.

"Well, I guess she *wouldn't* discuss this with you. She knows we're good friends…"

"No Mike. She just doesn't do it. Ever."

"How do you know?"

"Look. She's seeing someone else. And it's going fine…But even before that, she never moped or anything. She works hard and she goes out a lot. She *isn't* depressed. But *you* are…"

"I'm not. I'm just—spiritually unemployed."

"What's that Mike? *New* New Age? Or did you make it up yourself?"

Mike stopped and stared at her.

"I'm just saying—I've been pounding the pavement, and every door gets slammed in my face."

"What are you? A Jehovah's Witness?"

CHAPTER 35

▼

Mike sat cross-legged on a library straight-back, flipping through Cavell's book on melodrama, looking for Capra references. He didn't find any. He stretched and started on the introduction. A girl with soft olive cheeks, a mole, and a shaved head sat down across the table. She squinted at him.

"You're in Frazetta's Film Epistemology class."

Mike nodded.

"It's true."

"Yeah you talk a lot. It's usually interesting."

"I'm glad."

She shrugged.

Mike closed his book and said: "*You* never talk. I thought maybe you objected to the structure of the class or something."

She sighed.

"You think I'm an activist because you can see my skull?"

"Well..."

"I wasn't trying to make any kind of statement. I just got tired of brushing...And getting hit on..."

"Oh."

"It's not really working out. Although now I hear a lot about patriarchy. Right before men offer me drinks."

Mike laughed.

She smiled: "Listen. I need a cigarette. You want to get a coffee?"

"Maybe. What time is it?"

She looked at her watch.

"Seven."

"Really? How 'bout after next class then? I think I'm late for something..."

"Okay."

"See ya."

Mike shoved the book in his bag and rushed through the magnetic
gates. He dropped a quarter in a payphone and dialed his answering
machine. He fast-forwaded past stale messages, waiting for the new
lisp. He found it and leaned against the wall to listen.

"Hey Mike. It's Heidi. So...I guess this means you're already downtown. I'm almost dressed and out the door to meet you! Seven-thirty
latest—I promise...Just get another coffee and I'll see you soon! You
know what I look like, right? Well...I think I'll recognize you...Bye!"

Mike hung up and used another quarter. He chose option 2 from
the Dial-A-M8 menu and entered Heidi's box number.

"Hi. This is Heidi. I'm twenty-seven years old. I'm about
five-foot-four and weigh about one-thirty. I have black hair, pale skin
and hazel-green eyes. I live with my cat and I love him, even though
he's a bastard. I'm a creative-type; my life is a work of art—one of
those dark depressing things that critics enjoy...I love to talk when I'm
in the mood. And I like meeting people who can love. Box #22879."

Mike walked five blocks in the rain to "Jitters", an arcade/cafe in the
Alexis-Nihon shopping mall. It was a large room full of empty tables,
lit by flickering "game over" screens. He walked up to the counter and
asked for a double-americano. The woman at the cash smiled: "You
like Mrs. Pac-Man? We got Mrs. Pac-Man."

Mike paid for his drink and left a dollar tip. He found a booth and
started reading Cavell. A woman in a black velvet dress came in just
after seven-thirty and approached the booth. He marked his place in
the book and looked up.

Heidi waved uncomfortably and clutched her chin. Damp burgundy streaks dripped from her bangs. She closed her eyes and wiped her forehead with a napkin, which she crumpled into a ball. Then she sat down and blinked at Mike.

"Cheap make-up."

He grinned.

"Better for sunny days."

She nodded: "Except I always wear it on dark ones."

Mike used his napkin to clear a mascara slick from her cheek.

"It's pretty bad out there."

She breathed in phlegm.

"Yeah…Thanks."

Her blacklight stare spread to fill the space left by the make-up. Her skin was red from the napkins. Her purple lips parted nervously. She pulled a pack of DuMauriers out of her purse and lit one. She took a couple of drags on the cigarette, coating the base in lipstick. Her smoking hand had a skin-graft scar near the thumb-joint. She touched Mike's arm with the other hand.

"I'm glad I made it."

"Me too."

"You want to go somewhere else? I didn't realize this place was so bad."

"I don't know. It's nice and empty."

"Sure. I hate crowds too. But I think I want alcohol. And they don't sell any…"

"We *could* go back to my place. But that would be a little…"

"Strange?" she smiled. "I know I can trust you."

"Okay."

Mike finished the coffee and packed his schoolbag. Heidi put out her cigarette. They took the metro to Verdun and picked up wine on the way to his place. He gave her a quick tour of the rooms and introduced her to the cats. Eric wasn't home. They sat down on the couch and Heidi poured herself a drink.

"The last guy I dated wouldn't tell me where he lived."

"What?"

"He was a baker. He'd show up in the morning, after work, with all kinds of cakes and baguettes. We'd have breakfast and make love. Sometimes he'd stay and I'd lie next to him, tracing over his tattoos. Usually though, he'd leave, and he never invited me along. Then I followed him to a building and figured out his apartment number, but I didn't actually buzz him or anything..."

"How long did that go on for?"

"A month, a month and a half. Something like that. I broke up with him the day after I trailed him. I started to think he was married..."

"That's the only reason you broke up with him?"

Heidi shrugged.

"It was *fun*. For a little while. But this is better."

"This?"

"I think you're beautiful."

She kissed him. Her lips were naked. Mike fell back on the couch. She curled into him.

Mike whispered: "Thanks."

The next morning, Mike made coffee and Cream of Wheat. Heidi put on Canada AM and they had breakfast in the living room. She told him about her support group and he started explaining his thesis.

Heidi shook her head.

"It's just an essay Mike. It's for other academics. I wrote a lot of A papers on Poe, but I don't expect you to care...As far as I'm concerned, anything you can analyze isn't worth thinking about..."

"You think my work is useless?"

"Not if you like it. But it *isn't* sex..."

Mike shrugged.

"Fine."

"We'll watch the movies together sometime. That would be fun."

The front door rattled and Eric stumbled up the stairs. He kicked off his boots in the hallway and collapsed on the living room floor, in front of the television. He waved slyly and said: "I'm not in the way, am I?"

Mike stood up and made introductory gestures.

"Eric—Heidi."

They shook hands. Eric pointed at Heidi's Cream of Wheat.

"Are you done with that?"

"Sure."

"Thanks. I've been dancing all night."

She scowled.

"Techno?"

"Uh-huh."

"Oh you crazy students…"

Mike squinted at her.

She shrugged: "I'd better let you get on with your day."

"I guess so."

Mike helped Heidi find her things and kissed her at the door. When he returned to the living room, Eric had taken over the couch. His eyelids slid down over wide pupils.

"She's pretty strange Mike," he yawned.

"I like her."

Mike brought the dishes into the kitchen. He put on Fleetwood Mac's *Tusk* and started washing. The Cream of Wheat stuck to everything. The phone rang and he left the mess to soak.

"Hello?"

"It's me," Heidi lisped. "I'm at the metro station."

"Should I have come with you?"

"Don't be silly. You're not going anywhere."

"That's true."

"I just wanted to ask you—are we gonna be monogamous?"

"What?"

"It's important to me Mike. I need to know."

"Well…I always am. And it's important to me too."

"Okay. The metro's coming."

The line clicked.

CHAPTER 36

▼

Mike leaned over the laptop, with his legs curled to avoid the pools of spilt coffee on his blanket. The computer clock read 11:03 AM. He clutched the mouse and scrolled through the pages.

The essay had begun as an investigation of the ontological status of the "Pottersville" sequence in *It's A Wonderful Life*. Was it a delusion? An alternate reality unveiled by divine decree? Or a "noble lie", told by a determined agent of salvation? The important question was: did it accurately depict George Bailey's world, minus George Bailey? Mike had quickly concluded that it did not. Around page five, he had ruled the entire line of inquiry irrelevant and set about undermining his own introductory paragraph.

As far as Mike could tell, the remainder of the argument went as follows:

Generally, modernist solipsism festers in the scum-pools of memory and imagination, or shines with the certainty of original impact. The "Pottersville" sequence is unique—a murky flight from experience set ablaze by its own contradictions. An illustrative comparison can be drawn between George Bailey and Walter Mitty, a superficially similar character. Both men are trapped in the gerbil-wheel of the Protestant Ethic and yearn for release. However, where Mitty projects a daydream wonderland onto his drab surroundings, Bailey abstracts himself from "reality" and appears in a neon-lit film noir cliché. He drifts through Pottersville as an enigmatic stranger, clashing with the shades of characters he knows and has helped, ravenous for just one look of recognition.

Contrary to the critical consensus, George Bailey is not an "everyman" but a god—an immanent one. The fabric of Bedford Falls is held together by his divine presence. "Pottersville" is the negative image of an impossibility—a creator lost in a creation that could not exist without him.

Mike scrolled back to the beginning and rewrote the introduction. He saved the essay and printed it while he took a shower. He got dressed and slammed a staple into the top right-hand corner of the hot stack of sheets. Then he refilled the cats' bowls and rushed off to class.

Mike sat down in the seminar room, with a coffee, at 12:50. Heather—the bald non-activist—walked in two minutes later. She dropped her essay on the table, next to his.

"Well, that's it," she muttered.

"I'm sure it's great," Mike yawned.

"You'd better work on your pep-talks man. That sucked."

"Sorry. I didn't sleep."

"No kidding."

"Do I look messed up?"

"You look fine. Just kind of lazy…"

Professor Frazetta and most of the students arrived just after one o'clock. Mike half-listened to the voices for two hours. When he spoke, he repeated passages from his essay.

After class, the group decided to celebrate at the Red Lion, a dark pub that served cheap beer and Chinese food. Mike ordered another coffee and a plate of vegetable fried rice. Heather chain-smoked and split a pitcher with Anne, who was sorry to see the semester end.

"I always feel like I could've learned more."

"Sure," Heather nodded,"but summer's pretty cool. You can read without a highlighter and plan to do great things in the fall."

Anne's blue eyes widened and she flashed a slightly buck-toothed smile.

"That's kind of nice."

Heather sank back in her chair.

"Everyone thinks I'm so fuckin' negative..."

Anne laughed, swishing her red hair from side to side.

"No I don't! It's just, well, I guess I always see you in crisis mode."

Heather blushed.

"I have trouble settling on paper topics..."

"What did you write about anyway?"

She shrugged.

"The character switch in David Lynch's *Lost Highway.*"

Mike leaned forward and asked: "What did you argue?"

"Nothing really. I kept changing my mind. I just found it interesting."

"Why didn't you just pick a viewpoint and stand still? It's a good exercise."

Anne frowned: "That's pretty cynical Mike. Shouldn't we try to get *ourselves* into the work."

"I don't think so. Our thoughts, yes. Our selves, no. I don't see how you can do it...The idea is to focus your mental energy on one point and make an impact."

Heather turned to Mike.

"Actually, *that* sounds kind of naive. You think you can affect people with an *argument?*"

Mike grated his knuckles on his chin.

"Well...I hope so."

Anne poked Heather.

"I still wanna know what you wrote!"

Mike got up to use the washroom. He walked into the dirty stall and stood under the blinking neon, holding the flimsy door shut with his free hand. He skimmed through a debate about racism on the wall behind the toilet. Then he washed his hands and called Heidi from a payphone.

"Hello?" she answered.

"Hey."

"Mike! What's up?"

"I just finished my last class and I'm at the Red Lion…"

"I could come meet you."

"I'd rather go to your place. I haven't slept in two days…"

"Come over then. I'll make tea and we'll lie down together."

"You don't mind? You weren't doing anything?"

"No. Nothing. Masturbating."

"I'll be there soon."

Mike grabbed his schoolbag and said goodbye to the group. Everyone mentioned staying in touch over the summer. He took down a few numbers and left. Heidi lived ten minutes away, at the bottom of Atwater hill. He put his head down and walked quickly.

Heidi answered the door in an open purple housecoat. She set Mike up on the bed with some herbal tea. He collapsed on the pillow. She snuggled up to him, naked. He heard the news on TV. He pointed at the screen, bleary-eyed: "What's going on?"

"Nothing."

She pressed mute and pulled his shirt off.

Mike laughed: "I'm pretty out of it Heidi. The essay's still in my system."

"That's okay. You're here."

"Am I?"

She got on top of him.

He raised his head slightly.

"Is anything…happening?"

Her cheeks were flushed.

"Uh-huh."

"Good."

Sweat collected on his eyelids.

"I've been thinking a lot Heidi."

"Uh-huh."

"I hope you're happy."

The bed stopped moving.
"Of course," she whispered.
He heard the news again.

CHAPTER 37

▼

Mike jabbed his key into the lock and twisted it. He opened the door. Eric stood on the other side with a vacuum.

"Cool. You want to do some of this?"

Mike shrugged: "In a minute."

Eric switched on the power.

Mike took off his shoes and walked into the living room. Diane was stretched out on the couch, petting Marbles. She shook her head.

"You're gonna let Eric clean the whole place by himself?"

Mike looked at the VCR clock. It was 6:56 PM.

"The party's not until eight."

Diane sat up quickly.

"Are you okay Michael? You look…"

Mike sat down.

"I'm fine. I just broke up with Heidi."

Diane put her hand on his shoulder.

"Oh. Okay."

"What's okay? The break-up, or me not caring?"

"Both, if you want to put it that way. She didn't make sense Michael."

He frowned at her.

"Why're you here so early anyway?"

Diane shrank back.

"I came straight from work. I wasn't gonna go back to Laval for nothing."

"Oh."

Diane looked into his eyes.

"You *are* upset."

He shrugged: "No. There's just been a lot of crying, that's all."

Eric wandered in with the vacuum.

"Did you say you broke up with Heidi?" he yelled.

Diane stared at the machine until he turned it off.

"Yeah," Mike nodded.

"Finally."

"You guys didn't give her a chance."

Diane crossed her arms.

"She wore Cleopatra make-up to mom's house Michael!"

"*You've* worn stuff like that. I've seen it."

"Never in that *situation*."

Eric nodded.

"Part of growing up is learning to appreciate context."

Mike's head shook.

"*Sure*…What happened to rising *above* context and seeing the whole?"

"It's a privilege reserved for teenagers and madmen."

Mike glanced sidewise at Eric.

"Congratulations. You *have* grown up."

"So have *you*, man. You're already onto the mid-life crisis!"

Diane smiled: "He's right Michael…"

The doorbell rang.

Eric answered it and let Tina in.

She peeked into the living room.

"What's going on in here?"

"What did you think of Heidi?" Diane asked.

"Did?"

"What *do* you think of her?"

Tina curled up in the armchair.

"I don't really have an opinion. I only know what Mike told me."

"You've met her."

"Once. She scared me."

She blinked at Mike: "But maybe she's too lonely to be friendly. I can see that too."

Diane sighed.

"You can see that in *anyone*, if you look for it. That's what Mike does."

Mike cleared his throat.

"I don't see it in any of *us*..."

"So you found yourself a gem," Eric smirked. "Why'd you break up with her?"

"She really needed me, I think. Anyway, she hated me to leave. But I just lost track of her, when she wasn't around. I couldn't think of her, alone in that apartment. And maybe she liked it that way...It's kind of nice to almost bring someone to life like that. Except you almost kill them just as often."

Eric took a deep breath.

"Jesus."

Diane muttered: "It's a life-support system."

Mike stood up.

"Unplugged."

Tina leaned forward.

"It *sounds* like you got what you *wanted*. What you say you had with Dawn."

"Maybe it *seems* that way. But it didn't sound the same at all."

Mike brought the cats into his room and crashed on a mattress full of books. The vacuum roared on.

The doorbell rang repeatedly.

Mike crept out to make coffee. He cleaned the machine and put it on a burner. Then he leaned against the stove and waited.

A group of Eric's friends passed a joint around the kitchen table. A red-headed guy in a dress shirt asked: "You want some?"

Mike shook his head. He poured espresso into a cup of scalding milk. He inhaled the steam.

A woman in overalls counted famous American hemp farmers on her fingers. The rest of the group called out names—many of them more than once.

"Stop it guys!" she laughed. "You're confusing me!"

In the hallway, Tina leaned against the wall, squinting up at a vaguely familiar guy. She finished her drink and opened a cigarette-space between two fingers. The guy slid one in and lit it. Tina smiled and blew smoke into his chest and neck.

A multicolored disco ball hung from the living room ceiling. The soundsystem pumped Chemical Brothers. A few dancers carried the coffee table away. Heather and Anne studied the bookshelves, expressing hoarse opinions. A man in leather pants gawked at sports updates. A couple next to him on the couch played tic-tac-toe with a broken red pencil and a stack of post-it notes.

Eric and Diane sat on the balcony, drinking beer and observing the people on other balconies. Diane's shoes lay upside down near the railing and her toes curled toward Eric. His fingers drummed the wood in time with the music, just next to her thigh.

"Hey!" Nathaniel Snell's voice interrupted. "They said you went to bed."

Mike turned around.

"I did."

"Couldn't sleep?"

"I don't know."

"Brooding?"

"For a while. But I didn't want to miss anything."

"We should meet to discuss your progress. Maybe Wednesday morning?"

Mike nodded.

"I'll try to wake up."

CHAPTER 38

▼

Mike tossed aside the liner notes for *End of the Century* and turned up the volume. A notebook lay open on his pillow. The streetlamps shut down for the night. The Ramones hollered: "I can't hurry and you can't wait. It doesn't matter 'cause we're already late. I can't get off the telephone. It always rings when I'm alone." Mike drew the curtains and went back to bed.

Page one bore the title: "Notes for Snell Meeting". Beneath this was a point-form recap of his Film Epistemology paper, which worked toward the conclusion that:

> The Pottersville sequence is a typical product of American existentialist thought—an inversion of Emersonianism, or rather, an Emersonianism which has lost faith in itself. The whole world remains compartmentalized in a corner of the subject's mind — only now it is a dark corner.

Mike traced over the letters until the pen went through the paper.

A few pages later, he found a dense swirl of scrawl around the idea that: "Pottersville's relationship to the film as a whole is analogous to film noir's place within the Hollywood tradition." Incomplete word-spokes jutted at odd angles from the center:

"Capra aligns Romantic Comedy with Melodrama."

"(Tries to)"

"Christmas bells resolve the irresolvable."

"(No)"

"George learns to appreciate the world he's created—but he'll just get lonely again, after the credits."

"Clarence is fun, but why give him wings?"

"They're for the director, actually."

On the next page, he had written:

> Ever since James Agee, critics have been unable to resist comparing *It's A Wonderful Life* with Dickens' *A Christmas Carol*. Unfortunately, the discussion has usually centered upon the Christmastime setting, the use of flashbacks, and the supposedly simple "conversion" narrative. In fact, there is very little similarity, on the level of plot, between the two works.
>
> It is often argued that Capra merely rewrote the story for a more democratic age, making the clerk a hero and the miser a fixed referent; but there is very little logic in this comparison. The protagonists face fundamentally different problems. The agents of Scrooge's "conversion" come unbidden to force him back into society. Bailey, on the other hand, feels crushed by the weight of his relationships, and prays for some reassurance that his sacrifice has meant something. Scrooge's ghosts show him that a joyful world exists just beyond the confines of his isolation chamber. Clarence confirms that George's "reality", without George, would be a nightmare.

Mike flipped forward to a passage on the Christmas Present segment of the *Carol*:

> This chapter contrasts strikingly with the Pottersville sequence, although they purport to represent the same thing—"reality" untainted by the subjective presence of the protagonist. Clarence tells George: "Each man's life touches so many other lives. And when he's not around, he leaves an awful hole." In a key scene, Fred explains to his dinner guests that "the consequence of [Scrooge] taking a dislike to us, and not making merry with us, is, as I think, that he loses some pleasant moments, which could do him no harm. I am sure he loses pleasanter companions than he

can find in his own thoughts" (reference?). There is so much less at stake for Scrooge's world. It has a substantiality that Bedford Falls/Pottersville lacks. Even the Cratchit household, despite its poverty and Tiny Tim's illness, functions autonomously, with enough agency left over to fuel a gratuitous toast to Scrooge. <u>These objects pull him into their orbit.</u> George Bailey, on the other hand, is a sun on the verge of supernova.

He ripped out pages until he came to:

...but the undeniable kinship between *IAWL* and the *Carol* exists on a level beneath these trivialities—in the fleeting glimpses they offer us of the omniscience available to the artist, or God, or a trio of spirits. The possibility of relating to past, present, and future, all at once...

Mike tried to scribble in: "Both works offer the possibility of viewing past, present, and future all at once, from a perspective (non-perspective?) beyond the need to relate"; but the words jumbled together.

The CD surrendered to a droning alarm, which had gone off at ten. Mike turned it off and put on a Fastbacks mix. It was 10:21 AM. His fingers paced through the spoiled pages of the notebook. He found a fresh space on the inside of the back cover and wrote:

Forget the protagonists...Get through them, beneath them, above them...<u>I don't mean the God position!</u> The Dickensian Spirit...Past: "*That they are what they are don't blame me*"...Present: "My life upon the globe is very brief. It ends tonight."...Future: a grave filled with memories...Minefield of experience...

Mike called Snell's office. The answering machine picked up. He traced circles around the cluster of words, explaining:

"Hi Nate. I'm sorry, but I'm not coming in today. I'm still thinking this through..."

Mike hung up the phone and turned off the ringer. He curled up on the bed. A punk-thrash chorus of "Whaddya say?—You're wrong! Whaddya say?—So wrong!" melted into a guitar-hymn, and two female voices almost whispered:
"You say you think you're the king,
and you're wrong.
You say you say everything.
You're so wrong…
You're the one,
that's enough for me,
to know where I stand.
You're the one,
that's enough to see,
I don't stand any chance…"

BOOK FIVE

CHAPTER 39

"Uh, hello, my name is Mike. I'm twenty and kind of inexperienced. I'm five-foot-five and weigh about one-thirty…I have dark hair and green eyes…I'm into old movies, jazz music, Charles Dickens, my cats…I'm pretty nervous and I guess I just hope there are some nice women out there…Send your messages to box #5070. I'm listening."

"Hey Mike. This is Joanna. I've got some advice for you: don't waste your money on this system. You sound like too nice a guy. And don't send me a message okay? I'm blocking you…"

*   *   *   *

"Hey sweetie! *I'm* a nice woman and I'd *love* to meet you—I mean, we should talk. I'm a little older than you are, but that's probably a good thing…My box number's #3456. See ya…"

*   *   *   *

"Mike, Mike, Mike. What are you trying to prove?"

*   *   *   *

"Hi Mike, this is Donna. I'm thirty-nine, five-six, in good shape—work out three times a week and my ass looks great…I've got curly blonde hair—on my head…I hope I'm not scaring you off. I've got a feeling about you—a tingling sensation, actually…We could have fun. Leave me your phone number at box #10090 and we'll take it from there…"

*   *   *   *

"I don't understand what you're *looking* for Mike, but if it involves Dickens and your cats, that's *fucked*…"

*   *   *   *

"What's your favourite movie Mike? Mine's *The Graduate*. Box #3456."

*   *   *   *

"Hi Mike. I think you sound cool, but you're not my type…Like my ad says—I'm five-ten and I'm into Formula One racing…Anyways, I know this is weird, but I think you'd be perfect for my friend Jen. She's got a small cute body and beautiful eyes. She's really shy too. I don't think she's ever even kissed a guy—and she just turned eighteen…The thing that sealed it is the old movies. She loves them too. You know—Ginger and Fred. All that stuff…Maybe you're meant for each other. Who knows? I'm at box #4457."

*   *   *   *

"Why the Heli is this ad in the intimate encounters section?"

*   *   *   *

"Man, you are *hopeless*."

*   *   *   *

"Hey Mike. It's Heidi...So you're in a new box. At least some of you is...It's kind of interesting. But don't get carried away babe. It's still just a box..."

*   *   *   *

"You need a hooker buddy. Or maybe a pimp."

*   *   *   *

"Okay Mike, here it is: I'm an attached woman in her forties. A little chubby in all the right places and with energy to spare. My husband knows I do this and we've agreed not to talk about it. He's not as young as he used to be, and he gets distracted easily—out of focus really...I get that way too, but I like it sharp sometimes. You wouldn't be nervous with me, Mike—I'm very nice; and I'd take care of everything...Box #5328."

*   *   *   *

"Fascinating. You don't sound like the kind of person you're pretending to be. But you don't sound like you'd bother pretending...I wonder what kind of messages you're getting? Don't tell me. I don't care. And don't tell me you're nervous either. There's no way...People like you make this system what it is. But I don't have to pay for it— you do."

CHAPTER 40

▼

Eric's skin was red under the phone. He switched the receiver to the other ear and whispered: "What the fuck?"

He stared out of the living room, listening.

"Yeah, he just got in…I don't know, he just rushed past…He had the video camera again…Sounds like he's making coffee."

Eric paced to the bookshelves

"What do you want me to do, Di? You know what he's like."

He rearranged a few books.

"Why don't *you?*"

He turned around.

"Mike. Diane wants to talk to you."

Eric shook his head and whispered: "Nope…I'm sure it's fine…Can we talk about something else?"

He settled back onto the couch.

"What channel?"

He reached for the remote.

"Ah. We don't get it."

He smiled.

"You know we can't afford cable."

He sat up quickly.

"Hey! Did I tell you I'm teaching at Dawson in the fall?"

He yawned and sank back.

"Oh, you know, volunteering...getting ready for the new job...playing a lot of board games—I've read through half the library's chess books..."

"Honing my skills, perfecting an attack—it's important...But *Mike's* not too helpful these days. I mean, he's not even playing, really. I swear he sees more in the square-patterns and the dead pieces than the game."

"I don't like to win easily. I'd much rather lose. Wouldn't you?"

"I know, I know. But metaphorically..."

"I'll try, I'll try..."
The sound faded out...

...and back in again.
"...wait a sec Di. I think, uh...oh I guess it's nothing. Go on..."

"Of course, but that's not the point is it? I'm talking about..."

"Do you? I think you're just saying that."

"You can't separate it like that—I can't."

"Okay, there's *that*. But I don't see..."
Eric laughed.
"Pericles and Aspasia."
He laughed again.
"I didn't! You're crazy! I'm serious now. We..."

"I just happen to be reading about them right now, that's all."

"Of course not. There's more to life than chess. Or, maybe, there's more chess in life than on the board."

"Yeah, I know. I'm not going to change. But, hopefully, I'll keep getting better. You certainly do."

"Ah! But that has nothing to do with…"

"Okay. I concede the point. But still, you have to admit…"

"We're much better at this than we used to be."

CHAPTER 41

▼

A brush-cut sax player blew smoke through the roof of the Red Lion. His bandmate on guitar ignored requests to tone down his amp. Pitchers rolled off the bar and the funk gurgled on. Fresh students and the usual old drunks filled the room. Outside the open front door, inaudible cars sped by, leaving their fumes behind. Summer humidity clung to the small dark cellar.

Most of the American Documentary seminar had reassembled at a round table near the dart area. Chalk misted off the board each time a dart thudded into it. A drum solo rattled the table. A used fork dried in plum sauce on the class syllabus. A wrinkled hand with a tarnished gold ring on one finger brought clean ashtrays.

Heather picked up the syllabus.

"I'm pretty excited about this Pare Lorentz stuff," she yelled.

A guy with slick black bangs and a plaid shirt angled his head toward her cheek.

"Are you serious? I mean, that stuff...I'm sure it's just there for contrast."

She took a sip of beer.

"Hunh?"

"Well, come on—*The Plow That Broke the Plains*? It's pretty melodramatic..."

She shrugged.

"Life *is* melodramatic sometimes, don't you think?"

He shook his head.

"I think you can get what you need out of reality without grafting a soundtrack onto it."

"Fine," she smiled, "but I'm saying the soundtrack is just as real."

The band took a break.

"Not now," he grinned.

Heather shrugged: "What's your name again?"

The jukebox played Led Zeppelin's "When the Levee Breaks".

The dance floor cleared and Anne rushed to the pool table. She picked up a cue stick and rolled her sleeves over pale freckled arms. She looked directly at the group.

"Isn't anyone gonna play with me?"

The bass player, a chubby guy in a Milwaukee Brewers cap, grabbed the other stick.

Anne sighed and broke the triangle.

He clapped and made some kind of joke.

She took another shot and sank a green-striped ball, but the white fell in with it.

The bass player pointed out a tough combo shot and missed it.

They both laughed.

Heidi sat at the bar, next to an old man in a rumpled brown suit. She glanced back, once or twice, but the pitcher was in front of her. The man sagged forward and put his hand on her bare knee for support. She brushed it off gently.

Heidi stared wide-eyed at the man and said something. His lip curled and he gestured at her chest. She blinked. The man's nose started running and she stopped it with a napkin. He lurched forward again and this time she stood up to let him rest his face against her shoulder.

Anne drilled the eight-ball into a side pocket. She put the stick down and gave her opponent a hug. The rest of the band tuned their instruments. The bass player hopped up to join them and they started the next set.

A guy with long graying hair, wearing a black top hat and fish-hooks in his ears, came in off the street. He walked straight up to Heidi. She invited him to sit at the stool on her right. He licked his lips, eyeing the old man to her left. Heidi lit a cigarette and watched the smoke blend into the atmosphere. Neither man moved. She finished her glass and walked out. The new guy took her seat. He ordered a pitcher and two glasses.

The syllabus had rips in it and beer drops on top of the plum sauce. Each date had a corresponding presentation topic and a hand-written name next to it. Anne put her finger on September 9th and muttered: "How did I get stuck going first?"

She looked up and smiled brightly.

"Anyone wanna switch? It's just an overview."

Heather smirked at the guy next to her.

"Sorry. I really want to do Pare Lorentz. Anyway, I'm second, so it wouldn't help you much."

She touched the guy's arm.

"Maybe Jack?"

He scratched his head.

"I don't know..."

She turned around.

"Or Mike?"

Anne blew red bangs out of her eyes.

"Yeah *right*. He's doing Capra's *Why We Fight* series."

Jack slapped his palm onto the table.

"I'll do it! Get it out of the way early..."

Anne beamed.

"That's so *cool.* Thank you."

"No problem."

He got up.

"How about a game of pool? I liked watching you play before. And the band's wrapping up."

"Sure."

They went to claim the table.

The Jukebox played Guns n' Roses' "Rocket Queen". Heather folded up the syllabus and put it in her bag. She looked out onto the street and muttered:

"I wonder if the metro's still running?"

CHAPTER 42

▼

The fork slid through Tina's lips. She put it down on a clean plate. A waitress cleared the dishes. Specks of tomato sauce glistened off white checks on the tablecloth. The waitress brought coffee. Tina sipped brownish bubbles off the black surface. Steam rose to her smile.

"This one's different," she said. "Completely."

The waitress brought dessert—tartufo and rice pudding. The back of a dirty beige trench coat smeared against the window. The stiff blond man inside it mouthed the words to his line at a couple of tourists crossing Stanley: "Could you spare ten cents; a quarter? *Not* for *alcohol*—for food, hot coffee, a place to stay…" He started over when the next couple passed. Out of the corner of his eye, he watched Tina's spoon enter her mouth. Italian disco music played in the background.

"I'm not kidding," she continued, "this is what I've been *waiting* for. I don't mean I love him madly or anything like that. You *know* what I think of *that*. But, it just *works*. He gets inside me without ransacking the place. At least he hasn't yet…That's all I've ever asked for—but it seems like the hardest thing on earth to find. People can't just spend time together—they have to make a damned *impact*. I don't mean they want to change each other…*Everyone* knows that's bad. But no one likes to feel *extra*.

"It's too bad—'cause that's exactly what they are. I don't mean *worthless*; just not *essential*…Everyone's either *serious* or playing games.

Most people can't be *casual* and *sincere* at the same time…I've never been anything else—and it seems to drive them crazy."

Behind Tina, a balding man's crown moved in time with crunching teeth. Across the table, a woman with long blondish hair tilted blue eyes downward at a plate of bruschetta crumbs. The bald-spot spun out of view, revealing a tense mouth. The woman whispered something. The man removed his glasses and wiped Alfredo sauce off the lenses.

"Paul's got the best *timing*," Tina explained, "he always catches me in the mood: for talking, for sex, for being alone. I never minded being close, you know—but you can't fill the hours that way…We communicate in fits and starts."

The blondish woman excused herself and backed away from the table. The man opened a newspaper and started reading. He didn't see her leave the restaurant. The woman slipped a crumpled bill into a pocket of the beige trench coat and kept walking. The man at the table consulted his watch, shaking his head. The woman's red sweater had fallen on the floor. He picked it up with ink-stained hands.

Tina counted coins into a pile on the table.

"That was good."

She paid her bill at the cash.

The man in the trench coat said in a sing-songy voice: "Have a good evening…Bonne soireeee…"

His jaw continued to move.

Tina asked him: "Got a piece of gum?"

The man nodded and handed her a stick of cinnamon Trident.

"Thanks."

"You're welcome mademoiselle…"

Cold wind freshened Tina's cheeks. She headed toward Ste-Catherine street.

"Let's go this way."

A crowd of smirks gathered around a man with charts explaining the alien origin of civilization. He pointed at a drawing of a goggle-eyed creature on a cross. His voice throbbed.

Tina crossed the street, muttering:

"Wow. That's dumb. I mean, I understand wanting to believe in something. Aliens, sure. Christianity, fine. But both?"

She sat at a bench in Phillips Square. Cashiers in thick sweaters closed up gourd and knickknack stalls for the night. Tina massaged her arms with her hands.

"Oh, what do I know? I'm no visionary either, these days...I'm really starting to need this guy. Not *need* him exactly. But need some- one like him around, part-time...I used to just zone out and hum the New Age standards to myself. And it was good. More and more though, I think about Paul and the things we do together. It's just more interesting. I still need time alone, but it's not the same...The *reality* is: he may be an extra, but I'm through with simplicity."

She shrugged.

"I guess it's a dumb thing to worry about. The memories are made, right? And I know how to make new ones..."

She smiled.

"I don't know why I'm telling you all this. It doesn't matter."

CHAPTER 43

▼

To: "Mike Borden" <me25@hotmail.com>
CC:
From: "Nathaniel Snell" <ProfSnell@U.qc.ca>
Date: Monday, October 25th, 1999
Subject: Why?

Mike,

I don't understand the decision you've made. I don't even think this *qualifies* as a decison...Who ever said that an undergraduate Communications thesis had to account for every aspect of human existence? Or any thesis, for that matter? You say yours doesn't. Well, that's not exactly news Mike, but I was still looking forward to reading it.

The whole point of academic journals, and the larger community of scholars they feed, is that no one has access to the larger truths you're talking about. All we can do, as a discipline, is build toward a provisional understanding of things, using the little discoveries each member makes every day.

I shouldn't have to explain this to someone like you. In fact, I know I don't. I'm pretty much writing this for myself. I know the stance you're taking. There's nothing original about it. We used to call it *hybris*. A lot of bright students have made similar exits. A lot of dumb ones have too.

What I want to know now is—what will you do instead? You say academics play games. You're right. That's part of it. But at least there's some kind of communication going on. Maybe you don't get anything out of critical essays (frankly, I don't believe that's true), but many people find the dialogue stimulating. And what good can you possibly do, sitting in your room, waiting for some gnostic truth-bomb to explode in your head?

Okay. Fine. You're not here to "do good." But you have to admit there's something a little bit useless about the life you've got in mind. It's true, you can go blind from squinting at minutiae. But you can die from exposure at the altitude you're reaching for.

I'm not worried about that. Something will trip you up. It's probably already done. Despite the things you say Mike, there's nothing ethereal about you.

I guess that's as good a place as any to let the matter drop. I've really enjoyed working with you Mike—although, as you know, I've always had qualms with your approach...Precisely because it leads to this kind of renunciation.

Anyway, if you want to come for dinner on Friday, we'll make something vegetarian.

Take care,

Nate

CHAPTER 44

▼

Thick smoke wafted toward cracks in the kitchen ceiling. Wet globs of plaster drooped over the room in lava-lamp formations. Muddy shoes criss-crossed the floor between the six-packs and the ashtrays. Ants scurried for cover under loose black linoleum drenched in cat-piss. Someone opened the back door.

"Jesus! There's a hole in the balcony! The wood's all splintered!"

"Yeah, the railing's not too steady either."

"Stay close to the wall."

"Don't try to use those stairs."

"Man! Fresh air…"

"Good party…"

A light drizzle started again. More water breezed into the dark kitchen.

A girl with bright green eyes and magenta hair asked Patrique, the dépanneur clerk, if he liked his job. He shook his pony tail.

"It's tough. They robbed me twice, and I had to stand there doing nothing."

He stretched his fists out and looked down at them.

"These things are dangerous. I'm not allowed to use them unless my life is threatened.

The girl squinted at him.

"Don't do that."

A drunk guy skidded his dirt bike into the microwave table. The thin metal legs buckled. A group of people helped the appliance onto the floor. The cyclist sat on it and wiped his brow.

Tina's dark lashes came down over glossy browns. She whispered something to herself. Paul stood close by her side, laughing. He passed her a joint making the rounds. Tina took a puff and handed it to the next person. She straightened up and crossed her arms. Paul stepped in front of her. A pale hand reached for keys in his back pocket.

A stray cat slunk in from the balcony, following a scent-trail to a locked door. Voices squeaked and fingers snapped the air. Bodies crowded into the room. A bowlful of fresh milk cracked into sloppy pieces on the floor. The cat curled up on the microwave, next to the drunk.

The current flowed back into the hallway, eddying around a man with a goatee and a professional look in his eye, down on all fours, snapping pictures of the hardwood. A National Geographic map of the world flapped off the wall.

"Hey this thing's out of date. Where's Macedonia?"

"There's a piece of mold shaped like it on the bathroom ceiling."

Eric and Diane sat in the living room, with a chessboard between them, on the coffee table. She took his castle with a satisfied smile. He put her in check. She squirmed out of it and glanced at the clock. He reached for a piece, nodding. She caught his hand. He got up and stopped the music. The speakers hummed. Eric's chest swelled.

"Uh, hello, well…I know I'm better known for starting arguments; but tonight, I just have a flat statement to make…Um, Epicurus said that 'a pleasure shared is a pleasure doubled.' At least, the axiom's been attributed to him. Of course, he also spoke against romantic entanglements of any kind, so perhaps my use of him here is in bad taste. I can't help *that*. I think polite speech is an oxymoron…"

Diane reached under his armpit and pulled him close to her body. A crimson trail blazed up her arm to her lips.

"We're getting married everyone," she said.

Eric beamed into her eyes.
"And we're *going* on a honeymoon."
She bit his neck.
There was clapping and the smiles closed in.

A ring of heads swirled around mute gestures in the skylight.

CHAPTER 45

▼

Images of Mike Borden, on a video screen:

Sitting on a black leather couch, wearing cords and a black T-shirt, next to a woman in a purple body-suit; each looking straight ahead, stuttering over the first syllable of a yawn.

She swings her right ankle onto the middle cushion. He turns slightly. She tosses curly blonde hair and points at the wallpaper. His eyes lag after her. She rubs her left thigh with clipped fingernails. She touches his arm. His skin just sits there—not pale, not red.

She jerks her head to the left, looks at the telephone, gets up to answer it. Mike puts on his gray coat.

Wearing the same clothes, cross-legged—with a much younger girl, in a dress, sitting much closer to him, on a flowery love seat. She plays with a TV remote. Her bare feet are riveted to the carpet. She swallows hard, puts down the remote, near his knee, and leaves her hand there. She watches the screen. He just breathes.

In a gray sweater, hunched over a table, having his palm read by a woman with long red hair and a bit of an overbite. A stick of incense sends up smoke. Her fingers trace over his lines. She squints into his eyes. They're wide open.

On a bed, bare-chested, rubbing petite, olive-skinned shoulders. The woman buries her face in the mattress. Hair falls away from her neck. Mike's hands roll forward, circling lazily. She brings her head up, catching three knuckles inside her body. The fingers keep moving. Her dark lashes part. She sees him, in the mirror, reading her bedside-globe.

Lying under a dark blue comforter, next to a red-cheeked brunette with creases under her eyes. Gauzy white curtains; a table full of cosmetics, glinting in the sun; a Monet reproduction hanging over the pillows; a man's shirts and ties in the shadowy cupboard. Her arm curls around his neck. She leans over his mouth. The bed shrugs. She falls back on one elbow, with her chin in her palm. Mike gets up, naked, and walks straight ahead, getting larger. Perspective collapses.

The screen goes blue.

CHAPTER 46

▼

Earth-coloured leaves clung by their stems to cracks in rock-stairs. Balled-up bread bags and nutshards collected in the rot. Running shoes and squirrel tails brushed against them, crunched them.

Rows of gray-brown trees formed a dense, slanting wall. A flat path halved by yellow lines curved around it. Bicycle reflectors flashed red and orange.

Dark tunnels cut upwards through the branches. Dirt crumbled out from under root-steps. Moonlight fell on apple cores and condom wrappers. Birds and people made noise behind the wainscoting.

Another layer of pavement cut into the woods. Women in jogging suits squeezed water-arcs from a fountain. Liquid ran down their chins into a rust-basin. Pink and green signs pointed the way to Beaver Lake, to the Cross, to the Chalet/Observatory.

The city reflected off glass doors in a cement clearing. Wide beige steps descended to the courtyard. Seed-cases spiked out from gravel flower-beds. Large metal viewmasters peeked over thick railings.

Neon text filled the black sky, painted the river. Cars rolled up the steep streets, and sped down to the bridges. Dim light came out of university buildings and office towers. Passengers got off buses at the foot of the mountain. The air moved.

A flag spiraled around a pole on the roof of the chalet. The shadow of the stone building fainted back into evergreens. A seagull rummaged through leaves near a picnic table. Stubbly brown grass sloped downward over groundhog dens. A small bridge passed over the ditch. Traces of old storms led to a moss-covered drain.

The ground was cold and hard under Mike's back.

CHAPTER 47

▼

Mike sat down with a coffee and a video. He called Dial-a-M8. The robotic woman read off the menu. He pressed "4" to listen to his ad, then fast-forwarded to the delete option. He yawned, looking at the VCR clock. He got up to put the video back on the shelf.

The phone chattered into a cushion on the couch. Mike picked it up to listen. Recordings by all of the women using the system played in a loop. The familiar voices put a comfortable grin on his face, until he heard a click, a quick breath, and an alien sound.

Mike stood up and let the words come:

"...spasms and orgasms, poetry and roller coasters. I'm not looking for stupid thrills. So don't get on my nerves. I do my best, but I'm not *on* all the time. I'm not here to amuse anyone, except maybe myself...but that doesn't mean we couldn't have fun together, even if it happens by mistake. What else can I say?"

Mike cleared his throat:

"Hey. It's me. Uh, I don't know if this ad is serious or a joke...I know you won't answer me...I guess it doesn't matter..."

He paused to sip the coffee.

"No. It *does*. But, I mean, there's no tragedy here. Never was, was there? Do you realize Di and Eric are getting *married* next week? I'm supposed to see them tonight. Maybe..."

He noticed the time.

"Anyway, it's good to hear your voice again—brings back your teeth and your throat, and the parts of you I could never...*can't* imagine what you're doing now."

Mike brushed some of the dirt off his jeans and changed into a green sweater. He filled the cat bowls and smiled goodnight.

He walked to Verdun metro, paid the fare, and squeezed onto a car. He stared into the plexiglass, contemplating his reflection, wondering if he had pressed "#" to send. The image flickered as the train pulled into a well-lighted station and the doors lisped open.

About the Author

David Fiore is 28 and lives in Verdun, Quebec. He really likes it there.

0-595-22303-6

Printed in the United States
4626